THE FEAST OF BACCHUS

I0612524

Ernest George Henham was born in London in 1870 and as a young man travelled to the New World, where his sojourn in the Canadian Northwest provided the inspiration for some of his early works. As Ernest G. Henham, he published *Menotah: A Tale of the Riel Rebellion* (1897), *God, Man & the Devil: A Novel* (1897), the weird Gothic horror novel *Tenebrae* (1898), *Bonanza: A Story of the Outside* (1901), *Scud: The Story of a Feud* (1902), *The Plowshare and the Sword: A Tale of Old Quebec* (1903), *'Krum': A Study of Consciousness* (1904), and *The Feast of Bacchus* (1907).

Suffering from ill health, he moved to Dartmoor around 1906. In the words of a contemporary, "It is one of the strangest facts in literary history that a man, who had defined his place as a writer of fiction with nine novels or so, published under his own name, should have seen fit to begin his career afresh and write a long series of commercially unsuccessful novels under a pseudonym." However, this was what Henham did, publishing *A Pixy in Petticoats* anonymously in 1906 before adopting the pseudonym John Trevena in 1907 for *Furze the Cruel*, the first in a trilogy of novels focusing upon Dartmoor life, followed by *Heather* (1908) and *Granite* (1909). He continued to write prolifically, achieving widespread critical acclaim but little commercial success. His notable works include *Bracken* (1910), *Written in the Rain* (1910) (short stories), *Wintering Hay* (1912), which the *Los Angeles Times* ranked with the works of Turgenev and Dostoevsky, *Sleeping Waters* (1913), and *Moyle Church-Town* (1915). Trevena's life is so shrouded in obscurity that at the time of this printing even his date of death was not known, though he is believed to have died around 1946. Until the Valancourt edition of *Furze the Cruel* in 2010, all his works were out of print, despite the near-universal critical consensus during his lifetime that his works would live on among the classics of English fiction.

Gerald Monsman is Professor of English at the University of Arizona in Tucson. He is the author of *Pater's Portraits: Mythic Pattern in the Fiction of Walter Pater* (Johns Hopkins, 1967), *Walter Pater's Art of Autobiography* (Yale, 1980), *Confessions of a Prosaic Dreamer: Charles Lamb's Art of Autobiography* (Duke, 1984), *Olive Schreiner's Fiction: Landscape and Power* (Rutgers, 1991), *H. Rider Haggard on the Imperial Frontier* (ELT, 2006), and the editor of Haggard's *King Solomon's Mines* (Broadview, 2002). Recently, his work has focused on rediscovery of Trevena and the South African writers Bertram Mitford and Ernest Glanville, and he has prepared scholarly editions of six novels by Mitford and four by Trevena for Valancourt Books, as well as editions of Pater's *Marius the Epicurean* and Haggard's *Nada the Lily*.

By the Same Author

AS ERNEST G. HENHAM

Menotah: A Tale of the Riel Rebellion (1897)
God, Man & The Devil: A Novel (1897)
Tenebrae: A Novel (1898)*
Bonanza: A Story of the Outside (1901)
Scud: The Story of a Feud (1902)
The Plowshare and the Sword: A Tale of Old Quebec (1903)
'Krum': A Study of Consciousness (1904)
The Feast of Bacchus (1907)*

AS JOHN TREVENA

A Pixy in Petticoats (1906)*
Arminel of the West (1907)
Furze the Cruel (1907)*
Heather (1908)
Granite (1909)
The Dartmoor House that Jack Built (1909)
Bracken (1910)
Written in the Rain (1910)
The Reign of the Saints (1911)
Wintering Hay (1912)
Sleeping Waters (1913)*
No Place Like Home (1913)
Adventures among Wild Flowers (1914)
Moyle Church-Town (1915)
The Captain's Furniture (1916)
Raindrops (1920)
The Vanished Moor (1923)
The Custom of the Manor (1924)
Off the Beaten Track (1925)
Typet's Treasure (1927)

* Available from Valancourt Books

THE FEAST OF BACCHUS

A Study in Dramatic Atmosphere

BY

ERNEST G. HENHAM

With a new introduction by

GERALD MONSMAN

VALANCOURT BOOKS

The Feast of Bacchus by Ernest G. Henham
First published London: Brown, Langham & Co., 1907
First Valancourt Books edition 2014

Copyright © 1907 by Ernest G. Henham
Introduction © 2014 by Gerald Monsman

All rights reserved. The use of any part of this publication reproduced, transmitted in any form or by any means, electronic, mechanical, photocopying, recording, or otherwise, or stored in a retrieval system, without prior written consent of the publisher, constitutes an infringement of the copyright law.

Published by Valancourt Books, Richmond, Virginia
Publisher & Editor: James D. Jenkins
20th Century Series Editor: Simon Stern, University of Toronto
http://www.valancourtbooks.com

ISBN 978-1-941147-07-8 (*trade paperback*)
Also available as an electronic book.

All Valancourt Books publications are printed on acid free paper that meets all ANSI standards for archival quality paper.

Set in Dante MT 11/13.2
Cover by M. S. Corley

INTRODUCTION*

The Feast of Bacchus (1907) is a threnody both for a world of nature lost to modern progress and for a sacred power absent from fashionable turn-of-the-century culture. But Ernest Henham's novel also finds an unsuspected drama within nature, a hieratic force that can invade civilized life. Although Henham's era was one of arrogant scientific confidence in which Lord Kelvin was quoted as saying that "the grand underlying principles" of physical reality "have been firmly established" and all that remains is "determining values to a greater number of decimal places," Henham preferred another school of scientific investigation: the respected Society for Psychical Research, co-founded by Henry Sedgwick and Frederic Myers at Trinity College, Cambridge, to examine hypnotic, psychic, and spiritualistic occurrences. In case "G 274 'Apparition'" in the Society *Journal* (1903-1904), Henham reported a ghost he encountered in 1899 of a well-known deceased woman while bicycling through Oxford. (This was, of course, the era of the bicycle "revolution" which brought liberation to the congested city-dweller and speed and freedom to the villages.) In *The Feast of Bacchus* Henham incorporated ideas of "influence" and "secondary personality" from W. H. Myers's *Human Personality and its Survival of Bodily Death* (1903), particularly the belief that an alien personality with different behavior traits and mindset can take control of the primary personality, rendering it an involuntary puppet.

All the characters in the novel deny the presence of spectres; that is, ghosts seen causing the current happenings. But set in an isolated landscape of dwindling rural population, such as the West County environs of Dartmoor, *Feast* depicts mythic undercurrents, great static deterministic patterns of consciousness that dictate the individual's happiness or tragic fate. Henham's readers must forget the aim of conventional mimetic fiction to hold a mirror up to the solid fabric of material reality. Here, a mystical

* Publisher's note:—As the Introduction discusses many important details of the plot, readers may wish to return to it after finishing the novel.

sense of powers beyond the physical world centers in the orchard-garden of a country house (a moated grange) called "The Strath." The prolific flowering and blooming of its garden puts interlopers under its influence and is 1907's equivalent to the Bacchic or Dionysian vineyards of ancient Greece. Those ancient vineyards and this present garden both are expressions of the physical earth in its annual changes, nature's eternal flux from which humanity's experience of the sacred emerges. In antiquity Bacchus was a projection of primitive mankind's sense of the seasonal cycle of summer and winter—water, wind, and light as coalesced into an anthropomorphic god of the vine, a power beyond social control. Modernity is thus shadowed by the survival of an unsuspected divine-natural force in which life and death, beauty and horror, eros and anteros ceaselessly pass into each other.

The dramatic arc of Henham's modern social drama of flirtation and infatuation is divided as in Greek plays into five acts, with prefatory scenes, an introduction of characters, key events, and then falling action and the "exodic march." What anchors this dramatic schema is not the idea of the dead hand of the past in contestation with progressive modernism, but of a *living* hand from the past somehow invading an up-to-date twentieth century—specifically the power of Destiny (i.e., of fate or necessity, the ultimate power in ancient life by which even Homer's gods were bound) that had been a key conception of Greek thought. By turns joyous and cruel, but also subtle, impalpable, and indestructible, Destiny or "the custom of ages," was both outside and within human life. Henham's novel, subtitled "A Study in Dramatic Atmosphere," turns the actor and his role on its head. The actors' impersonations of imaginary or mythological figures that ordinarily create an "atmosphere" for modern drama are in this story not assumed to be fictitious. The eight central characters become puppets of mind and flesh, no longer inhabited by their former personalities but by some inescapably greater corporeity, essence, or "thing" that invades their modern personalities. This ancient and primordial force connected to the worship of Bacchus is the apodeictic "doer" or controller of the novel's "atmosphere." As the mundane and dream-like interweave throughout, the line blurs where reality ends and something else—undeniably fantastic—begins.

Henham suggests that ancient religion and art sprang from the symbolism of the wine god Bacchus (originally called Dionysus in ancient Greece), who in the Strath's garden is an ironic epiphany of a post-Christian paganism. The author may have been aware of Walter Pater's "A Study of Dionysus" (1876) and his imaginary portrait, "Denys l'Auxerrois" (1886), about a Bacchic denizen of ancient Greece who finds his way into medieval France, bringing a golden age of natural and artistic bounty as well as tragedy. Like the Greek coffin in "Denys," the Strath is a "dry body," "a tomb," and its cellar "an open grave"; like the lively green wine flask found in the coffin, its garden is enchanted, while near the Strath gipsies set up a pleasure fair in the spirit of the land's renewal. Under the garden's influence Dr. Berry's academic rendering of the ancient Aeolian poets "escaped from the trammels of prose and became itself poetry." His translations of the poets are a recrudescence of the sensuous sun and sea-wind of Lesbos: "When we read their poems, we seem to have the perfumes, colours, sounds, and lights of that luxurious land distilled in verse," observed J. A. Symonds in *Studies of the Greek Poets* (1873-76). Berry's pen at times even guides him in divination or "spirit writing" where his words come from bygone spirits beyond his conscious control. Drawing on recent psychological and anthropological investigations and on classical textual scholarship, Henham structures his romance as a more explicit parallel to ancient myth and drama than did Pater in his story, coordinating apposite dramatic divisions, theatrical images and analogues in order to interpret or to find significance in the contemporary social scene: "Had the double crime which wrenched her heart," inquires Henham of a mother who fancied she had killed child and husband, "been committed in a past age, by hands long vanished into earth?" As in the "shedding of kindred blood" in *Agamemnon* or *Medea*, *Feast*'s use of such ancient drama is a method that W. B. Yeats, James Joyce, and others would pursue later.

The spectre of cosmic influence (for Henham, I suspect, it was no fantasy) develops so inexorably that the reader willingly suspends disbelief in actual possession by alien spirits. Henham pilfers from common details the Strath's extraordinary magical realism that the minor characters, insensitive to the unseen world, apparently find ordinary or merely disagreeable. He is at his uncanny best with his sharply drawn main characters who either resist or are forced to let go of their ingrained notions of themselves to embrace new attitudes and relationships. As they find or lose happiness, their elemental transformations are like the dawning of spring's rebirth or the encroachment of winter's death. But although highlighting the ineffable power of spirits in eternity, Henham does not neglect the portrayal of human foibles or the satirizing of conventional motives, events, and situations. This tapestry of everyday life side by side with the fantastic, in which the ridiculous and the profound underpin humankind's alienation in a world they only think they control, is superb. When, however, Henham supplies heart-broken extracts from a journal, recounts a sermon on paganism (as amusingly eccentric as it would be from an actual pulpit), narrates a lonely child's pathetic love, or gives an extract from a poetic drama on the madness of King George (eighty some years before that subject became a popular hit both as a play and a movie), he may need the indulgence of his hasty reader. More happily, he engages his other readers by novelizing ideas commonly treated either in analytic discourses—such as Plato's dialogues—or, considering Henham's integration of anthropology, religion, and folklore, modernist fiction structured by mythic parallels. Thus apart from its perhaps playful Aeolic iambo-trochaic scansion patterns, the George III excerpt recalls Pentheus and the influence of the god of wine and madness.

At the story's outset, two young beauties, Flora and her friend Maude, who married a stockbroker for his money, languidly discuss love's emotional entailments. Maude is worried she is losing her considerable physical charms to encroaching age. Flora confesses her incapacity for emotional warmth and believes herself capable only at best of a mental relationship with men. In Flora, Henham seems to illustrate—ultimately to reject—those ideas of changing social roles for the New Woman advocated by "advanced" thinkers in the 1890s—as illustrated, for example, in Charlotte Perkins Gilman's "The Yellow Wallpaper" (1892) or Olive Schreiner's "The Buddhist Priest's Wife" (c.1893; 1923). Flora has overheard herself described as an "asymptote"—a curve approached by a line in which the point of contact continually recedes. As an asymptote, Flora's incapacity to "touch" love blocks her daily life from being infused by the irruption of a power or force beyond the self. Henham fictionalizes this psychological or spiritual reality in which the actants undergo a stripping away of social conventions as their selves come under the control of more primal and dangerous instincts from above or below the rational and the civilized. These ancient forces become active in Henham's story via the faces of a criminal and a comedian embodied in the twin theatrical masks of Comedy and Tragedy, points at which nature's cycle of renewal-and-destruction touches the line of eternity for either good or ill. The masks' perilous pagan knowledge and power replaces the short-sighted conventions of the ordinary world. Like the contrasting masks, the villages of Kingsmore (living) and Queensmore (moribund) are linked by the Strath's garden in the hamlet of Thorlund, a contact point ("a spark of vital element") for the disembodied spirits outside common reality.

Dr. Berry, the dreamy local rector, disregards his parishioners as he translates the poetry of the Aeolians, while the "neglected garden" and orchard of the moated grange next door, unlived in for the last century, has an irresistible attraction to him. As a "garden of Eden grown wild," it encourages freedom without rules or restraints, projecting an overpowering and addictive sense of wild gaiety and a lifting of inhibitions more characteristic of ancient pagan Bacchic ritual—though after the Judaeo-Christian Fall perhaps containing a larger capacity for melancholy. Dr. Berry's surname is a satirizing pun on the grape and on Bacchus as the spiritual form of the vine since the grape as a fleshy single-ovary fruit is a berry. His fictional role as grape/berry is to be a reincarnation of the Greek drama's *exarchus*—the leader or poet-character speaking to a chorus grouped around the altar of Bacchus. The novel's uniqueness and complexity emerges particularly in its structural parallel of modern life with great classical drama. Like the later major modernists who sought to reconfigure myths that could make sense of contemporary history, Henham uses classical motifs sometimes as mock epic satire and at other times to suggest the potential for heroism forced upon life. In the creation of theme, character, and structure, *Feast* is perhaps the most allusively mythic narrative before W. B. Yeats, James Joyce, and T. S. Eliot. We don't know what scholarship on Greek drama Henham may have consulted for the *modus operandi* of his novel, but he was classically educated at St. Edwards School, Oxford. Well before Jane Harrison's famous *Prolegomena to the Study of Greek Religion* (1903), K. O. Müller's *History of the Literature of Ancient Greece* (1840) discussed the Bacchic festival with its masks, which seems to be paraphrased in Dr. Berry's sermon (Act 3, Scene 4). Henham's novel also makes reference to J. W. Donaldson's *Theater of the Greeks* (1844) in connection with a word Dr. Berry finds on page 61, ΚΑΣΣΙΤΕΡΟΙΟ (*kassiteros*: "tin" or "pewter" as in *Iliad* 21:592).

The Aeolian Greek writers that Dr. Berry translates include Sappho and Alcman, of whose works only fragments survive. Sappho flourished c.610-c.580 B.C., lived at Mytilene on Lesbos, and supervised a school devoted to the cult of Aphrodite and Eros. Alcman, from the 7th century B.C., was an Aeolian-Doric choral lyric poet from Sparta. Henham's readers who have not read A Level classics may find some names or terms unfamiliar, though the relative import is clear enough. The relevance of antiquity's living presence arises one day when a new owner, Henry Reed, appears from America with plans to fight the Strath's "unholy influence" by turning the grange into a modern agricultural estate that will nullify its uncanny omens. Dr. Berry finds himself expelled from its garden and his thirty years of private dreaming are seemingly at an end. Without citing the actual translation, Henham writes that Berry recites to Reed "his" version of Alcman's "Night." Here the author slyly brings into play William Mure's romanticized nineteenth-century rendering since a few paragraphs later in the text Reed mentions disparagingly Alcman's "busy bees" and "feathered tribes." Mure's images had been: ". . . the busy bee / Forgets her daily toil. . . . / And all the feathered tribes, by gentle sleep subdued, / Roost in the glade, and hang their drooping wings." This over-embellished effort might lead Henham's reader to sympathize with Reed's dismissive attitude were one to suppose Alcman's unheard and sweeter melodies were similarly the silliest of clichés—but more likely the reader is meant to judge Dr. Berry's work as akin to this inapt translation. Whichever, Reed's brutish cultural contempt for the classics is his death sentence.

As the *exarchus*, Berry somnambulistically and "without shame" strangles him as a "man hated by the immortals" who, defiant of "destiny," epitomized progress and modernity without respect for tradition. The police, of course, can identify no suspect.

Charles Conway, a handsome but dissipated young Londoner, now inherits the Strath from his mother's side of the family and falls promptly under its spell to become the manor's reincarnated Bacchus. Meantime, Conway's literary and impoverished friend, Drayton, alarmed at his disappearance from town pawns a pair of Conway's heirloom masks of comedy and tragedy for ticket money to get to the Strath. These antithetical masks of Bacchus were copies of "uncanny" eighteenth-century originals, presumably destroyed but in fact now hidden at the Strath—made, we later learn, from the skins of actual human faces. These original masks are the avenues for the hostile or benign "influence" of spirits upon the visitors. At Conway's invitation, shortly after his own arrival, Flora and her uncle Mr. Price, the rector of Kingsmore parish in the next village over, visit the Strath. Dr. Berry is also there and the spirit of comedy causes all of them to dress up in the eighteenth-century clothing of the last occupants, the Branscombes, who had abandoned the house in mid-feast. We are never explicitly told why the Branscombes' banquet is interrupted (merely, "arrival of ill news") but now this Bacchic feast is resumed without interruption as though it were still the eighteenth century. Continued in a later age, this reenacted past becomes drama in the present. The modern group at the Strath cannot remember what occurs during their masque because it is like a dream in which they have been the *dramatis personae*: "Inside the Strath they were puppets; outside they resumed . . . their normal selves."

Originally, back in the eighteenth century before the house had come into the Reed family by adverse possession, Sir John Hooper, a highwayman, and his abused daughter Winifred, had been the last true owners. Unbeknown to Winifred, Sir John had killed her lover Geoffrey on the highway, and this crime turned Winifred's life into an endless wait stripped of purpose. Conway, finding her hidden diary, immerses himself in her grief for her absent soulmate. In this perpetual longing she ironically does not know she is worshiping an already dead ideal. Her situation here symbolizes the dawning of the modern cultural condition—waiting for a salvation that never comes, a loss of meaning in which the purpose of life becomes the unrelenting reality of tragedy's "goat-song." If Winifred's journal is an unearthed voice of anguish from the past, Maude, who meantime has rented a nearby cottage, successfully flirts with Dr. Berry. Not unlike one of his semi-deponent verbs, dead from the waist down, Berry now develops a hilarious and almost childlike infatuation with her "soul." Emotionally, if not physically, self-transformed, he makes a threesome with Maude's donkeys pulling her cart. Another path of transformation is that of the young woman, Nancy Reed or "Lone Nance," a figure of rural nature's comedic "wine-song," who dances on the mountainside like a mad priestess or votary of Bacchus. A pure pagan unaffected by historic Christianity, her "wild beauty" represents the antique summer harmony of body and spirit. Under the benign comedic influence of the Strath, Nance is installed in Winifred's room, regains her sanity, and Conway functions as if he is Winifred's regained Geoffrey. Because these two resume the roles where their eighteenth-century antitypes left off, Nance can describe the secret burial of Geoffrey, the absent object of Winifred's unrequited passion. But when the group at the Strath descends into Winifred's crypt, they find only the sleep of body and senses with no agency of nature's renewal. Winifred, the grieving earth-goddess without her consort, Geoffrey, god of the summertime vines, only return in their new *personae* as Nance and Conway.

The second and final masque at the Strath climaxes when the original masks of Comedy (worn by Drayton) and Tragedy (Conway) fight for supremacy in the lives of the other six characters until a new arrival, Biron, the great-grandson of an earlier occupant of the Strath who "had entombed the horrible things" in the cellarage, renders the spirits powerless. When those faces are finally thrown in the fire, their influence is at an end and the characters return to reality from their anagogic personalities as human puppets. But they are released back into the social order of what Thomas Aquinas would have called *homo sibi relictus*—"man left to himself," abandoned to his own devices without spiritual knowledge or *gnosis*. The collapse of the tottering Strath, echoing Poe's powerful denouement in "The Fall of the House of Usher," suggests the cloak of Gothic fiction was Henham's profoundest way to prefigure or deploy personal and cultural anxieties of this lost revelation within nature and society. Neither homage nor parody of Poe, the similarities within these two scenes stimulate the reader to think about how Poe's falling house sheds light on emotions of which the outlets are sealed, turned in upon themselves in a strange and delirious way. An observation of T. S. Eliot gives insight into Henham's subject: to be saved "from the ennui of modern life," he said in his essay on Baudelaire, "what we do must be either evil or good; so far as we do evil or good, we are human; and it is better, in a paradoxical way, to do evil than to do nothing; at least we exist" (1930).

The antithetical masks thus enkindle and shape the ignored or forgotten human reality of damnation and salvation, an awakening that Aristotle calls the *anagnorisis*, meaning a "discovery" or "recognition" when a protagonist suddenly gains insight, especially into his/her own self. This denouement for *Feast*'s diverse characters, after they have been reacquainted with the sacred, ends for each variously—happily, absurdly, terrifyingly, insanely. The ceaseless interaction of comedic and tragic is the human condition, a dialectic of Destiny from which Henham's figures at first see no escape—unless like Dr. Berry one simply becomes delusional. He had lived too long in the dream-world of the Strath to evade its spell on his mind. Plato, of course, would not allow his escaped prisoners to remain in that upper world of the "islands of the blest"; they must return to the world of shadows sharing their beatific wisdom for the good of mankind. Dr. Berry knew that "the bridge which separates the inspired from the diseased mind is perilously narrow and frail." So, given his addiction to the visions of his long dreaming sleep, he goes fully insane with the colossally fantastic illusion that he is Zeus, god of the gods. More happily, after the destruction of the masks Conway becomes a decidedly purposeful man. Earlier, Flora had found him too much in the grip of that "awful shadow of some unseen Power" (as Shelley called it); but then when she found him with Lone Nance in the garden, she became murderously jealous. With the help of Nance as an angel with a bent sword, Conway expels Flora from the Strath and although his love for Flora belatedly flames up anew and he abjectly proposes to her, Flora out of the garden is too independent and eccentric. She rejects him, becoming a missionary, then a convert to Buddhism, and finally is never heard of again. Lone Nance, away from the Strath, loses her equable balance and returns to the hills but no longer as socially out of touch. Maude, who imagined she had destroyed her family as in classic Greek tragedy, embraces her Destiny and finds fulfillment and happiness in becoming a dedicated housewife and mother. Indeed, this may be Henham's sly and deliberately conservative analogue in an age of unbelief for a credible miracle akin to Leontes's joyous recovery of wife and daughter in Shakespeare's *Winter's Tale*—a reclamation for Maude less powerful than fantasies from the Renaissance or antiquity but, triggered by her experiences, nevertheless a transformative leap of self-understanding.

The accent of Henham's literary vision rests upon a profound sense that man can neither reach spiritual salvation by his own reason nor attain to happiness by modernity's agenda. Henham is much like Romantic writers who are stranded in an irresolute synthesis between the brightness of a glimpsed vision needed to thrive in the real world and darker misgivings that those epiphanies are fleeting figments. Though the Romantics objectively suspect the visionary may be a delusion, such glimpses are what prop up and nourish daily life. Thus when theorizing they often appear to define their symbols as unproblematic avenues of transcendence promising an escape from painful self-confrontation. Among the nineteenth-century definitions of the Romantic symbol's capacity to enfranchise the self are those of Coleridge—"A symbol is characterized by . . . the translucence of the Eternal through and in the Temporal" (1815)—and of Thomas Carlyle: "In the Symbol . . . the Infinite is made to blend itself with the Finite, to stand visible, and as it were, attainable there" (1836). Blending the eternal with the temporal, the infinite with the finite, the Romantic symbol enables the self to see the external world as no longer foreign but as potentially that in which its own higher identity consists. In that nature has so many facets and faces, at least in some of his fiction written afterwards Henham suggests the possibility of a more widely benign Destiny, perhaps as ordinances of a divine plan within the flux of things and thoughts. In these later works the discords of a *diabolic* state of tragedy (Gk *dyo* two > *dia-* across, apart + *ballein* to throw apart) seem mystically balanced by this *symbolic* capacity to envision order (*syn/m-* together + *ballein* to throw together), the broken made whole in and through transcendental symbols of an ultimate Reality. This derives historically from "the One and the many" of Plato and his Allegory of the Cave. Yet for Henham as for Plato, this beatific vision beyond the world of shadows is always darkened at its source by earthly eyes initially adjusting to or returning from the supernal light. Thus in *Feast* the walled garden and the house with its moat is man's shadowy world of facticity's givenness, here dramatized by the ceaselessly interacting masks of happiness and sorrow in human affairs.

Henham's mordant portraiture of this pre-World War I British society seems so effortlessly paced and witty that a devotee of action-adventure fiction may think little is happening because the author doesn't seek to achieve any conventional balance between situational events and his fiction's speculative implications. But a thoughtful reader will find moments of sublimity and irony as the romance's storyline spins off subtleties that incrementally explore and expose the timeless elements of our irreducible humanity. *Feast*'s bold plot hypothesis offers a spiritualistic alternative to the quiet desperation of conventional rationalism and a gratifying narrative suspense as to how ancient patterns will express themselves in modern social roles. This challenges the premises of literary realism and naturalism that humans exist in one and only one sensory environment, their destiny (lower case) delimited wholly by heredity and objective circumstance without a spiritual dimension. As the central characters gradually capitulate to the overwhelming presence of antiquity's mythological life, the plot displays Henham's awareness of contemporary anthropological thinking (E. B. Tylor, James Frazier, the Cambridge anthropologists) and demonstrates his connection to the dawning of literary modernism. By envisioning Tylor's primitive "survivals" as able to reanimate contemporary society, *Feast* both anticipates the modernist's search for a recovery of lost spiritual vitality and foreshadows T. S. Eliot's exposition of modernism's "manipulating" of myth as "a continuous parallel between contemporaneity and antiquity" (1923). The reader of *Feast* could do worse than recognize in Henham an anticipation of W. B. Yeats's cultural swings of destruction and renewal, of Apollonian and Dionysian phases, and of visionary "automatic writing" dictated by the spirits in eternity. A line from Yeats's *The Cutting of an Agate* (1912) seems especially apposite: "All art is dream, and what the day is done with is dreaming-ripe, and what art has moulded religion accepts, and in the end all is in the wine-cup, all is in the drunken fantasy, and the grapes begin to stammer."

GERALD MONSMAN
University of Arizona

January 8, 2014

The Feast of Bacchus

PRELUDE

When an unnatural idea possesses a woman bitterness flows from her tongue.—*Euripides.*

The silence upon the river was broken by a vivacious voice,—

"My lady, out of the depths of your wisdom define for me the word asymptote."

"Spell it," murmured beauty in laziness, from a heap of pink cushions.

The vivacious voice did so, inaccurately.

"Never heard of the thing," said indolence.

"Then I must search in the dictionary," answered vivacity.

A moment later the punt lurched violently, there was a splash of water under the bank, a nodding of tall rushes; and beauty in pink closed her pretty eyes and tried to forget she was Maude Juxon, wife of a rich stockbroker, and mother of a three year old child whom she had not seen for more than six months.

Some evening clouds were reflected in the smooth river. Swallows darted to and fro, and fish were splashing after ambrosial gnats. The atmosphere was languorous. A single jarring note, necessary to make the surroundings earthly, was supplied by an impatient owl hooting from an elm before its time. Down to the river sloped the garden of widowed Mrs. Neill, burning with the flowers of June. The sleepy occupant of the punt heard far away the snip of the gardener's iron scissors. This, the only, sound of human labour made her more contented with the lot which had fallen to her in an easy ground.

The punt lurched still more violently and Mrs. Juxon was again awakened to the troublesome world. Flora Neill, the widow's only child, and bosom friend of the little lady in pink, settled herself, at the other end of the boat, and balanced a drab volume upon her knees.

"Will you be pleased to refrain from sleep for a few minutes, my lady?" she asked. "Because I have a desire to talk."

"Don't call me my lady," said Mrs. Juxon irritably. "If you do I will go to sleep at once. Have you found out what that thing is?"

"I am just going to," said Flora, who was a tall fair-haired girl, endowed with more than average good looks, but unmistakably "narrow atween the eyen," and possessing a chin which her bluff old uncle, the vicar of Kingsmore, had described as a walnut-cracker. "Before I begin you may look into this letter which has just come. And, Maude, I found mother reading an incoherent epistle from uncle. It appears I am expected to make my annual appearance at Kingsmore, the week after next, to criticise pigs and bring the scent of the footlights over the hay for the benefit of my reverend relative who is about as much at home in London as you or I would be in Timbuctoo. Here! catch your letter." Flora tossed the missive across the punt, and her indolent friend was sufficiently curious to lift her head and glance at the handwriting.

"Only from Herbert," she sighed disappointedly. "What a ridiculous thing it is to have a husband who writes to you every day! I know exactly what he says," she droned, pulling the envelope open.

"When are you coming home? I find the evenings very dull without you. Couldn't you have Peggy at home now? I don't like the idea of her being farmed out. She isn't farmed out," cried Mrs. Juxon indignantly. "What a nasty objectionable phrase to use! Peggy is with a very good nurse, who will bring her up much better than I ever should. What is the good of being a rich woman if you are to be bothered with your baby? And as for going home—well, I'm quite happy here."

"You would rush into matrimony and motherhood, my child," said the fair-haired girl, who was not more than four years Maude's junior. I warned you, and now—"

"I'm driving my husband to drink, prophetess," laughed the pink lady.

"Or to some other woman."

Mrs. Juxon tore the letter into fragments which she snowed daintily over the water with a tiny white hand.

"I couldn't have worked for my living," she said. "And nice men are poor. What's that you are reading?"

"An asymptote," read Flora, "is a line which approaches nearer and nearer to a given curve, but does not meet it within a finite distance. It is an astronomical phrase. Now do you know what an asymptote is, Maude?"

"It is a line," recited the pink lady, in her frivolous way, "which—which does something or other to a curve."

"Don't worry that little head," said the maiden. "I won't ask you to repeat the definition. I wanted to see if you would be personal. My dear, I have been called an asymptote, and no longer ago than yesterday."

"I can't think out things," said Maude pettishly. "It makes my head ache. Who ever called you that thing? I can't pronounce it."

"I overheard the compliment," Flora answered. "So I went up to the culprit, a wicked old clergyman who dabbles in astronomy, and demanded an explanation. He laughed, and said, 'It is a mathematical way of calling a lady a flirt.'"

"Do explain," said a voice which suggested slumber.

"I will, if you listen," said Flora. "Are you awake, Maude?"

"I will be, if it is not going to be too hard," said the pink lady.

"It is quite easy," said Flora. Then she began to read,—

"The asymptote is more than a mere scientific expression. It is a term which may be applied to many of Eve's daughters. The human asymptote has her being amongst us both in country and in town. The observer is made to feel her presence, as she may be seen approaching nearer and nearer the man who is her given curve for the time being, he prepared to respond to the influence, and she equally determined never to meet him until they reach infinity together. She is no beautiful figure, despite all her surface charms. Her blood never responds to the natural call of sex. But admiration is to her as the breath of life, and she will beguile as wantonly as any of the Sirens of old. Equipped with a ready brain, which has never been dulled by the mastery of love, her power of seduction is complete. She throws down a cold heart and a scheming brain to challenge a true nature and real affection. But so soon as the human curve leaps out of hyperbola to meet his asymptote repulsion assuredly must follow.

"Our asymptote may be graceless, but she is never a fool. She knows indeed all that a girl can know. She has opened all the books of dangerous knowledge and loves to indulge in unrestrained speech. She will discuss the tenderest relations flippantly, because they are nothing to her. She will converse upon matrimonial matters with the carelessness of the child blowing soap bubbles. She passes through life lonely, though to an outsider she may appear the centre of a crowd. She is happy enough to all outward seeming, and finds a vast deal to interest her. She is not often dangerous, because when all is said she remains little more than a rattle, and if she marries at all it is late in life, and then not because she has met her curve—for that is scientifically impossible—but rather because she finds she must have a man of her own to plague. When thus settled she may still, if the fates be kind, happen upon some foolish youth ready to play the curve to her asymptote. One does not pity her; but a sigh may well be spared for her husband."

Flora gazed thoughtfully along the river, her mouth determined, and a strong light in her eyes. Her companion, who was by this time wide awake, had no imagination; but she could not help feeling that behind that face there was a will which might carry its owner rather too far.

"Are you really like that?" Maude demanded, nodding in the direction of the book of knowledge.

Flora nodded seriously.

"Then I think you are a wicked person," said Mrs. Juxon virtuously.

"My dear little Maude! Do you really believe what I have just read?" laughed the fair-haired girl. "It is rubbish. It's a fairy-tale written, as a warning for very young men, by some snuffy old philosopher who never found a woman with whom he could agree. You needn't stare at me with those big blue baby eyes. I am a far better girl than you will ever be. I don't meet my curves, but you have become hopelessly entangled in yours."

"I am not an—I can't pronounce it," protested the pink lady. "It's nonsense to rail against matrimony. A girl without money must either earn her own living, which is altogether disgusting and impossible, or she must marry."

"Suppose she shrinks from the idea, as you would from a cold bath on a winter's morning?"

"Flora, a girl must marry if she wants comfort and liberty. Of course it's silly to marry for love. That doesn't last long after marriage anyhow. You may say what you like, but matrimony will always be a girl's one aim in life, besides it is nice and proper. Really," little Mrs. Juxon concluded, "I am quite clever this evening."

"Your wisdom has not supplied you with an answer to my question," Flora went on. "It's true I shrink from the thought of matrimony, but I won't be called an incomplete woman, though I have my one little antipathy. I cannot touch or smell a rose. But that's a matter of temperament. In other things I am as complete as you are. I love admiration, but what girl does not? Perhaps my blood is a little bit cold, but then men and women no longer meet only on the ground of sex. Thank Heaven for that. I really think that in time I might love—in a spiritual sense."

"Men don't appreciate that kind of love," said Mrs. Juxon decisively.

"Because they have never been properly educated. We shall train them to higher things in time. Why, Maude, the spiritual union is the perfect state. We are not animals, to increase and multiply, at this stage of the world's history. We are nervous sympathetic beings, and love properly developed should be a reaching out of the soul for larger and wider sympathies. And a man will hold and squeeze a girl, and call her idiotic names, if she will let him. Call that spiritual love! The state of the man and woman in the garden was the sympathy I crave for."

"And they fell from it at once," cried the other joyously.

"Because they were ignorant. The world is older now and we are wiser. We shall advance to platonic marriage. Matrimony, as it exists to-day, deadens the sympathies. The state of the soul which demands a perfect union cannot under present circumstances be attained. In your case, my dear, nature, after attaining her end, has snatched away the veil which hid the coarse reality, and you know you don't love your husband. As a matter of fact you never did love him."

"Herbert has always been good to me," argued the pink lady. "And he is so well off that I should have been very silly if I had refused him. Mother assured me love would come after marriage. It didn't, but that is not my fault. I am quite a model wife; I don't quarrel with my husband, I let him kiss me sometimes, and I never interfere with his business. When he gives a dinner he shows me off with ridiculous pride. And when he is unreasonable I come away and visit my friends, while he writes every day for me to go back. You see it is not a bad marriage."

"What has the soul got to do with it?" demanded Flora.

"Nothing," Mrs. Juxon laughed lazily. "This little body is quite enough for me. I don't worry about souls or sympathies."

"The sympathies will not be ignored," the fair-haired girl threatened. "If you are married without love some state of the soul will assert itself. That is always the punishment for a marriage of convenience."

"I won't sit here and be persecuted," said Mrs. Juxon with some spirit. But, while she rebelled, her face became sad and her eyes full of thought; because she could not help recalling the memory of one in particular with whom she had once experienced, as she thought, that state of the soul, and in whose arms she had cried to say farewell. "Why have you such a rooted objection to matrimony?" she went on quickly.

"Because it is abominable and tyrannic," said Flora. "Because the wretched girl becomes completely absorbed by her husband, if she gives herself up to him entirely as she is supposed to do. She has not even her identity left. She is compelled to think as the inferior half of somebody else's mind. She actually grows to resemble her husband in face and manner. The man takes everything from her, not only her name and her individuality, but her health and her beauty—"

"Flora, I won't listen. You are horrid and coarse. You'll be saying it is wicked to have children next."

"It is sometimes," the out-spoken young woman retorted. "You remember what a beauty Gertrude Norton was, and how everyone used to rave over her?"

"Yes," admitted the stockbroker's wife.

"She has been married only three years, but who would rave

over her now? Nobody would call her even nice-looking. Only a few seasons ago she won a tennis championship, or something equally good, and she would think nothing of cycling fifty miles or more in one day. Now she is the mother of twins, and a confirmed invalid. She is a model wife, I daresay, and a perfect pattern of motherhood, but her dancing days and her tennis playing are over. And she is not twenty-five."

"Her husband is very fond of her," said Mrs. Juxon pathetically.

"I know a man who says he is very fond of me," replied the fair-haired girl. "But I do not intend to spoil my life while I retain my senses."

"He wouldn't be fond of you if he could hear you now. I declare," shivered the little lady, "I'm getting quite afraid of you. I wonder what you really think of me. Am I falling off at all, Flora?"

"Horribly," said the girl, rising and swaying the punt. "It is nearly dinner time and it is getting chilly. Let us go in."

"I am beginning to feel not only cold but old," said the pink lady, as she gathered in her skirts to step ashore. "But I cannot be ugly. Whatever may happen I cannot be ugly. It is heavenly to feel upon coming into a drawing-room that men cannot take their eyes off you. What is the secret of preserving beauty, Flora?"

"You must be spiritual," said Miss Neill.

"I have Peggy," murmured Mrs. Juxon, as she stepped upon the bank with her studied daintiness of motion. "I really have done my duty as a wife and a mother."

"Do you hear the owl?" exclaimed Flora, as they walked away from the lazy river.

"Yes, the beast!" replied Maude spitefully. "I am always superstitious when I hear owls!"

OVERTURE

Inasmuch as Nature tells us there are Gods, and we know, by reason, what they must be like, so, with the consent of all rational beings, we believe souls to endure everlastingly; where, however, these spirits exist, and what they are like, we must discover by investigation.—*Cicero*.

The reverend Doctor Berry concluded to his satisfaction the single paragraph which was the result of a morning's thought, wiped his pen, fingered the sheet of manuscript tenderly, and placed it carefully in a drawer of his desk, then rose and walked across to the open window.

The sun was setting upon beech woods, and a deep haze flecked with dust and white butterflies shimmered across a strip of garden, bright with poppies and cornflowers, which divided the rectory from the churchyard; the main portion of the garden stretched away behind the house, down a slope which ended in an orchard where a stream ran bounding the glebe in that direction. A crumbling wall, completely covered with ivy, marked the line where the consecrated ground ended; on the rectory side grew docks and nettles and red sorrels among the altar-tombs and mossy slabs, with here and there a black yew striking its roots deeply into the resting places of the dead. An unfrequented road passed beside the church, to become a mere cart-track upon the downs, where the white-thorn was being shed like snow and the shadows of the beech wood were lengthening fast.

"It is a glorious evening," the rector whispered, "I will go and walk in the garden of the Strath."

Taking a great key from an oak bracket he walked out of his study, placed a straw hat upon his silvered hair, and stepped into the glories of the failing day.

The ecclesiastical parish of Thorlund, scarcely worthy of being dignified by the title of hamlet, consisted of a wooded valley watered by a stream. Far down and buried amid elms were tiny church and parsonage; and hard by rose the inexplicable house, its garden surrounded by a time-worn wall, known to all as the

Strath. A few cottages upon the Kingsmore road were passing into an advanced stage of decay. A few in a more habitable state were dotted singly, or in pairs, beside the grass by-paths or upon the lower ridges of the downs. The entire parish was moribund. Nothing flourished except the trees and strong-scented wayside weeds. No dignitary of the church had entered the valley for hard upon a century. A deadening influence prevailed over the church, pastor, and people. There were not thirty adults in the parish all told, and the nearest school was at Kingsmore four miles distant across the downs. A few peasant farmers clung to the chalky slopes because they lacked the means to go. The labourers were agricultural machines; the wives went out to work afield beside their husbands; and by day the sun smote across an altogether deserted prospect, where a lone cat slept on the dusty green, and a caged blackbird listened sadly and silently to its free brethren singing in the weird garden of the Strath.

Thorlund had in common with the world the sun which warmed it, the moon which ruled its night, the rain which coursed in milky rivulets down its stony roads, and the storm which broke its beeches and its elms—but nothing more. It was a peaceful, but not a happy valley. Its sleep was not a healthy one. Once, no doubt, Thorlund had lived, and in a sense flourished, then death came, but a spark of vital element had crept back to the body, diffusing itself throughout its entire system, and lending to it a semblance of life. It was from the long abandoned house known as the Strath that this vital and dramatic element proceeded. Dr. Berry served as the intermediary between the incomprehensible spirit of the Strath and those human beings who had their habitations near. He had remained untouched by the noise and trouble of the world. His life had moved smoothly from the cradle, and promised so to continue down to the grave. He had always been happier apart from others, living his own life which consisted in striving to materialize rather than dispel that atmosphere of mysticism which gathers around a scholar's solitary existence. At Oxford he had worked for classical honours, not for the sake of reputation, but for the pure love of knowledge; and when at the age of twenty-five he had been offered the living of Thorlund, which nobody else could be induced to accept, he had merely asked, "What is the population of the parish?" The answer, "Fifty at the last census," which had frightened away every one else, satisfied him. The stipend of forty-five pounds per annum was not a serious consideration, as he possessed means of his own. After passing through the divinity school with his customary display of polished scholarship, he accepted the 'benefice'; and thirty years had passed him there, as so many uneventful weeks, while he built up slowly the work which it was his intention to bequeath to posterity as a justification for his existence, an analysis of the lyrical poetry of the Aeolians.

A drowsy rustling of foliage was blown with the chalk dust across the unused road to the parish church, as the scholar made his way through the churchyard towards an old oak door set into the grey wall, nearly twenty feet in height, with a coping of tiles the majority of which time and storm had worked awry. Pushing the key into the antique lock he opened the door communicating with the churchyard, and immediately found himself standing in the shadows of the old garden of the Strath.

Neither building nor grounds had been touched by the hand of man for more than a century. The romantic house, which bore the date 1670 above the arms of an extinct family graven upon a stone let into the masonry above the hall door, was of no great size; high rather than wide, and completely enveloped in ivy and other creepers from cellars to chimney stacks. The garden and orchard comprised six acres, bound by that great wall which had in no place fallen completely out of repair. The grass waved like corn along what had once been the drive, and the iron gates leading from the Kingsmore road were red and glued together with rust. Through these gates children often peered to catch glimpses of the sad house through the tangled growths; to watch the birds and insects sporting as in another and a stranger and more restless world. No one ever entered there except the rector. That wall could not be climbed. The old people of the hamlet would stare through the forbidding gates, and observe to each other that the flowers were extraordinary that season in the Strath—there were blooms in those jungles such as they had never seen elsewhere—or that the odour of the garden was wonderful, or that the Strath was noisy; and when the latter statement was in their mouths they realised dimly they were hinting at what they could not understand.

Yet the place had no evil reputation; the reverse rather. Mothers would quiet fractious children by promising that they should enter the mysterious garden some day, or threaten that if they were not good they could never hope to go to the Strath when they died. No wild stories dealing with phantasms or spirit lights were passed upon the village green. Not a tongue had ever been so bold as to suggest that the spiritual world had acquired a perpetual tenancy of the wild old place. The Strath had simply remained unentered and unused for over a century. The flowers and weeds fought together, the trees increased, the bushes spread, fruit formed, ripened, and dropped to rot year after year. And yet there was something about the place which made it unlike other deserted houses; something which did not appear to have its origin in the weedy circlet of water—for the Strath was a moated grange—nor in the jungle-like garden, nor in the damp and darkened house itself; but which had its being in the air, and in the clouds above, and in the wind around.

"No, Sir," said Simcox the sexton, when Dr. Berry questioned him many years ago. "There ain't nothing what you might call gruesome about the old place that I've heard tell on. But it seems to me, Sir, that sometimes when the sun is bright 'tis wonderful happy in there, and when the wind is noisy 'tis awful solemn-like. I've been cutting that nettle patch along churchyard wall in summer, and had to stop and laugh out loud, and all for nought, Sir. And I've been sweeping leaves in autumn under the wall, and felt that miserable I could almost have cut my throat, or maybe somebody else's throat, begging your reverence's pardon for saying it."

The young rector nodded his head gravely, and because he had a strong desire to obtain entrance into the mysterious garden, instituted a search for its owner. He succeeded in part. A firm of land agents in the neighbouring town supplied him with the address of a London lawyer; and when next in the metropolis Mr. Berry, as he then was, found his way into a stuffy office hard by Goldsmith's memorial, where he was received by an old fashioned attorney, who replied in the affirmative when the rector of Thorlund asked whether he represented the owner of the Strath. As a result of that interview the rector was granted permission to enter the garden by the gate from the churchyard, on the condition that he would not lend the key, which was given him for that purpose, to others. He also received the information that the owner was abroad, and that the house was neither to be sold nor let.

"I will write to the owner, informing him that I have given you permission to use the garden," the lawyer had said, as he accompanied his visitor to the door, "and if he objects you shall hear from me."

Years went by, but the lawyer never wrote; and Dr. Berry walked in the garden every day, until the glamour of the place made him its slave; and after walking there, as along the unknown ways of another world, his work on Aeolian poetry escaped from the trammels of prose and became itself poetry, pierced through and through by the strange lights of romance; and he became still more a recluse; and the present world went away from him and was shrouded in the mists of unreality.

On many a bright day, when nature was revealed at her best, the poet would laugh and applaud, and even dance grotesquely along the paths of the Strath, his feet in time to a music which was in his brain but not in his ears. Was this mere animal enjoyment of life, or was it influence? Decidedly the latter. The odour of flowers and the giddy dance of insects were also controlled by that vital and dramatic element, to which the scholar could only give the name of comedy, a happiness tinged slightly with the knowledge of mortality. And when the day was sad with wind, the opposing note of tragedy was struck throughout the garden; and that fatality which dominated the Attic drama, the struggle of terrible human passions in the wind and rain, the falling of life before unpitying destiny, controlled his sensitive mind. Dr. Berry had suffered when the elements fought above his head, blending with the influence, which bade him seek out the man hated by the immortals and slay him without shame. Then was the knowledge swept upon the poet that he was an intermediary between seen and unseen, and thus an agent for the effectual working out of the tragedy of justice.

The influence at work within the high wall which fastened about the Strath was therefore twofold, that of the sun, and that of the storm; the former a comedy, elevating if bizarre, tempered by a sentiment suggesting the presence of melancholy beneath the motley; the latter a tragedy, wild and extravagant as the passions of a Lear, yet redeemed from absolute despair by the thread of hope chased through the scheme. Comedy was in the air that evening, a riotous happiness which inebriated like wine. Singing noisily, although unconscious of it, Dr. Berry gambolled towards the house, under the rose bowers, along the track which his own feet had worn into the semblance of a path, beside the acacias with their grape-like bunches of bloom bursting into pink or white. He passed below the sun-dial, which rose altar-like above a mass of tottering masonry coloured with flowers, through the herb garden, and on until the jasmine and the honeysuckle wafted their fragrance at him from the worm-eaten porch. A blackbird flew past screaming. He looked up, annoyed at the interruption, and straightway shivered, because he saw the figure of a man standing among the high grass near the front of the house. Indignation possessed the dreamer's mind when he beheld a material presence in his garden. His life had become so intimately connected with that of the Strath that he was unable to think of the garden as another man's property. So, he reflected, the iron gates had been forced apart at last, and a master was visiting the bewildered place after the silence of a hundred years—for the thinker was convinced that the elderly man, standing in the ripening grass, was the owner—and now the garden was to be his no longer, and his dreams were to be brought to an end. The stranger lifted his hat and bowed grotesquely. The rector returned this compliment, after a more dignified manner, and they approached, making old-fashioned salutes at every step.

"The learned and distinguished Doctor Berry?" said the stranger, holding out his hand, and laughing with what beyond the wall might have appeared to be unreasonable mirth.

The scholar laughed also as he replied, shaking the hand offered him in conscious tune to the persistent music in his brain.

"My lawyer has told me about you. I am Henry Reed, the owner and master of the Strath. It pleases me that you should have used my garden. I trust that the inspiration of the place has benefited you."

It was the first occasion on which Dr. Berry had spoken to a fellow-being in the garden. He could not rid himself of the fantastic idea that he and the man before him were characters of a comedy playing the parts which had been assigned to them.

"I assure you I have found this place a veritable wonder-world," he replied. "It has made another man of me—"

"The Strath has made you a dreamer," broke in the owner sharply. "Men who dream perform nothing. What an overpowering atmosphere is here!" he went on, removing his hat and laughing again. "I can scarcely breathe. Only a few minutes ago I entered upon this property of mine, a tired and solemn man, and now I am as merry as a clown. Do the bees always buzz so musically? Are the flowers always sending forth this fragrance? Ah, you laugh at me."

"I laughed in spite of myself," the rector answered. "No, the music is not always soft, as it is this evening. When the wind changes, and the sky becomes dark, and the clouds fall low, you shall perceive a difference."

"The place is haunted," the owner shouted.

"Not so," said the rector happily. "There is nothing here which could terrify a child. Like us the Strath has its moods. Sometimes it is happy, and often it is sorrowful. It must either laugh or groan. And now you will change it all," he went on bitterly. "You will restore the house, dig up the garden, prune the orchard, mow the lawns, gravel the paths, and lay the Strath out like a dead body."

Again the owner laughed. "Let me set your mind at ease," he cried, turning himself as though he would address the house. "Even if I desired to destroy this picture I could not, for I am a poor man, and the expense of restoration is beyond my means. I have come to live here, but I beg you to use my garden as you have done in the past. And now shall we enter the house?"

Very gladly the rector accepted the invitation. He had often pushed aside the creepers, to stare at the windows, heavily obscured with dirt and blinded by close-fastened shutters, longing to visit the rooms which were in darkness beyond. He passed with the owner of the Strath towards the bridge which spanned the black water; and as they walked they went on laughing.

"Will the bridge bear us?" questioned the master, testing the damp green wood with a nervous foot.

"Let me cross first to convince you," said the scholar.

Reed's mood changed when they stood beside the door; and

it was with signs of fear he produced a key, a feather, and a small bottle of oil. "The light is fading rapidly," he muttered as he lubricated the lock. "And I have brought no lamp."

"There may be candles inside the house," the rector murmured, although he had no good reason for saying so.

The bolt crawled back with a scream, and wood dust rained upon their heads as the door creaked open. They passed side by side into the dampness of the hall, while the master muttered, "This house has not been entered for a hundred years."

"So it is furnished, as I have seen it in my dreams," the rector murmured.

Their feet sank into the dust, which in places had drifted to a depth of several inches. Stairs, carpets, and pictures were coated and muffled; a mildewed growth shewed in patches on the walls; a stunted nightshade struggled around a quaint eight-legged table, its roots sucking nutriment from the damp rottenness of the wood. A circle of fungi occupied the centre of the hall, and some bats flickered up and down the stairway.

"My inheritance," said Reed, shivering as he ploughed his fingers through the silky dust.

"The garden is your inheritance," replied his companion. "That is the soul of the Strath. This is the dry body."

Walking as he spoke to a door, before which a moth-eaten curtain hung in shreds, he sought for the handle and pushed inward. The door gave unwillingly, pressing the dust into a high ridge, and the rector groped forward holding a lighted match above his head. Their eyes encountered no repulsive sight; and yet they hesitated before making an entry, because the past was brought before them, and it is the custom of men to waver when they open a tomb.

They looked into a dining-room and saw a long table, decked out with plate and glass, with what had been flowers and fruit, and decanters caked with wine; around the table chairs were grouped, or pushed aside, as their former occupants had left them. They beheld the concluding course of a dinner one hundred years old, as the long dead diners had left it, interrupted and startled by the arrival of ill news.

"I will go in and open the shutters," said the rector firmly.

"You hear nothing?" muttered the owner. "Nothing?"

"There is nothing to hear, except the chirping of the birds."

"I thought I heard footsteps, and a woman's voice."

"No," said the scholar. "There will be no tragedy while this weather lasts." He went on hurriedly, feeling Reed's eyes upon him, "Your imagination is playing with you. You think you hear voices of the men and women who have dined. They are not here. Their bodies are as the dust which lies upon their table and their chairs."

Lighting another match he passed in, and leaning over the table dug out the wicks of the candles and lighted one after another, until he had converted each of the seven-branched candlesticks into a row of stars. Then he turned and beheld Reed at his side, staring up and down, sweeping the cloth with his great beard.

"You are my guest," he laughed with a hollow note. "In the face of your knowledge of this place I had almost forgotten that I am master here. Will you sit down at my table and taste my old wine?"

"Let us have air," said the rector.

Unfastening the shutters he drew them back, and immediately a tawny glow mingled with the candle-light. The windows were encrusted with dirt, and black ivy stems were matted against the glass. The iron window catch was rotten and snapped when the rector tried to force it back. He strained at the casement, but the hinge remained immovable.

Reed stood beside the table, fingering one article after another. That heap of dust had been once a flower, that was an orange shrivelled to the size of a walnut; here was a snuff-box standing open, there a half-smoked pipe leaning against a box which still contained bon-bons. Near him a glass had been overturned in the days when it was the custom of men to drink hard, and when he cleared away the dust with the flat of his hand he could distinguish the stain of wine upon the yellow cloth. He picked up a lady's glove, black and full of holes, and bringing it to his face detected the faint fragrance of her who had dropped it. Another pile of dust resolved itself into a powder puff, and yet another became a scrap of paper. These had presumably been dropped together. Reed unfolded the paper, shook it, and holding it near the candles read as much as he could decipher aloud:—

"I will wait near the sun-dial until you come. Do not wear a mask. Dear, do not tempt fate by even thinking of a mask here . . . to father, if there be a storm this night . . . Thomas flogging a horse, and I felt no pity . . . This atmosphere is . . . to rejoin my ship . . . Nelson against the French. I shall not be at dinner . . . later on."

"What does it mean?" cried the rector, as he stumbled towards the table.

"I cannot trace the signature," muttered Reed. "It means, doctor," he went on, "that the Strath is controlled by some unholy influence which has kept it empty all these years."

"No," cried Dr. Berry fervently. "That is not true. Consider how safe, and happy we are. Neither you nor I suffer the slightest sense of fear. Hardly a day has passed and not found me in the garden during these past thirty years, and I am a wiser man than when I came. It is true I have felt at times the influence which that dead hand suggests. But it has done me no harm."

"It has aged and saddened you," said Reed curtly. "It has caused you to forget how a man should live."

"The Strath has been my happiness, my pleasure, as well as my inspiration," said the scholar, clutching the back of a chair, and scarcely noticing when it broke away in his hands. "You will admit as much when you read my translations and restorations of Sappho. No unholy influence could have prompted me to that work. Knowledge has come to me while walking through the garden, amid the fragrance of the flowers, the song of the insects, the music in the air—"

The master of the Strath interrupted with a shout of discovery. Following the guidance of his hand the rector saw a dark face grinning at them from the opposite wall, over the glow of candles and the tawny light from the half sealed window, through the grime that a hundred years had placed upon it.

Dr. Berry hurried forward, mounted a chair, and removed from the wall what proved to be merely a grotesque ornament, a brown mask, with the leering mouth, great nose, grinning eye-sockets, and arched brows of comedy. The mask was made of wood, stained a deep brown, and inside cut upon the surface appeared the words, "Copied at Nuremberg by Jos. Falk."

An impulse, which could not be controlled, seized both men, and they laughed until the old house rang.

ACT I

Scene I.—SATIRIC

Bah! I do hate bainting and boetry.—*King George II*.

The influence changed, as was usual at the approach of darkness. The power compelling them forth became irresistible. It was a new sensation for the scholar, but his sensitive nature suggested that the resentful force was directed against his companion, and not against himself. He extinguished the candles and walked lingeringly to the hall door, following Reed who had escaped into the twilight of the garden, having no desire to explore further that night. Nor had the owner any intention then of sleeping in the house. He had indeed when proposing it to himself forgotten that every room would be buried deep in dirt. When the scholar joined him with a hospitable invitation to the rectory he accepted gladly. They passed together towards the iron gates.

A few country folk had assembled upon the road, to discuss that great event the opening of the gates of the Strath. One man stood leaning upon an iron bar, which he had used at Reed's request to force those gates apart. Their voices ceased when the rector was seen wading through the grass, and gnarled hands went up to pull gravely at the brims of dilapidated and picturesque headgear.

After having engaged two men for the next day, to wrench open doors and windows, to cut away the creepers, and to clear the interior from its accumulated dirt, Reed secured the chain, locked the padlock with his own hands, and giving a good night to the rustics turned away. For a hundred yards not a word was spoken, then Reed pulled himself upright, and brushed the dust from his heavy beard.

"It's all nonsense," he said roughly, and his companion shrank at the change in the stranger's voice and manner. "It's sheer folly to suppose that the Strath is different from any other old place, apart, of course, from the fact that it has not been inhabited within the recollection of living man. I'm just thinking I may have made a fool of myself when we were in that garden, Professor. I don't know what possessed me. I'm a practical man, level-headed as the best of 'em ordinarily, but in there I felt—well, I'm not much of a talker, and hang me if I can explain it, but I felt as if I had taken a little more drink than I could manage. I might have been playing a part. Ah, that's it! I might have been an actor, spouting words that some other fellow had written down for me."

"You need not explain," said the rector gently. "I can enter into your feelings."

"Well, I'm going to change all that," went on Reed. "I'll clean the place out from cellar to attic, sell off the old stuff, get in some decent furniture, tear down the creepers, cut the garden up, sell the hay for what it is worth, and get the place into as good shape as I can afford. I mean to start a small poultry farm and make a bit that way. I come from America, Professor, and I'm not afraid of work. Lucky I'm not, for I reckon it will take all my time to get that garden into anything like order this summer."

The rector shuddered. The stranger had changed indeed now that the influence of the Strath had loosened its hold upon him.

"You said you would not alter the place," he reminded him quietly.

"Did I say so?" Reed answered with a hoarse laugh. "Well, I must have been crazy. I'm not in a position to spend money, but I'll soon show you what one pair of hands can do. Before autumn you won't recognise the rotten old property. I shall start with the house to-morrow, and when that is clean I'll root up the bushes, drain the moat, and go for in fruit and poultry."

"The Strath will not let you," the rector cried.

"What's that?" said Reed.

"You are not strong enough to fight the place," replied the rector boldly.

Reed regarded his companion with open-mouthed astonishment, and presently his beard began to wag with laughter. "'Scuse me, Professor," he said. "Hope you haven't got the idea into your head that it is not legal for a man to make his own house habitable? I tell you what it is," he went on in his blunt fashion. "You have lived out of the world too long, and have roamed around that old wilderness of mine until you have picked up some queer notions. Wait until I show you how to breed turkeys."

Then Dr. Berry realised that he hated this little bearded man who had come to destroy his happiness. He wished with all his heart he had met him in the first instance outside the Strath and there discovered his true character. Had that happened he would assuredly never have invited him to the rectory. Gazing ahead at the wooden spire of his little church he said quickly:

"There is the rectory. You see I am a very near neighbour. I have always been accustomed to enter your garden by the churchyard, through that gate which you see yonder in the wall."

Reed shrugged his shoulders, and, muttering into his beard, followed his host into the cool house.

A very plain supper was the evening meal at Thorlund rectory; and afterwards the poet sat in his garden to dream upon matters which were too great for him. That evening he brought two chairs upon the lawn. When they were seated Reed plunged at once into business and asked the rector if he could recommend a suitable housekeeper and a man with some knowledge of poultry. "Poultry and poetry sound a bit alike, eh, Professor?" he said jocosely. "But there's a heap more money in my line than in yours."

The rector shrank from the jest as from a blow. He answered the questions of his thick-skinned guest as fully as he could. Then, prompted by curiosity, he asked Reed how long the Strath had been in his family, and why it had remained desolate for so long.

The other pulled at his pipe with a frown, as though resenting the other's natural desire for information. At last he put up his hand, stroked his beard, expectorated—again Dr. Berry shrank from him—and said:

"I don't know much about yonder place. The Strath was owned in the first place by a family called Hooper. You can see their arms carved upon a stone over the entrance. They held the property until the middle of the eighteenth century. The owner was then a baronet who lived there alone. He was a pretty bad lot, I've been told, and was hanged at last for murdering his servant."

"There was another and more serious charge against him, according to the opinion of a time when gentlemen were permitted to use their servants like dogs," the rector interposed. "Sir John was certainly hanged, but it was for highway robbery. Local tradition declares that the rope which was used for his execution is now used for ringing the single bell of Thorlund church. If this statement were to be proved I should certainly have the rope removed. But I do not consider that it has been proved."

"You know more about the Strath than I do. Perhaps you can tell me how it came by its queer-sounding name?" said Reed; and he raised his pipe to his mouth as a hint that the rector might proceed.

"About the name there is nothing remarkable," came the answer. "Strath is a gaelic word signifying a broad valley. For a time, I have no doubt, the whole of this neighbourhood was known as the Strath; though glen, also a gaelic word and meaning a narrow valley, would have been more accurate nomenclature, as you may see for yourself by ascending one of the hills and looking down. There is an ancient, although undated, document among the parish records which alludes to the village of Strath hard by King's Moor. The name of Thorlund, which means the sacred grove of Thor or the Thunder God, was at some later date attached to the hamlet, the name of Strath being retained by the manor house alone. But to return to the Hoopers. According to oral tradition, which I have generally found reliable, Sir John became a notorious highwayman after his wife's death. It is said he had one child, a daughter who lived with him at the Strath, but whose name is not mentioned in the register of deaths. It is also said that he treated her most cruelly. Indeed, if report concerning him be true, Sir John was altogether bad, a robber and a drunkard in his country life, and when in town a habitual frequenter of the gaming houses which at that time were plentiful in the neighbourhood of St. James's. Probably his midnight escapades upon the road were instituted to obtain money for the payment of debts thus contracted. One night Sir John was tracked to his house after a more daring venture than usual; his reeking mare was found in the stable; his body servant, one Thomas Reed, was discovered in the saloon mortally wounded, the baronet believing, it is supposed, that the man had informed upon him. The old fox had fled, having escaped by crawling out of an attic window and letting himself down the side of the house by means of the creepers, but he was found that same night hiding in a hollow tree. In due course he was hanged. What happened to the daughter I have never been able to discover."

"I suppose you want to know how we came into the property. You will have guessed I am a descendant of the murdered servant," said Reed. "Well, I'll tell you. The Strath doesn't legally belong to me. It is, or it was, Crown property. But as by some oversight, the Crown never seized it, the Reeds did. They were on the spot, you see, and when they saw the place was abandoned they thought they would have compensation for Thomas's murder, and so they stepped in. They were never turned out, and no questions were asked. But the Reeds were only village folk, and couldn't afford to occupy the place. So they let it to a man named Biron who had spent most of his life in Germany. When he gave it up the Strath was taken by a family called Branscombe who for some reason left suddenly. It would be the last dinner party of the Branscombes that is still set out in that dining-room. Since their time not a soul—" he paused, then added with a grin, "I should say not a body, has entered the place until this evening."

"But what have the Reeds been doing all these years?" asked the rector.

"They emigrated. My grandfather took no interest in the place. My father sent over enough money every year to satisfy the local rates, always hoping he would make enough to enable him to retire and come back and play the gentleman. The old man died twelve years ago at the age of eighty, and I went on with the business until it was ruined by a trust. Then I realised, and shipped back with the notion of spending the rest of my life at the Strath."

"Were there no attempts made to let the property?"

"Not for the last fifty years," Reed answered. "After the Branscombes left, and why they did so before their time I can't tell you, the place had a bad reputation, and no one would go near it. But I have come at last," he went on in his coarse voice which sounded unpleasantly through the garden. "I'll soon clear away all that unhealthy nonsense. We Americans don't hold with the conservatism of this old country, which makes everybody tumble into a trade error or a crazy belief one after the other, like sheep following the bell-wether through a hole in the fence. I'm not a gentleman in your sense, and I don't pretend to be. I'm a practical man, the great-grandson of a farm labourer, and a free-thinker from my youth. I don't believe in what you call occult influences, and if I can't take up my quarters at the Strath and do what I like with the place I'll eat my hat. And now, Professor," Reed concluded in his familiar manner, "what do you say to a small glass of whisky?"

The rector rose without a word, and went into the house to find the bottle of spirits which he kept for use in an emergency; but while he groped in the cupboard there was a mist upon his eyes, and his usually gentle spirit was shaken with disgust and anger as he murmured, "He shall not lay a hand upon that garden. I hate the man. He has inherited my Paradise, and would take it from me and make it a desert."

Early in the morning the visitor left for the Strath, entering the grounds by the gate in the churchyard, and the rector did not see him again until evening. He did not receive any invitation to accompany the master in these explorations; and the key, his property for the past thirty years, had been taken away. During the afternoon he walked along the front, noticed that the iron gates were ajar, and breathed more easily when he saw the long grass still waving in the wind. Returning, he fell in with one of the men in Reed's employ, who touched his hat and would have walked on; but the rector stopped him and enquired what he had done.

"Opened the doors and windows in yonder, Sir," said the man. "Some of the frames were that rotten they broke like paper. I scraped the dirt from the panes, and cut off nigh a truck-load of ivy to let in the light. But I ain't going in there again, Sir."

The rector asked for an explanation.

"Well, Sir, it's what they've always said about the Strath," the man went on, "It ain't healthy in there. I don't know whether 'tis because such a powerful lot of strong-smelling plants grow there, or what it is, Sir, but I do know a man can't help making a fool of hisself when he's there. I was a-laughing and a-singing while I worked, and feeling just as though I was tipsy, though, as you know, I'm a sober man, Sir, and when I looked inside there was this Mr. Reed laughing at summat like to hurt hisself, and I don't know if you'll believe me, Sir, but I saw him join 'ands with Bill Vyner, and them two danced round the room, kicking up the dust awful. They seemed to be fair enjoying of themselves, Sir, but now

I come to think quiet-like it was a horrid kind of sight, though I liked it well enough at the time, and stood in the door whistling a tune for them to dance to. You see, Sir, it ain't proper for a gentleman like Mr. Reed to be so familiar with such as me and Bill. And Bill says he ain't going there no more neither."

Dr. Berry resumed his walk with a dreamy smile upon his handsome face. His sensitive mouth quivered as he repeated the famous satire of Archilochus addressed to his own soul. "Nature does not change," he murmured. "The lampoons of Archilochus caused the daughters of Lycambes to hang themselves for shame. How will the influence of the Strath use Henry Reed?"

It was twilight when the man came to the rectory, sullen and discontented. He had little information to give, and when the doctor enquired whether the work of restoration had begun he curtly replied, "Not yet," and went on to ask whether he might spend another night under the parsonage roof.

"I will try him," said the rector to himself when they had supped; and going to his study he extracted from a drawer his little manuscript book of translations. "I will see if this man has a soul which can respond to the unseen world. If so there is a chance for him; if not the Strath must conquer."

He came out upon the lawn where his guest was chewing the stem of his pipe restlessly.

"Allow me to read you a translation of mine," he said; then seating himself a little behind his guest he read the description of peaceful night written by Alcman the Lydian slave and poet, who lived and sang a hundred years before Daniel interpreted the writing on the wall for the lord of Babylon.

As the poet concluded, dropping his musical voice to a whisper over the last iambic, he drew forward, watching and excited, his own spirit thrilled by the magic of those lines. Reed appeared to be abstracted; with wild hope the scholar put out his hand and touched him.

"Oh, done?" muttered the bearded man. "Queer, fellows should waste their time writing that stuff, ain't it? Suppose they're good for nothing else though. I was thinking while you were talking that what my place wants is better air. It's too much shut in, you see, and no one can live without lots of fresh air. I shall cut down the elms along the road. It will be all profit to me, as the timber is big, and ought to sell at a good price. Have you any idea what figure elm is fetching now?"

The rector groaned as he pushed the book of treasures into his pocket. He had been prepared to follow up any success he might have gained by reciting a song of Arion, who, the legends say, was brought into Taenarum on the backs of dolphins. But his test had failed. The man beside him was base earth, with a mind impervious to the world's music.

"Will you permit me to say something?" he asked nervously.

Reed swung his head round, and his small eyes twinkled maliciously.

"Whatever you like, Professor. I can guess what it is. You want me to spare those trees. Well, I tell you right now they must go."

"I do not ask you to spare the trees," said Dr. Berry earnestly. "The genius of the place can take care of them. I am going to entreat you to save yourself."

"What?" ejaculated Reed. He frowned and crumpled his beard. "What foolery is this?" he muttered testily.

"You will not understand me," the scholar went on. "You laugh at my warnings. Remember I have studied the Strath for thirty years. It has been kind to me, and more than kind, because there is sympathy between us. We are both dreamers. I have been the sole character of its drama all these years. I have tried to be its friend, and it has regarded me as such. But you—you are opposing it. You are its enemy."

Reed dropped his pipe and planted each hand firmly upon his knees.

"I'm an ignorant man from your point of view," he said in a grating voice. "I can't write or talk about busy bees forgetting their daily toil and feathered tribes hanging their drooping wings, and I'll be hanged if I want to. I can go better than that, Professor. Put you and me down in the world to live by wits, and I would build up a business, while you would sink to the poor-house. Ignorance? Well maybe. Have you ever heard of a millionaire who could read Greek? I don't follow you in your talk about dreams and warnings, and if you will excuse my saying so I don't intend to listen to any more of it. If you have any suggestion to make about the property

I'll be glad to listen. But when you say that a man can't live on his own place because it has taken a dislike to him—well, Professor. It's moonshine."

"Explain to me one thing," Dr. Berry urged. "Tell me how it was when I came upon you in the garden yesterday evening you were as different from your present self as my house is different from the Strath?"

Reed stirred uncomfortably. That question rankled.

"If we were sitting in that garden now," impressed the rector, taking his mild revenge, "and I were to read you those lines of Alcman, which you despise, you would listen eagerly. Explain why your mood should be different there?"

"Maybe it is you that change," suggested the other unamiably.

"Come into the garden with me now."

But Reed declined emphatically.

"You and I have got to be friends, Professor," he went on with attempted heartiness. "You're the parson and I'm the squire, and it seems there is no one handy to act as peacemaker. We had better not quarrel, and if we are not going to quarrel we must agree to differ."

"I have done my duty," said the rector quietly. "I had to warn you that if you insist upon opposing the Strath you will be made to suffer. If you refuse to be persuaded I cannot help you."

Reed stretched out for the bottle and helped himself generously.

"How in the name of common sense can I be made to suffer?" he muttered; but there was in his voice for the first time a definite note of awe.

"There will come upon you the last punishment which can befall any man," Dr. Berry answered.

"The Strath will destroy you."

Then he removed his hat and wiped his forehead; and walked slowly into the house.

Scene II.—SKETCH

He sette not his benefice to hire,
And lette his shepe acombred in the mire,
And ran unto London, unto Saint Poules,
To seken him a chanterie for soules,
Or with a brotherhede to be withold;
But dwelt at home, and kepte wel his fold.—*Chaucer.*

Dr. Berry never learnt whether any phenomena occurred within or around the Manor of Thorlund immediately subsequent to that evening when he had been constrained to issue his warnings, because Reed came no more to the rectory. The scholar reasoned that it was not any feeling of indignation which kept the so called master of the Strath away; nor was it fear lest he might be compelled to listen to more ominous forebodings; it was, more probably, shame at defeat.

The gate which admitted from the churchyard was open to the rector no longer; but every day he passed along the front, both at morning and evening, anxious to see if the work of demolition had been commenced, and from each of these walks he returned with the same triumphant smile. Not a tuft of grass had been mown, nor had the axe been laid at the root of any of the elms; not a bush had been removed, not a flower or weed uprooted. The garden remained unaltered in all outward essentials, except that a pathway had become beaten out from the iron gates to the bridge across the moat.

When the rector questioned sexton or shepherd he learnt what he might have guessed, namely that the owner hardly ever left the place; that he had given up searching for men to work there; that he lived alone, attending to his own requirements in colonial fashion; that his baggage had been brought from the distant station across the hills and taken by the carrier into the house; and the tradesmen of the small market town seven miles away had been instructed to call for orders not more than once a week.

"Will he also become a dreamer?" the scholar wondered, as he gazed longingly upon the old grey wall. "Can it be possible for the Strath to give him a soul and take him to itself as it received me? Will his poultry farming become poetry making after all?"

He laughed sleepily at the quaint idea and approaching the oak door turned the handle and pushed timidly. He had done so every evening since Reed had left him, hoping rather than expecting to feel the barrier yield. It was the same then as upon other nights; the door was locked.

During the tension of that long week, when the garden was closed to him, Dr. Berry for the first time realised the loneliness of the Thorlund valley.

His single churchwarden, a peasant farmer who signed his name with difficulty and without legibility, had his dwelling place almost a mile from the church. The nearest gentlefolk lived four miles away at Kingsmore across the white road of the downs. The only houses in the valley were the rectory and the Strath. Half ruined barns, standing in a disused yard which sloped towards a pond where sheep were sometimes scoured, hedges, grass-roads, and a triangular green where a whipping-post was preserved, comprised the remainder of the hamlet. In such a place the talented Greek scholar had been content to pass his time upon earth.

The rector found himself using that past tense unconsciously while he mourned for his lost Eden. After thirty years of a strange sleep he felt stirring within him a desire for more breadth and motion and some human sympathy. The small voice of the world was calling him; the natural human passions, long latent and drugged by the influence which had dominated his life, struggled to reach the surface. The sluggish calm had been disturbed by expulsion from the garden. He had entered there to dream; and now that the gate was closed he became conscious of the thorns and thistles of the world.

This restless mood grew upon the scholar as the days passed, the long dry days of midsummer when the spirit of comedy prevailed around him. His belief in the ultimate triumph of destiny was as deeply-rooted as that of any ancient Greek. The Strath had long ago suggested to him the theatre with its rites and mysteries and the open stage where characters came and went, speaking their messages through either the comic or the tragic mask. He himself represented the chorus, and had merely played his part of exarchus in warning Reed. He did not require to turn to his Aeschylus, or to his Sophocles, to learn the fate of that man who thinks himself strong enough to fight destiny. Reed's fate was fixed, as assuredly as Agamemnon was doomed to death when he returned to his palace in Argos. But destiny must strike with mortal weapons; and it was impossible to believe that any human instrument in the neighbourhood of sleepy Thorlund could be so wrought upon as to strike the fatal blow.

Although the scholar had never been a sociable being, he felt it a relief when Mr. Price, vicar and squire of Kingsmore, rode over on the Saturday and invited himself to lunch. This reverend neighbour was a simple-minded man of seventy, bow-legged with much riding, hearty in manner, an excellent judge of beasts, and somewhat of a connoisseur in wine. He would shout a jest at every rustic, and touch his disreputable hat to every dame in his village, address his labourers as equals, and throw coppers to the children who passed him as he rode. He had long ago forgotten what little learning he had acquired; and it was to be feared that, good man though he was, his farming interests were not infrequently placed in front of his spiritual duties. He could indicate all the good points in a horse at a glance; but it might be doubted whether he could have quoted verbatim any one of the thirty-nine articles.

"Good-day to you, Berry," he shouted in his hearty manner, as he crossed the rectory lawn while his dogs hunted the scholar's cat into the shrubberies. "I was saying to myself this morning that it was a long time since I had eaten roast beef at your table, and as I know you have a sirloin on Saturdays I thought I would ride over and help with the under-cut. So the owner of the manor has turned up at last. My village is full of families with his name. The place was a swamp originally, I'm told, and they say the name came into existence on account of the number of reeds which grew there. Any truth in that, do you think? I believe in tradition. It's the only thing I do believe in nowadays. If your squire turns out to be connected with our Reeds, as they say he is, I'm afraid he won't be much of an acquisition."

"He is connected," said Dr. Berry. "However you may be able to agree with him better than I can ever hope to do," he went on with unintentional maladroitness. "He has actually proposed to me a plan for altering the Strath and breeding poultry there."

"God bless my soul," exclaimed his brother cleric, pushing an end of his soiled white tie beneath his collar. "There's no money to be made out of poultry in this part of the world. I can't dispose of mine so as to cover expenses. He should go in for pigs. I'll call on him after luncheon, and tell him there's money to be made in pigs. I have some good sows for sale."

"Pigs!" murmured Dr. Berry in anguish. "Pigs at the Strath!"

"They ought to do well," said the farmer-vicar of Kingsmore. "There's plenty of grass at the manor, and pigs do well on grass. Ah, you're afraid of the smell. But pigs don't smell, if they are properly kept. We will call on Mr. Reed this afternoon. I am very anxious to see the inside of the place."

"I cannot accompany you," said the rector of Thorlund a trifle coldly. "Mr. Reed and I have not made any considerable advance towards friendship."

"That won't do," said the other, shaking his head seriously. "You must pull it off with your squire, even if you do have to lower yourself a bit. You and he are alone here, and when two men are cast upon a desert island they can't afford to quarrel. Now I'm quite prepared to call on Mr. Reed, and be friendly, though he is distantly connected, I suspect, with my head-carter. Every man is a vote, as my dear uncle, who was member for this division under Lord Derby's administration, used to say; by which he meant, I fancy, that every man can do you either good or harm, and you may as well earn the good at the sacrifice of a little pride. But look here Berry. For the hundredth time I want to know whether things are as they should be at the manor?"

The scholar smiled somewhat feebly as he replied, "Is it possible that everything should be in order with a house that has stood deserted for a century?"

"You know what I mean," said Mr. Price. "I have asked you many a time if the place is haunted, and I have never been satisfied with your answers. I believe in haunted houses, because I once owned a farm which was troubled by a tiresome old woman in a plaid shawl and a poke bonnet, and I had to pull the house down to get rid of her. You have always declared that the manor is free from anything of that sort; but I think there must be something you have kept from me."

"Come indoors," said the doctor. "It is hot out here, and dinner will soon be ready. I will tell you what I know about the Strath."

The old gentleman followed his reverend brother into the study, and seating himself beside the window listened to what he had to say, his white head on one side, and his eyes blinking incredulously.

"Berry," he said gravely, when his mind had been sufficiently perplexed. "If this is what our progress has brought us to I am glad I am nearly seventy-one. I have always said that the world is going ahead too fast. When I was a boy we lived very much the same as they did a couple of thousand years before, and then in just fifty years the whole world changed. First came steam, and after it the telegraph and electricity, and now we have reached a stage when we can send a message from one end of the earth to the other in about the time it takes to write it, and hear the voices of dead men speaking out of phonographs, and we are talking of travelling a hundred miles in the hour, and there is no hell and very little fear of death nowadays, and—God bless my soul! we can't even have a respectable ghost, but our old houses are to be haunted for the future by this electricity and magnetism; and they say messages are coming from people who are dead and ought to be decently at rest, and we are learning something about the next stage of existence, and a future state can be proved, we are told, not through the Bible, which was good enough for everyone in my young days, but by certain phases of human consciousness which I refuse to believe in and don't profess to understand, and—I'm very glad I shan't live much longer."

"There is surely nothing much older than the idea of a house permeated with some essence of mystery," the scholar continued quietly. "Read again your Greek drama, and refresh your memory by the references of Aeschylus to the palace of Argos, whence odours issued like the breath of graves. There you have a house, haunted, to use your word, like the Strath by an inexplicable and invisible presence working its influence upon the affairs of men."

"You go beyond me," said Mr. Price perplexedly. "I never could translate Aeschylus, and the only way I got through at Oxford was by learning the crib by heart and getting the selection right by luck. I always thought it a waste of time to learn Greek, and I think so still. Give a boy a good commercial education. Teach him French and German, and elementary science, and American methods. Give him a chance to make his way in the world."

"And deprive him of the finest literature of all time, and the knowledge of human nature as it is revealed to us through the classics," added the scholar quietly. "Is that fair?"

"Bah," said Mr. Price. "There are always translations if they are wanted, and there are Shakspere and our grand old Bible."

"Shakspere could only model his tragedies upon the Greek drama," the scholar protested. "All that he could do was to clothe the old thoughts with his own unrivalled speech and introduce additional characters and scenic effects. The dark thread of influence runs through all his tragedies. We know from the outset that Lear must die, that Hamlet must fail, that Othello must fall through his frightful error. As for the Bible permit me, with all reverence, to say that much of its early lore is apocryphal, and much more of later date derived from the thinkers and writers of ancient Greece. You talk of sustaining your student with stagnant water taken far from the fountain head."

"I never could argue with you," said Mr. Price sadly. "You swim right away, while I sink like a stone. Though I am an old-fashioned Englishman I do my best to be modern. I have recently bought a mechanical foster-mother to rear my poultry, I have stocked my farm with American implements, and now I'm seriously thinking of employing gramophones to frighten the pigeons from my peas. It's no use trying to fight progress, as the savage who charged a locomotive discovered, and destiny, or whatever you call the thing that is haunting the manor, will find that out. This Reed comes from America. If I were a betting man, I would lay you what you like that he will improve the place according to his plans, and clear away that atmosphere which you say has settled over it. The Strath wants a thunderstorm to freshen its air, and I wouldn't mind wagering that the American will play the part of thunderstorm to perfection."

"If I were a betting man, to borrow your expression, I would take you," rejoined Dr. Berry with a strained smile. "But now let us go and eat our beef."

"Talking of thunder-storms," said the squarson of Kingsmore, as he followed his host into the dining-room. "I am reminded that the glass was falling very rapidly when I left home, so I shall pay my call upon friend Reed and get away as quickly as possible."

SCENE III.—TRAGEDY

Circles and right lines limit and close all bodies, and the mortal right-lined circle must conclude and shut up all.—*Sir T. Browne.*

While the two clergymen were in the dining-room the expected change in the weather occurred. When Mr. Price rode away, having decided to postpone his visit to the Strath, the sun was wrapped up in dense clouds, there was no sky, and the light was fading rapidly.

For some time Dr. Berry sat with a book in his study. Then he ventured upon the lawn to observe the heaving clouds, which each moment threatened to burst into lightning. There was not a breath of wind. The trees in the garden beyond were entirely without motion; the walls appeared to have no substance, and the very house seemed to float away into unreality. Afar the watcher sighted the chalk-pits on the downs, their white sides glowing fiercely against a sombre background.

"It is the hour of tragedy," he murmured.

Here, as in the ancient drama, the actors played their parts in the open air, in order that their passions might blend with the fury of the elements. The proscenium, as in old time, was made by nature. The wall of the Strath formed the back-scene; the theatre was the garden; the orchestra that mound on which the sun-dial stood. Already the storm-cocks were chattering there, and their notes came into the doctor's ears like the piping of flute-players.

"I must go," said the dreamer with a slight shiver.

Passing back to the house he quickly reappeared carrying a small wooden box. He crossed the churchyard, where the sexton was digging a grave, singing hoarsely as he shovelled up the dirt. The man touched his hat and said, "Looks like a storm coming up yonder, sir. But the sun shines above Kingsmore."

The rector hesitated, and asked absently, "Whose grave is that?"

"'Tis for old Jim Reeve, sir. Him as died a Tuesday, and is to be buried to-morrow."

"Ah yes," the doctor murmured, adding to himself as he passed on, "I thought it might be the grave of Henry Reed."

The door in the wall was unlocked. Dr. Berry had felt assured that it would be so. He entered and stood within the influence of the garden.

The air no longer thrilled with the note of mirth, the intoxicating happiness and the exuberant laughter were gone. Instead of the sunshine sorrow brooded, and the flowers were shut, and a moaning came from the rotten gables of the house. The tragic note was dominant, and all the grotesque sounds of mirth were stilled.

Fully possessed by the influence, the priest ascended the mound and extended his white hands over the dial, which represented to him no longer a recorder of the flight of time, but an altar sacred to Bacchus. He opened his box, scattered its contents upon the metal slab, and applied a light. Then, as a filmy cloud of incense rose in a long thread into the gloom, he tramped slowly round the knoll reciting an Argive song.

No sane voice spoke from his inner consciousness to remind him that this was worse than folly; that he was offering sacrifice to a mythical deity. He was merely playing the part which had been allotted him, and reciting those words which were suitable to the occasion as they presented themselves to his memory. The impending storm was, he believed, about to break upon the house; and it was not to be dispelled until the last words had been spoken, the tragedy accomplished, and the stage abandoned.

The rain came, and the lightning, and then strong wind which sent leaves whirling across the knoll. But there came no sound from the house. Through the rain and the thunder and the wind moved the old atmosphere of fate and despair and the conquest of unbending human will. The Thymele streamed and smoked no more; but the elements fought on as the accompaniment of the drama, and the piping of the invisible storm-cocks became shriller and more stern.

Again the mood changed, and Dr. Berry was driven forth like a villain to the hisses of the wind. Instead of returning home he took the field path which led beside the beech wood; and ascended until he reached the summit of a grass hill where larches were odorous in the hot sunshine. Pausing there he looked out, and saw the growth of sable cloud above Thorlund and the lightning crossing it and the white steam of the rain ascending.

A rabbit bounded among the larches into the open, and after it came a female figure, young and lithe, her face tanned by exposure to the weather, her great eyes unashamed. At first sight she was beautiful; at the second pathetic, because the light in her eyes lacked reason. She bounded up to the rector, flung herself at his knees, and burst into a noisy incoherent prayer.

"Get up, girl," cried the scholar, dragging her almost roughly from the grass. "How often must I tell you this is wrong?"

"Here are flowers for you," cried the girl, pressing a quantity of pale-blue and white harebells, warm and withering, into his hand. "They are always ringing, and I am tired of their noise. Take them and curse them. They will stop that wild nodding of their heads for you. Why will you not let me touch you? There is force coming out of your fingers, and when I hold your hand I see no longer the strange things in the wind. I have been among the larches, and in the white chalk-pits, and down by the stream, and in the churchyard, but I still see the strange things coming down the wind. And you too walk alone. Do you see figures? Have you seen the masked man running, and the white woman crying into the lilies? Do you see them in the garden in the valley?"

This girl, a well-known character of the neighbourhood, lived at Kingsmore with her grandparents, but was seldom to be found within the cottage of her relatives. Her real home was upon the grass hills, or in the dry beech wood, or down in the valley. Nancy Reed, Lone Nance as the villagers called her, passed about the country like a will o' the wisp, talking to the birds and the creatures of her imagination, revelling in wind and shouting through storm. Yet for all her wild speech she was as gentle as a child, although perfect reason had been withheld from her all the twenty-four years of her life. She was sane enough to know that she was not as others, and her one desire was to become perfect and womanly; but relentless nature continued to bear her from place to place against her will, flinging her body about the hills like drift wood tossed upon the sea.

"You go into that garden with a book in your hand," she cried, pointing into the vapours. "I watched you come out, your lips moving, and your face as white as that chalk. You saw and heard a great deal in that garden, and you were wondering what you had missed. If I had been nearer I would have told you."

"You have never been in that garden," said Dr. Berry sternly. "And you must never go."

The girl laughed noisily into his face.

"That house is filled with sounds which you cannot understand. But if you go there much more, and sit under its shadow a few more years, you will begin to understand. And then you will come out and call for me, and we shall chase the sunbeams into the valley."

The rector drew away from her. The note of inspiration was there and he had recognised it. It was true he had felt a slow unloosening of mind from body, an exaltation of the brain, and a tingling of each sense, while he had tarried in that garden. He had called this the birth of higher knowledge and the stirring of genius; but when the girl spoke he remembered that the bridge which separates the inspired from the diseased mind is perilously narrow and frail.

"I cannot keep away from the place," he muttered, forgetful that Lone Nance was his listener. "I cannot stop my ears. I must go there, to sink into sleep and dream. It is good for me. The Aeolian poets walk at my side. I can describe their land, their speech, and their manners, as though I had lived in that far off time. Their language is as familiar to me as my own. I can enter into their moods. I can see where history has erred. I can make the crooked places straight. I can see the outlines of their figures and describe the very texture of their raiment. I can even detect the odour of Sappho's anointed hair as she passes along the road to Mytilene."

He stopped, remembering the status of the wild girl. She was looking beyond him into vacancy, her hands locked behind her back. The dark clouds were lifting from Thorlund, but the vapour still ascended like the mist of the genie from the fisherman's vessel.

Twilight was trailing over the land as Dr. Berry descended, and the beech wood became a black sea, tossing and moaning with the voices of life. A labourer cutting hay stopped from his work and leaning upon his two-handled knife pulled at the brim of his hat as he peered down from the strong-smelling rick.

The rector looked closely at the man, until his sluggish memory awoke and suggested a name.

"Was it not your father who was taken ill? How is he now?" he asked, with a dim feeling that he had neglected his very inconsiderable parochial duties of late.

"Broke," said the hay-cutter, abruptly and hoarsely. "Broke a week ago and been took. Sixty-one he wur, a good age for the likes of we."

"I do not remember burying him. When was it?" Dr. Berry asked.

"'E didn't not 'xactly die," the man explained. "'E was took to the 'ouse, and so 'e be done to we. Us all get broke, some sooner, some later. Us can't last for always. Father broke quick when 'e started, but 'is brother, my Uncle Tom as was, 'e took a terrible time. Us all said every fall, "'e'll get broke this time for sure," but 'e'd pull through and laugh at us. 'E went sudden at the last. 'E'd been threshing all day, and 'bout evening 'e couldn't carry. Tried time and time 'e did, but couldn't carry. 'E walked 'ome, and sat down 'e did aside the fire, and 'e said, 'I be broke.' 'E was took that month."

"Is he still alive?" the rector asked.

"Ay, sir. I saw 'im one day walkin' the yard, when I druve the waggon by, but I didn't want 'im to see I. When they gets broke they don't come back no more. Some on 'em lasts a powerful time yonder too. But they ain't of no account, and us don't talk on 'em. Us ain't got nothing to do wi' they. I'll get broke in my time. Us don't think on't till it comes."

"Would it not have been possible for you to have kept your father out of the workhouse?" protested Dr. Berry. "You are in regular work with good wages, and an old man does not cost much to keep."

The hay-cutter looked perplexed, and a trifle puzzled, at the scholar's lack of very ordinary knowledge.

"Father wur broke, sir. 'E couldn't earn no wages," he explained.

"So I understand," said Dr. Berry. "But did it never occur to you that you might maintain him? It should surely be the son's duty to support the father in his old age."

The labourer smiled more and more at the rector's ignorance.

"They that be broke be took, sir," he said heavily. "When I be broke I'll be took, and my son will say, 'Good-bye, father,' and wait for 'is turn. Wife and me 'ave six children, and another comin' 'fore harvest. I gets twelve shillun, and pays 'alf-a-crown rent and sixpence club money, and my wife and me live clear of charity. There ain't no room for old folk along wi' a big fambly. 'Sides, sir, it ain't proper. Them that be broke, be took. And them that works get wages."

"Good-night," said Dr. Berry abruptly.

"Good-e'en, sir," replied the hay-cutter gruffly.

"Broken in pieces like a potter's vessel," the scholar muttered as he walked away. "As we cast the sherds of shattered utensils from our houses, so are these men cast forth from their homes when their strength breaks and their utility as machines passes. There is matter for the thinker here, but it is colourless and cold. It lacks the warmth and glamour of the past."

One last sunbeam passed over the hills and slanted across the Strath. From a point, where the grass road swung round, a side of the old house became visible, and a single window blinking in the middle of the light. Dr. Berry watched with shaded eyes, and suddenly came to a stop. There was a white figure bending across the window, and as he saw it the question of the wild girl flashed back: "Have you seen the white woman crying into the lilies?"

The same minute he was smiling, because a breath of wind had passed, shaking the foliage, and the white figure rocked in unison and vanished, as the sunlight died away. The shape had been caused by the ivy and a certain arrangement of the boughs of an elm acted upon by the white ray. The rector breathed more easily when the window became blank.

Yet he knew that the people of the hamlet would be saying that evening, 'It is noisy in the Strath.' They who behold a tragedy see only the outward passions of the actors; of the influence which is behind they can see nothing. So one may watch the tree tormented by the wind, but not see the wind.

Supper was awaiting the poet, and he ate and drank mechanically. Then entering his study he spread his translations before him, and straightway became an Athenian, floating delicately through most pellucid air.

The poetic mountains breathed their influence into him over the deeps of time. Fragrant odours were in his nostrils, and in his ears the murmur of bees upon Hymettus. He passed restlessly to Olympus where the Gods were in council, and saw the Father aiming his thunderbolt, and like Menippus sat at the door whence issued the supplications of the world, and heard the petitions for wealth, honour, and long life repeated in shameless monotony. He heard also the prayer of Reed entreating that the terrible atmosphere might be dispelled, and he felt no sorrow when the frown on the thunderer's brow remained unrelaxed. Through all the shifting figures he dimly perceived the table before him and the passionate iambics of Archilochus spread upon paper by his hand, and aloud he read, "My soul, my soul care-worn, bereft of rest." And at that his head sank forward upon his breast.

The study window remained open, and moths and beetles blundered through to bombard the globe of the scholar's lamp.

It was ten o'clock when the housekeeper knocked as usual at the door, and receiving no answer entered softly with her master's bedroom candle and a cup of cocoa. Dr. Berry was leaning forward over the table, his face hidden upon his folded arms, a disabled ghost-moth floundering across his left hand. The woman noticed that the muscles of her master's hands were standing out like cords.

"Your reverence," she said.

The rector did not stir, and after repeating her call she muttered gently, "He's been and tired himself again." Then she turned down the flame of the lamp, drew it further from the sleeper, and retired softly, leaving the door ajar.

The tragedy was over; and the tired exarchus slept.

The next morning it became known about Thorlund and its neighbourhood that the owner of the Strath was dead. The woman who supplied him with milk had discovered the body lying across the threshold, its head towards the garden. Henry Reed had pitted his strength against the Strath and the influence of the house had triumphed.

INTERLUDE

He was nothing better than a consumer of the fruits of the earth. 'Dost thou then,' quoth I, 'imply that we should name such a creature as this—as we do the drone in the bee-hive—a blot upon the community, a mere drone at home, and abroad a disgrace to the state?' 'Even so, Socrates,' said he.—*Plato*.

The houses, which compose a street at no great distance from the trees of Gray's Inn, are for the most part occupied by authors, artists, actors, and architects engaged, like Icarus, in making wings.

The first letter of our alphabet originated it is said from the hieroglyphic picture of an eagle. Followers of the four professions beginning with that letter are, strictly speaking, not wanted. Everybody must need letter B as represented by baker and butcher. But letter A suggests luxuries. The picture of the eagle is therefore appropriate. Authors, artists, actors, and architects must learn first to fly, and then to soar well above smaller birds, before they can win success.

The side posts of each door are studded with an amazing number of brass knobs, intended originally to be in communication with bells upon every floor, but at present restricted seemingly to the duty of exposing lilliputian milk-cans to the public view. These great houses, which in the time of the Georges were occupied by people of title, have become brick-and-mortar masks, hiding the sunken eye and hollow cheek of poverty, in addition to the shame of rake and harlot, from the view of the town. On the ground floor of Number 15 a middle-aged man was brushing a long-haired terrier beside the open window of a wide room panelled with oak. It was close upon ten o'clock, but breakfast was still waiting. The interior was moderately well furnished, although with the typical middle-class disregard for art. The pictures were for the most part prints depicting scenes of sport. There were also a few German photographs in doubtful taste, and one or two engravings of river scenery in blurred and fly-spotted frames. There was not a book to be seen, except one which was open upon the sofa, and that to judge by its broken back was in continual use. Its title was Ruff's Guide to the Turf.

A well-built man of not more than thirty years, unbecomingly attired in a yellow dressing-gown and scarlet slippers entered the room. His haggard face, listless attitude, and general appearance of disgust with himself and his surroundings, suggested that he had been in the habit of guiding his life according to the traditions of the house. As the middle-aged man turned to welcome him, the profligate yawned profoundly and lowering himself into a chair pushed the hair off his forehead with an irritated gesture.

"So you're here again," he muttered. "Drayton, you're a regular vampire, always after money or food. I suppose you would suck my blood literally, if you weren't afraid of poisoning yourself. What is it this morning? Breakfast I suppose?"

The other—he was a poor scribbler, who made a precarious livelihood by contributing paragraphs to popular penny weeklies—stroked his stubbly chin, laughed, and removed the dog from the chair as carefully as through the animal had been made of precious porcelain.

"As a simple statement of fact I have slept upon your premises," he said, indicating the sofa. "Have you forgotten who guided your weary footsteps homeward during the early hours of the morning?"

The profligate bent over the table and picked up a letter which was addressed to 'Charles Conway, Esquire,' in copper-plate handwriting. He tore open the envelope, yawned again, and inquired of his companion whether at the time specified he, the questioner, had been very grossly drunk.

"A gentleman of private means never gets drunk," said the parasite. "We apply that term to costermongers and coal-heavers. But you were, I fancy, rapidly approximating towards that Bacchic state which in classical language is described as *vino gravatus*. Even the policeman at the corner of the street, whom for some reason best known to yourself you insisted upon greeting most fraternally, would never, I am sure, admit that you were more than footsore; but then you presented him with a shilling, thereby obtaining your commission as captain. You wasted that shilling. I would have installed you as a Field Marshal for half the amount."

"Eat the breakfast," said Conway, as he transferred himself

wearily to the sofa and unfolded his letter. "And don't talk so much. My head is tender."

Drayton hurried to the table and surrounded himself with victuals; but before beginning he looked across and suggested, "Better have something. Try a kidney and a piece of toast?"

"You can get me a bottle of beer and an apple," said Conway in his jaded manner.

Drayton bustled to a cupboard, bent his rheumatic knees, and after an interval approached the sofa in the capacity of waiter, bearing the desired refreshment.

"A glass of milk would be more appropriate, considering the time of day, only you might insist upon having whiskey in it," he said. "You will soon resemble Lord John Hervey, who, in this neighbourhood, and perhaps in this very room, breakfasted on an emetic, dined on a biscuit, and regaled himself once a week with an apple. Here is your ale—all white and yellow! You can imagine it is a poached egg."

The younger man gave no heed to the parasite's chatter. He was studying his letter with a frown. When it was finished he leaned back, drank his refreshment, looked at his watch, then read the letter again.

"Bring me the newspaper," he commanded.

The scribbler was making famine in the land. He believed in eating well, entirely mistrusting the French proverb, which associates a good stomach with a bad heart, and pinning his faith rather upon the creed which teaches that virtuous folk have hearty appetites. His own poor line of business rarely afforded him the means for more than one substantial meal in the course of the day, and too often not that; so when opportunity was given to kill a hearty appetite without lightening his pocket he was never wont to be backward.

Rising obediently Drayton opened the newspaper, folded it with the sporting intelligence outward, and so handed it to his patron with the remark, "There is no change in the betting."

Conway did not even glance at the sheet, which had been presented as a matter of course; but turning to the general news searched each column carefully. For several minutes there was silence, while the scribbler made ruin of the breakfast. Then

Conway threw the paper down and resumed his former attitude.

"Give me a cigarette," he ordered.

The other briskly left the table, complied with the demand, and as briskly returned. A coal cart rumbled by, and the Stentor in charge announced his business by a long ear-shattering yell.

The noise seemed to stir Conway into life. He paced across the room and set his back against the door. "Drayton," he said, "I have heard some extraordinary news this morning. My uncle has been murdered."

"Great Heavens!" exclaimed the writer, his jaws ceasing from their labours.

"Don't worry your brain to find condolences," said the other coolly. "I have never to my knowledge seen this particular relative, so I am in no need of sympathy, especially since I benefit by his death. But I want to know whether you have read anything of the murder of a Henry Reed? I see there is no mention in to-day's paper."

"Sympathy apart, it's an awful business," said Drayton, pouring himself out another cup of tea. "No, I don't remember to have heard anything. How did it happen?"

"It seems, from the bare narrative here, to have been a remarkable affair altogether," Conway answered. "My uncle returned from America only a few weeks ago, to take up his residence in an old house belonging to him which had not been occupied for ages. Last Sunday morning he was a discovered by the milk-woman, lying dead across the threshold of the hall-door. It appears that the house has a queer sort of reputation, and it was at first supposed he had died of fright. But at the inquest it was shown that he had been strangled. And the curious part of it is that no stranger had been seen in the place, and it is impossible to suspect any of the inhabitants of the village."

"The mystery of the haunted house," muttered Drayton professionally. "Perhaps there will be a chance for me to do something here. Where is the place, Mr. Conway?"

The younger man came away from the door without answering and walked up and down, swinging the tassels of his dressing-gown. Suddenly he sat down at the table and poured himself out some tea.

"That's right," said the scribbler approvingly. "Nothing half so stimulating as tea. I hope I have left enough."

Conway filled a cup and drank off the contents. While doing so he kept his eyes fixed upon two grotesque objects above the chimney-piece, one on either side of a picture which depicted Isinglass winning the Derby; and when he set the cup down he remained in the same posture, staring at a pair of brown masks representing Comedy and Tragedy.

"My head is full of wheels," he muttered. "Come and hit me, Drayton, that I may be sure I am alive. I must have played the fool badly last night. I remember coming back from Sandown, and driving to some restaurant in the Strand. The next thing I can recall is groping round my room for a drink of water. My body aches and pricks, and my head feels as heavy as lead, and my eyes—Great Heavens! are those faces laughing at me?"

The elder man had finished eating at last. He came round the table and placed his hand soothingly upon the profligate's arm.

"Come over to the window and get some air," he said quietly. "You have been making a hot pace these last few months. You'll be breaking if you don't hold up."

"Look!" muttered Conway, pointing at the masks.

"Turn your back on them," said the scribbler. "What are you going to do about your uncle's death?

Again Conway disregarded the question. Turning from the wall to the furrowed features of his poverty-stricken companion, he exclaimed thickly, "Sit down, Drayton, and don't bother me. Do you know why I have those masks hanging there? They are family heirlooms, copies I have been told of a pair made in Nuremburg, during the eighteenth century, by a crazy toy-seller. These belonged to my mother before her marriage, and her father had a pair like them."

"Where are the originals?" inquired the listener.

"They have been destroyed. There was something uncanny about them, but beyond that I know nothing. This is the crest of the Reeds."

Conway drew a ring from his little finger and held it out with an unsteady hand. The other took it and saw a white cameo, showing two masks, leaning together, a cap and bells over the forehead of the one, a dagger over the other. He returned the ring, with the grave remark, "But you are not a Reed."

"My mother was. The family emigrated to America, and there my mother married into the Conway family, and returned with her husband to England. My uncle leaves his property to me, not because he could have loved me, but I suppose there was no one else to whom he could leave it."

"Go down and see the place. The change will pick you up," suggested the elder man. "It isn't probable you will live there?"

"What, give up London to rot away in a lonely country house?" said Conway contemptuously. "Is it likely? If I cannot let the place I shall try to sell it. What are you doing with yourself to-day?"

"The usual thing," replied the man who lived by his poor wits. "The British Museum reading-room, in chase of a guinea. I have earned nothing this week."

"You shall have a guinea, if you will pack my bag and take it to Paddington. I am going to see my late uncle's lawyer, and will meet you at the station about noon. You can occupy these rooms until I come back."

The literary adventurer closed with this offer promptly; and a few minutes after mid-day a train drew out of London, carrying the profligate Conway towards the influence of the Strath.

ACT II

Scene I.—COMEDY

Drink, be merry! Life is mortal, short is the time on earth.—*Amphis*.

It so happened that the exit of Henry Reed made no stir beyond being the wonder of a week in the neighbourhood of Kingsmore. An inquest was held at the Load of Mischief, a wayside beer-house standing before an unworked chalk-pit at the entrance to Thorlund parish; the customary verdict of wilful murder against some person or persons unknown had been returned; and there the matter appeared to end, so far as the inhabitants were concerned. Officials whose duty it became to detect the criminal made a thorough investigation. They searched the house and grounds—the Strath being in its sunniest mood—and the entire district for material upon which to work, but not a particle of success crowned their efforts. The medical evidence clearly showed that the unfortunate man had been strangled by a strong pair of hands; the locals testified that no stranger had entered the valley; the principal witness, Dr. Berry, declared that he was the only resident who had been in the habit of using the garden. He admitted, in answer to a question by the foreman, that he had spent very much of his time beside the lonely house; and so soon as he had spoken the coroner inquired whether he had been upon good terms with the deceased.

"When in his garden we had no difficulty in agreeing," the scholar replied. "When in mine we differed, but without quarrelling."

"How do you account for that?"

"I attribute it to the influence of the Strath."

"The influence of your garden is then less elevating?"

"My garden is in the commonplace world," said Dr. Berry, speaking what was in his mind, and shrinking when he perceived the half-pitying smile with which his answer was received.

It was not until his housekeeper had given evidence that her master had not left the rectory during the evening that Dr. Berry realised, with a thrill of horror, that distrust had certainly rested, if only for a few moments, upon himself. And yet he was the only man upon whom suspicion could fall. The sensitive scholar was exceedingly pained that he should have been questioned at all. He could not remember ever having purposely deprived a living thing of life; he had refrained from digging in his garden after having inadvertently severed a worm with his spade; and he had passed a troubled week deciding how he might act without cruelty when a lazy cuckoo had deposited her egg in a favourite hedge-sparrow's nest.

Days passed, and already grass was flourishing upon a fresh mound beside the churchyard wall where rested the shell of the stubborn little man who had fought against the Strath and had died in the attempt. The master of the manor had quitted the scene unmourned. The sun went on shining in the valley, the old house settled back into a triumphant silence, the church bell jangled its summons on Sunday, and the incumbent soared in rhetorical flights above the souls of his tiny congregation. There was no change. Yet it seemed to the rector that his step was not so firm as formerly; and when he glanced into his bedroom glass he detected a whiteness above his brow which had not been obvious before the coming of Henry Reed.

One evening a young man, with dissipation signed upon an otherwise good-looking face, called and introduced himself as the dead man's heir. He went on to ask for the keys, which his agent had instructed him were deposited for convenience at the rectory. Dr. Berry surrendered his charge with a nervous glance at the newcomer, and after begging to be excused from accompanying him went on to ask permission to retain, as he had always done, the key of the gate in the churchyard wall. The young man's hearty consent thrilled him gratefully; and though, after his late experience, he dared not invite any relative of Reed to take up his quarters at the rectory, he remarked in his courteous manner that he would be pleased to make the further acquaintance of his new squire. Conway in boisterous slang replied that he would be delighted to have someone to speak to during his visit, and after promising to look in later that evening retired to glance over his property and to engage a room at the Load of Mischief.

That day was made notable by other arrivals. Flora Neill came from her riverside home to pay her annual visit upon her reverend uncle the squire of Kingsmore; and as dusk was settling upon the hills a line of dingy caravans proceeded at a walking pace along the bending road, accompanied by swarthy gipsies and the paraphernalia of the pleasure fair. These nomads invaded Kingsmore that night, and the following day all the village folk were making holiday; it being Mr. Price's kindly custom to follow a precedent established by his ancestors, and to free his farm hands from their usual duties upon that particular day.

Shooting-booths, swings, and trial of strength machines occupied waste spaces by the roadside, while a merry-go-round discoursed blatant music upon a triangular patch of turf where the parish stocks were still religiously preserved. The Kingsmore fair was as degenerate as it was harmless. There was neither dancing-horse, elephants playing at ball, Italian marionette, nor booth of classical play. But posturing, grinning through horse-collars, eating of hot puddings were to be witnessed, besides such natural monstrosities as a calf with five legs and a lady of prodigious adiposity.

During the afternoon the squarson himself drove into the midst of the animated scene, accompanied by his niece, with a view to discovering whether the pleasures of his people were as innocent as stated, or whether this was to be positively the last occasion on which he could allow the fair to take place. The rustics, who were compelled to give him their allegiance, were not in the least afraid of the old man, whose nature was very nearly as simple as their own. Mr. Price was one of the last of the plain country squires. He permitted his servants to address him with familiarity. From his position in the chancel he would scan his congregation and record the number of heads before commencing service. Should a grey beard nod in the course of his sermon, the vicar would break off his discourse and order that the sinner should be awakened. The tramp on the road he would greet as a worthless rascal and soften the charge with a shilling; and at Christmas he took care that no cottage should be without its beef and beer. As he then glanced at the swarthy faces of the proprietors of booths and stalls he felt certainly 'in some doubt whether he should not exert the justice of the peace upon such a band of lawless vagabonds.' But when it came to the test his heart was too kind to deprive anyone of his livelihood, or his own people of their pleasure. He was no new man, anxious to assert himself. Mr. Price knew his power, and therefore had little temptation to use it.

"Uncle!" Flora exclaimed. "Who is that man throwing at the cocoa-nuts? He was my travelling companion yesterday from the junction."

Mr. Price fumbled in the deep pockets of his disreputable driving coat for his spectacles; and when they were produced, together with a sample of wool and a bunch of twine, he pushed them on his nose. "Where," he asked. "Do you mean that elderly man in the brown gaiters? He is a sheep-farmer from the other side of Queensmore."

"No—the young man to his left. There! He's just going to throw."

"Why, that is Mr. Conway, the new owner of the Strath, I do declare," exclaimed Mr. Price, who having been called out on duty the previous evening had looked in at Thorlund rectory on his way home, to condole with his reverend brother upon his recent ordeal at the inquest, and there had made the acquaintance of the young man from town. "I am surprised to find him here, so soon after that terrible affair too. The squire of Thorlund throwing for cocoa-nuts! And not a stitch of mourning for his uncle—and smoking —and shouting! God bless my soul, Flora, the man's no gentleman!"

"He is young," said Flora indulgently.

"All the more reason why I should show him his duty," said the old squire.

He summoned a passing labourer to hold the horse's head; but as he was about to step down Conway sighted the dog-cart, and hurried across the dusty grass in the happy mood of a schoolboy enjoying a half holiday. Mr. Price sank back to his seat with an exceedingly guilty expression, and caught up the reins.

"So you are taking in the variety show," the young man cried, with an appalling bonhomie that set the immediate neighbourhood grinning. "I had no idea one could find such sport in a village," he went on. "I've been throwing for an old chap, who came to me with a penny, and said he wanted to take a nut back to his grandson, and couldn't throw himself, so would I? He kept his penny while I spent a shilling before I knocked down a nut. You seem to breed good business men down here."

"I am here to satisfy myself that no objectionable features have been introduced to corrupt my people," said Mr. Price severely. "I hope you will not mind an outspoken remark from an old man, Mr. Conway, but I feel that when one comes to take up a position in the country it is very necessary to keep up appearances. These simple people readily form a wrong estimate of character. Ah, yes! This is my niece, Miss Neill."

"Do you enjoy this sort of thing?" asked Flora directly she had been introduced.

"It's something fresh to a Londoner," the young man replied. "I have been round all the shows, I have smashed bottles, tried my strength and my luck, and found I haven't much of either, seen the fat woman, pinched her leg—"

"Did you sleep at the Strath last night?" broke in Mr. Price.

"No, I went to the pub. It's an awful hole," said Conway. "I started out to call upon you, as you were good enough to ask me to come, but when I got here I yielded to the temptation of the fair. If you are on your way back, I may as well walk on to the house," he added coolly.

"Mr. Conway might drive back with us," Flora suggested. "There is plenty of room behind."

Courtesy hindered the squire from objecting. The young man neither acted nor spoke according to his old-fashioned ideas of a gentleman. He appeared to be neither temperate nor well-bred. And here was Flora making herself agreeable, solely because there did not happen to be another man handy. The smoke from Conway's cigar passed across his face, and the old gentleman, whose constitution prevented him from appreciating tobacco in any form, coughed disgustedly.

It was a long mile from the centre of the village to the vicarage. As the cart jolted along the road Mr. Price shouted his customary little jokes to the people who passed on pleasure intent; while his niece sustained a running conversation with the new owner of the Strath.

"Uncle has told me all kinds of stories about your house," Flora was saying. "I have often wanted to see the inside of it. But I should be sorry to have to spend a night there."

"The parson at Thorlund swears it isn't haunted," said Conway eagerly. "I just looked in last night for a few minutes. It did make me feel a bit queer to see all the eighteenth-century fixings which haven't been touched for the Lord knows how long. The old garden by itself is enough to make a fellow imagine all sorts of things."

"Your poor uncle was not strangled," said Mr. Price, breaking into the conversation with a note of strong conviction. "That was only doctor's evidence to give the jury a chance. I shall always maintain that Mr. Reed was killed by fright."

"I do not believe that fright has ever killed a man," objected Flora.

"Nonsense, child. What do you know about fear?" said the vicar sharply. "At your time of life you ought to be asking questions, instead of arguing with your betters. If the Strath were mine down it would come," he went on, turning to Conway. "Of course it is haunted. You remember, Flora, my farmhouse and its spook of an old dame in a poke bonnet? Well, I had the place down, and out went the lady. You can't strike a bargain with unrepentant souls. You must employ drastic measures, and the only way of getting rid of a spiritual nuisance is by using fresh bricks and mortar."

Now that Mr. Price was mounted upon his hobby he talked freely, and the young people were compelled to remain tongue-tied until the vicarage was reached. There tea awaited them, a meal which Mr. Price took seriously, and when he was satisfied Flora asked Conway if he would care to see the garden. The townsman rose at once and accompanied the tall girl along the grass paths, above the valley and the stream winding in the distance, while the vicar uprooted plantains from his lawn, with an old table-knife. It was all delightfully old-world and simple. The profligate felt the charm of the soft evening and began to understand the pleasures of country life, as Flora, bare-headed and handsome, talked freely upon his limited subjects and laughed at his somewhat vulgar jokes. It was the sound of this laughter which caused Mr. Price to straighten himself and remember that he was the guardian of his fatherless niece, and that his guest might be able to claim some distant sort of relationship with his head-carter.

"Uncle," said Flora, who always insisted upon managing the

affairs of the house during her stay, as the old gentleman approached them. "Mr. Conway will stop and have supper with us."

"I really think I ought to go back," the young man said, conscious that it would not be wise to outstay his welcome.

"What, back to your Load of Mischief? No, you must follow the custom of the country. We will feed you and send you off to Thorlund by a poetic moonlight. Uncle, do go and wash your hands. They look as if you had been making dirt pies."

"A man has no need to be ashamed of soiled hands," said Mr. Price somewhat sharply, because he resented any allusion to his peculiarities. "I shall be pleased if you will share our evening meal, Mr. Conway," he added, turning to the young man. Directly he had spoken he went to his threadbare knees and expelled a huge dandelion from a bed of larkspurs.

"Mr. Conway wants us to go over to Thorlund to-morrow," Flora went on. "You will take me, won't you, uncle? I am longing to see the Strath, and he has promised to give us tea."

"I am not at all sure whether I shall be able to come," said Mr. Price, approaching Conway, with the dinner-knife in one hand, and the bushy dandelion in the other. "I don't like leaving Kingsmore while these fair people are about. They are an ungenerous lot, and sometimes repay my kindness by appropriating my chickens. But we will come if I can get away," he added, because he too was burning with curiosity to see the interior of the house concerning which he had heard so many strange tales.

So Conway stopped to supper, and Flora played hostess; while Mr. Price, his simple face shining from a generous use of soap and hot water, thawed out under the benign influence of a glass of port, and told all his anecdotes for his guest's benefit, studiously avoiding any reference to the Strath or to the Reed family, until his niece rose and left them. Then he pushed the decanter across the table, and from a dissertation upon the iniquitous corn-laws passed at a bound to the subject of oral tradition, and furtively inquired of his guest whether there were to his knowledge any letters or memoirs appertaining to Sir John Hooper in existence at the Strath. Seeing blank astonishment on Conway's face he went on to explain his question, by dealing with the known history of the defunct baronet.

"Never heard of the chap," declared Conway, assisting himself to wine.

"You may possibly find in your house some of those materials which help us to a knowledge of history," went on the old squire, who was by this time in his most genial mood. "Sir John had a daughter, an only child, who, it is reputed, was very beautiful, and he treated her, 'tis said, with great cruelty. A tradition exists in my family that on a certain winter's night the girl was discovered crying among the elms in this garden. My ancestor had remarked upon the noise made, as he supposed, by the owls, until a friend declared that the sound was made by human voice. They went out and searching in the snow found the girl. She was huddled against a great dog, and her eyes were fixed with fear. They carried her to the fire, but directly she found her strength she was gone. They say she had a lover, and that her father killed him on the highway."

"When did this happen?" Conway asked, reaching again for the decanter.

"About the time that Wolfe was chasing Montcalm out of Quebec. Hooper was hanged upon what is still known as Dead-man's Hill. Any villager will point out the spot to you. But I want to know what happened to that poor girl. Tradition in this village suggests that she was often to be seen, walking at night with the dog, always crying, and always dressed in white like a bride. It was considered bad luck to meet, or even to see her, just as it is thought unlucky nowadays to break a mirror or spill the salt."

"Is she supposed to haunt the Strath?" inquired the owner with more interest.

Mr. Price shook his head in a puzzled fashion, and bent low over the table.

"Your rector, who knows the place better than any man living, declares there is neither figure to be seen, nor sound to be heard, either in house or garden," he said, fingering the ends of his white tie excitedly. "And I must own that village opinion bears him out to the letter. Now as regards my farm-house, which was undoubtedly possessed—I saw the queer old Georgian woman myself, standing by a hay-rick, one raw winter afternoon—not a labourer would go near the place, and the stories I heard of red and green lights flashing across the windows, groans, and gnashing of teeth, though the poor old dame, I would swear, hadn't a stump left in her head, made me sympathise with the psalmist who declared, 'all men are liars.' Try the Strath for a few days, Mr. Conway. Don't mistake me. I wouldn't live there myself. I'm a churchman, but I have a horror of the unseen world. Is that decanter empty? There is another upon the sideboard. Yes, give the Strath a fair test. It has always been a place of mystery, but latterly seems to have broken out, if I may so use the expression. Enter into the mood of the influence and it will treat you well, Berry would say. Only don't let him get too strong a hold upon you, or he will whisk you back into an atmosphere of prehistoric days."

Nearly an hour later Flora, weary of her own society and nettled at being isolated, came glimmering round the house in her white dress, and played spy at the dining-room window. She saw the two squires, the old aristocrat and the young plebeian, leaning across the table, slopping wine amicably into each other's glass, the one talking perpetually, the other laughing in approbation. She heard her uncle announce that his father had died of gout, the blame being on the speaker's great-grandfather; and she also heard his companion's assertion that Mr. Price might therefore consider himself insured against the malady. Then she shivered a little at the grotesqueness of the scene, entered the house through the conservatory, and passing into the dining-room broke up the conversation by taking Conway out into the garden.

"If you decide to live in the country," she told him severely, "you will have to abandon your London habits. Uncle is an old man," she added reprovingly. "And it is wrong of you to excite him into forgetting himself."

Conway became penitent and apologetic. "A fellow living alone in diggings hasn't much chance of doing himself any good, Miss Neill," he said in deep humility. "It's too lonely of an evening to stay in, and the means of enjoying yourself are made so jolly convenient. I'm ashamed of myself—I am really, but your old uncle is such a jolly good sort. And, you see, I'm not a clever chap, Miss Neill," he rambled on. "I haven't got much learning, and I can't stand books. I don't know Shakspere from Robinson Crusoe. Don't laugh at me, Miss Neill. I can't help being a silly jackass. Perhaps I had better be going now. But you will come over to-morrow? Do come and see my house."

Flora was about to deliver one of her plainspoken remarks, when she was interrupted by a loud summons from the dining-room. Leaving the guest she slipped back into the house, and discovered her uncle, sitting erect and preternaturally stern, beside his hospitable table, which had been influenced that night by some subtle nerve of consciousness deflected from the Strath.

"Flora," he cried indignantly. "The man's no gentleman. I forbid you to contaminate yourself by speaking to him. He has drunk more than is good for him. And so have I."

"I fancy you once told me your great-grandfather never went to bed sober," said the girl.

"Customs were different then," snapped the squire. "Send Mr. Reed away, and remember please, he is related to my head-carter."

"If you mean Mr. Conway he is just going. Had you not better come into the drawing-room? The housemaid will be here presently."

"I shall remain here until to-morrow morning, if necessary," said the squire solemnly. "Supper has not agreed with me to-night. The soup was a failure."

"If my mother could see you, she would take hold of your poor old shoulders and shake you," cried Flora; and with that she ran out and rejoined the squire of Thorlund, who was standing near the gate, gazing penitently at the solemn stars.

"Miss Neill," he said tremulously. "There's nothing like the country. I was ill when I came here, but already, thanks to the beautiful fresh air, I feel a different man. I am going to walk back to Thorlund in this wonderful moonlight, and I shall admire nature all the way."

After an earnest appeal to Flora "not to forget to-morrow," the guest started off along the shining road. From a distance came up the mellowed noises of the fair, and the glow of naptha lamps became reflected against the rolling clouds.

Flora stood, smiling a little, in the shadow, flicking away the gnats from her forehead.

"That is one of the weakest men I have ever met," she said to a moth which hovered for a moment before her. "It would be amusing, and quite easy, to treat him in this fashion."

She wound her handkerchief tightly round her little finger, and turned with the action towards the house.

Scene II.—MYSTERY

Is it possible then that the soul—which is invisible and proceeding to another place . . . when it is separated from the body—is at once dissipated and utterly annihilated, as many men say? It is impossible to think so.—*Plato.*

When Conway reached the exposed road, leaving Kingsmore behind, a cool wind sprang up redolent of pines. To feel it the better he took off his hat and leaned against a moss-clad milestone. The unwonted exercise of walking along country roads tired him quickly. He watched the moonbeams playing across the ridges of short grass, and flinging shadows into the ghastly chalk-pits, until the solitude awed him. He found himself in a vastly different world from the noisy town which had surrounded him throughout his life. And yet he found himself longing for the grapes and pomegranates of his Egypt. He was incapable of feeling any true admiration for the splendid silence of the hills. The novelty of the experiment was still upon him; but the artistic temperament was not, and never had been, his.

Across the brow of the chalk a thin thread of road cut the highway at right angles, and here a spectral sign-post pointed with three arms; the fourth had been removed by storm, and its remainder was a sharp finger-like splinter. Reaching this point Conway crossed the patch of grass to make a short cut; but in passing the post his foot struck an obstacle, which proved to be the amputated arm. In idle curiosity he lifted the rotten board, and holding it in the moonlight made out the barely legible inscription, 'Queensmore. 1 Mile.'

There was nothing to be seen in the direction pointed at by the splinter, except ragged bushes and white stones, beside a weedy road which descended in graceful curves from the summit and disappeared far down in a clump of larches. There was no indication of a village down beyond; not a voice proceeded from the valley, nor tinkle of sheep-bell, nor snort of cow or horse at pasture. A barn owl slid across the firs and shrieked at the enemy; and silence settled down again.

Presently there sounded a rattle of wheels, a stamp of iron shoes; a stream of lamplight followed; and then a box-shaped cart topped the ridge, and came noisily to the rectangular section of the roads, the horse backing as he felt the decline.

"Like a lift, sir?" inquired a hoarse voice, proceeding from a muffled figure perched high between two goggle lamps.

Conway recognised the mail-cart making its journey towards the distant railway. Glad of the invitation he reached the flat roof, with the driver's assistance, settled himself upon a bag of newspapers, and, clinging to the iron rail, closed his eyes when the horse was given his head, because it appeared that any moment he might be hurled forward into space. The driver began to chat, and when his head had ceased revolving Conway found himself able to listen.

"I ain't allowed to take anyone up," the man explained. "And I ain't supposed to smoke neither, which is what I call a bit of stupid tyranny. But 'tis lonesome driving along these roads night after night. Would you mind leaning over a bit, and holding the reins, while I strike a light? Are you a stranger in these parts, sir?"

Conway replied, without revealing his identity, and as the cart jolted on he asked the driver to point out the site of Queensmore and the position of Deadman's Hill. The man immediately swung round, and extended his whip in the direction of the rapidly receding clump of larches.

"Deep down in yonder valley," he replied. "You ain't got property there, I hope, sir?"

"I have not," Conway answered.

"Queensmore is deserted and broke up. A very old village, they tell me, sir, built by these Saxons, and full of their remains, leastways the ground is. Go over and have a look at the place, if so be you can spare the time. It lies just at the foot of Deadman's Hill. That there is the hill, sir. A bit further back you can see the post which marks where the gallows stood. They do say it ain't healthy to be along these ways by night; but I've crossed this here country for years in all weathers, at Midsummer, Hallow's E'en, and

Christmas, and I've seen naught, but only owls and bats and glow-worms. Folks let a fancy get into their heads, and keep it there, and let it grow, until they come to believe it's true."

"How many people live at Queensmore now?" Conway asked.

"Not one. The last inhabitant—an old man, name of Jabez Tooke—died there five years ago. He wouldn't leave the place, and having a bit of money of his own he lived there by himself till he was ninety, and then he had to go whether he wanted to or not. They buried him in the old churchyard, and there's a stone over his grave, saying something this way, 'Here lies Jabez Tooke, the last resident in Queensmore, who wouldn't be taken from his native village till death took him.' Kind of joke on his name, you see, sir. Parson Price was angry when that stone was put up, they tell me. But it don't matter now. Queensmore has had its day, and now the owls have it to themselves. The wind is pulling it down bit by bit."

"What made the people leave it?" the townsman asked.

"Well 'tis a bad country for agriculture hereabouts, and when year after year the sheep did no good the farmers began to get out of it. Then, of course, the labourers had to move on, and after that the parish was joined on to Kingsmore, and that was the end of it. It wasn't ever what you would call healthy down yonder. Too much stagnant water, and they couldn't afford to drain. Flowers did well, but there's no money in them. All the village must be just blowing with roses now, sir, and any one as wants can help themselves. But 'tis a sad kind of place, with its tumbling cottages, and ruined church, and nobody seems to care to go near it."

The driver chatted on, glad of the opportunity to use his tongue, until the mail-cart approached Thorlund, and the great elms which surrounded the Strath could be seen against the sky.

"I don't carry no weapons," he said, in response to Conway's question regarding the dangers of the road. "I wouldn't know how to handle a pistol—shoot the old horse as likely as not. There ain't any real danger on the road nowadays. I was held up once, when 'twas thought I was carrying valuables, and I gave my gentleman strong medicine with this here whip. I'm tidy useful with a whip, and when a man gets a clean cut across the eyes he's had enough. Never got a word of thanks for saving the mail, but if I was seen carrying a gentleman I would be sure of the sack. I mustn't do less than my duty, sir, but as much over as I like. It's a hard life, because there's more foul weather than fair, and never a word of encouragement if I bring in the cart up to time all the year round. Yonder is Thorlund, and the Strath. Now that's an awful mysterious sort of place, if you like, sir, and it's a very queer affair about this Mr. Henry Reed."

"If you don't mind stopping here, I will get down," said Conway, when he discovered that the cart was turning away from the valley. "I am going to Thorlund."

"Are you though?" exclaimed the driver, with a sudden direct interest in his passenger. "Mind that step, sir. It's dangerous when you don't know it. Well there, I've been real glad to have your company, and I didn't ought to take anything, but thank you very much all the same, and good-night to you, sir."

It was not until the ancient yews of the churchyard appeared before him that Conway perceived he had somewhere made a wrong turn. He saw ahead a grey wall partly covered with ivy, and in his pocket he felt a key which would open the hidden door in that wall. A light streamed across the graves; a window beyond was open, and coming near he saw Dr. Berry seated at his table, and when he stopped there came upon the night the scholar's rich voice chanting a Greek lyric. It was an unknown tongue to the listener, but he was nevertheless fascinated; and as he stood, listening, a strange power fell upon him, his mind succumbed at once, and his feet passed the dark mound which marked the resting-place of his uncle's body, and entered the shadow. He fitted the key into the lock, turned it, and the door opened at a touch.

For an instant he held back. The wonderful garden spread away before him bathed in moonlight. Then he laughed with a sense of new-found happiness, and moved forward, drawn on by invisible bonds; and the door closed into the wall with a gentle vibration; and a hundred unknown energies made music in his brain. The house called to its new servant, and he went to it; and the guest's bedroom in the Load of Mischief remained unoccupied that night.

As the Aeolian harp is thrilled by every passing breath of wind, so the consciousness of Dr. Berry responded to every change in the influence of the Strath. He had not perceived the figure of Conway passing before the window, neither had he heard the opening nor the closing of that door in the crumbling wall; and yet he knew a material being had entered the garden, and he felt more strongly than he had ever done a power controlling his human organism, prompting him to take pencil and paper, and write—he knew not what.

The influence of the Strath was again strongly aroused. Since Reed's tragical fate the old house had remained quiescent. It appeared to have exhausted its power for the time. And now in one moment the scholar's tongue was silenced as he recited the complaint of Euphron. "God, as thou hast given us only a short life, why dost thou not allow us to pass it without sorrow?" and a cold breath went through the room, and his body began to pass into ecstacy; and he knew by all this that the power had returned, and that it was kindly and wished him well.

The impulse to write became overwhelming. Scarcely knowing what he did, the scholar took a pencil, and immediately the hand supporting it was guided towards a sheet of paper and there reposed with violent twitchings. The upper part of his body turned shudderingly away from the right arm, and settled, a mass of semiconscious matter, across the high support afforded by the side of his chair; but the arm, and especially the hand which clutched the pencil, were impatient, active, and mobile.

"What is this?" he moaned; for he could feel that his body was in pain, and there was in his mouth a taste exceeding bitter, as though he had swallowed hemlock.

And immediately his unconscious hand moved fiercely and rapidly across the paper, tracing out in ancient Greek the explanation:—

"We cannot command the elements, or would have come near before. Now you shall recognise our power. Give praise to the Supreme, for the permission afforded of proving to you the truth of the endlessness of life.

"We will answer the questions you have written down, though we work with difficulty, being compelled by the immutable law of Nature to communicate through your brain and your mind, feeling again, as we return to earth-state, the pains of our dissolution. The conditions are exceptional to-night. We have awaited such an opportunity for long. But being yourself in the body you will desire some proof of the presence of an objective mind. When you awaken go forth into your garden. Seven white lilies stand in a line beside the gate. The blooms upon the fourth we will remove as we pass from hence, leaving the green stalk bare. We will also read from a book and impress you of a word. Walk, when you are able, across the room, and your hand shall seek out a book, which, as you hold it, shall open at the one hundred and ninetieth page. The last word upon that is ΚΑΣΣΙΤΕΡΟΙΟ. It is enough. Thus you shall learn our power over matter.

"What is the meaning, you have asked, of this influence at the Strath? You have doubted whether this power could arise from the actions of certain earth-bound spirits. Also you have desired to know how it is that after years of quiescence the spirit of the house, as you have called it, should have become in so short a time thus mightily aroused. We answer you concerning these things. Those spirits, who, because of their grossness, are imprisoned near the earth, are ever struggling to make their presence felt. As the sea-bird flutters towards the light of some lofty tower, so do these discarnate beings struggle towards that incarnate mind, or towards those material objects, through whom, or by which, they may exert their will and proclaim their identity. Some of these spirits are harmless, but many are dangerous and all are undeveloped. There are in the Strath certain material objects by means of which these spirits are allowed great power upon the affairs of mortals who approach the place. You cannot understand, nor may we explain to you further, how this should be. Only beware, for there is peril in seeking out this knowledge, and the body endures not easily nor for long. You know not how the spirit may work, even through a ring, or a lock of hair, or may seek to impress its nearness through the bird or the flower. We say again, beware, for the spirits of the earth-bound, they who in the flesh have done murder, or violence to themselves, or have succumbed to the bodily appetite, are jealous of the happiness of those who have led the spiritual life in your condition. They shall retard your upward progress if they may.

"And now we answer concerning the present great activity of those who control the ancient house. It is your desire to seek into hidden causes which has made it possible for such energies to arise. That power will not be maintained, but while it continues we have fear for you, knowing the frailty of the incarnate mind. These undeveloped spirits have at length become skilled in managing the elements. It is necessary that a certain combination of circumstances should be formed, before such manifestations of spiritual power be possible, and because such a combination is rare you do not often find upon your sphere that influence, as you call it, which is now filling your mind with perplexing doubts. It is possible that the combination, which now exists, may not be made again. We would speak upon other matters, but your brain is unable to express those greater truths, and your mind is incapable of receiving them. Be satisfied now, and rest. You have very much to learn."

The inert body of the scholar stirred slightly and he groaned deeply in his trance. But, before he could awaken, his vitalised right arm, acting so strongly at variance with the remainder of his system, swept again across the paper, and his hand settled, and his fingers went on to write:

"A spirit lately arrived desires to communicate, and we are commanded to permit him. He will use our power to write in his own language, and will then depart from you, having given the evidence that is required."

There the sprawling Greek letters ceased, and the pencil went on to write in English, forming in illiterate unshaped handwriting the brief and blasphemous message:

"Damn you, Professor. You were right."

Some minutes passed before Dr. Berry came to himself and was able to comprehend what the intelligence had wrought through his undiscerning brain. It was close upon midnight before the message was deciphered; for despite his scholarship and skill in reading manuscripts, there were words and symbols in that script which were new to him. The communication was written in Attic Greek by an intelligence which exhibited a perfect command over the finer tones of that perfect language. No living scholar could have penned those lines, and possibly few modern Greeks could have translated them into their own decadent tongue.

Slowly and painfully, for his body was racked and weary, Dr. Berry approached his bookcase, and immediately his arm was raised and his hand guided towards a work near the end of the top shelf, a book bound in drab boards, entitled, "Theatre of the Greeks." That work was one of a parcel which had come to him during the previous year and so far had not been opened. The boards fell apart, but not the pages which he required, and on bending to discover the cause he found that the leaves had not been cut. Opening the page quickly with a paper-knife, his eye sought the concluding word upon page 190. It was ΚΑΣΣΙΤΕΡΟΙΟ.

Lighting a candle, the scholar walked out into the garden and the still dark night, until he came to a flower-bed, beside the gate which opened upon the graveyard. Six tall Madonna lilies lifted their heads of white bloom before the fence where at sunset seven had stood. Approaching, the scholar raised the candle above his head, and before a moth blundered against the wick and extinguished the flame, he perceived that the central lily, the fourth from whichever side the plants were counted, stood a bare green stalk, denuded of its blooms.

Scene III.—MUSICAL COMEDY

Light quirks of music, broken and uneven.—*Pope.*

When Flora awoke she discovered a pink envelope addressed in Maude's careless calligraphy, lying beside her morning cup of tea. She hurried over her toilet, made her way into the garden; and seating herself luxuriously in an easy chair beneath an arch of honeysuckle, read and laughed over the selfish sentences inscribed upon two sheets of perfumed paper.

The little lady was very miserable. London was dusty and desolate. She had read the new books, seen the new pictures, and heard the new plays; she had done everything and enjoyed nothing, because she was losing all her prettiness. Lately no one had admired her, at least no one had told her so, and it was because she was growing old. She felt perfectly convinced she would never attract anybody again. What would happen to her if she became a widow she dared not contemplate. As for Herbert, he was always in the city, which was of course the proper place for him, but he was bad-tempered when he did come home, and always declaring money was dreadfully scarce, which she didn't believe, but he had always been fearfully stingy. And he declared he would not take her into the country, so she had made up her mind to go away by herself, before her health was completely wrecked. And if Flora was staying for any time at Kingsmore, would she look out for a furnished cottage, upon rather high ground, but not in an exposed spot, well away from standing water, with a ice garden, which could be guaranteed free from toads and owls, with plenty of lavender bushes, and green blinds to all the windows, but not Venetians, which always broke directly they were touched. . .

Then a bell jangled in the house, and Flora rose at once, because she desired to find her uncle in a good humour; and she knew nothing upset the old gentleman more than being kept waiting for his breakfast.

Because it had been the custom of his ancestors, and Mr. Price was an ardent conservative, a service was held for the labourers early every morning in one of the barns. The squire had not only accomplished this duty, but had ridden round the farm and signed the death-warrant of several pigs, before entering the dining-room where his niece immediately joined him. The old gentleman kissed the girl on both cheeks, according to custom, and plunged into discursive talk which had nothing to do with the guest of the previous night, or the empty decanters upon the sideboard; while Flora, so soon as she was allowed the opportunity, told him of Mrs. Juxon's requirements, and read such extracts from the letter as were fit for publication.

"Bless my soul," exclaimed the squire, as he dropped a drumstick of cold chicken noisily into his plate. "What more will the woman ask for? Why does she not say at once that she intends to have the entire scheme of nature altered to suit her convenience, and engage angels for landscape gardeners. Lavender bushes and green blinds! I hope she may get them."

After sundry remarks on Flora's part Mr. Price stumbled into his niece's snare, and suggested that she should take the light cart and drive round the neighbourhood, with a view to finding a cottage sufficiently idyllic to suit the spoilt beauty. When this matter had been settled, Flora placed her elbows on the table, rested her chin upon her hands, and introduced a fresh topic with the statement, "I have been thinking, uncle."

"Have you, my dear?" the squire replied, adding with a chuckle, "You look none the worse for it."

"I think mother would be willing to let our house this year," Flora went on. "We have heaps of applications, on account of the river. And then she could come here, and keep house for you all the summer."

"Before agreeing, I shall require an undertaking that my liberty is not to be interfered with," answered the squire, who was in very good spirits that morning, despite the excesses of the previous night. As a matter of fact Flora's suggestion was entirely after his heart, and had been made by himself without success in former years. "You know, child, I will never consent to have my study tidied," he went on, "and the privilege of the latchkey I must retain. Your dear mother has a weakness for what she calls order, therefore, before admitting her into this house, I shall require a signed agreement granting me full licence to continue in my untidy ways."

"Oh, you shall have all your old privileges," said Flora. "I will write to mother at once, and then go cottage-hunting for Maude. Remember," she added carelessly, as she rose to go, "we are due at Thorlund this afternoon."

Flora had her way. At half-past-four the Kingsmore carriage entered the valley of Thorlund, bringing the vicar and his niece to visit the Strath. The old gentleman wore his best coat, which had left the tailor's hands not more than five years back. He had also put on a fresh white tie, which was already showing finger-marks, and had brought out his dusty silk hat, the wearing of which when visiting a neighbouring squire being a point of etiquette upon which he was particular. During the journey across the four miles of chalk hills he talked sheep and turnips, and was continually putting his head out of the window, to examine the state of the road, or to shout a simple joke for the appreciation of some passing son of toil.

As the coachman was unwilling to venture with the carriage through the high grass, which completely obliterated what had been the drive, the visitors alighted at the iron gates, and made their way along a faintly defined path to the house. The front door stood open, but there was no sign of any occupant, and their attempts to ring were frustrated by the corroded bell-knob, which remained immovable. Mr. Price shouted and stamped, and, when no one put in an appearance, stepped into the hall. He was the first squire of Kingsmore to enter the Strath since the beginning of the period styled by historians modern England. At the opposite side of the hall a huge fireplace yawned blackly, its iron dogs red with rust. Some old tables, stiff-back chairs, and sofas of tapestry, with a couple of tarnished sconces holding blackened candles, and a curious clock its dial made of white flowered glass, were the principal articles of furniture. The hall was paved with stone. Above, a rectangular wooden balustrade, sadly in need of repair, went round the building, and a few sombre pictures could be seen against the damp stained walls of the first floor. The frames were as black as dead walnut-leaves.

"It will cost the young man a great deal to restore the place," Mr. Price whispered.

"But where is he?" returned Flora. "I wonder if he is in here."

She led the way boldly into the drawing-room or saloon, the walls of which were hung with tattered crimson velvet. This room had been cleaned by the late owner with a good deal of care, until traces of what must formerly have been a richly gilded cornice had become here and there apparent. The extinct Hoopers had furnished their home well. There were tables and chairs made of mahogany, a new and expensive wood in the eighteenth century. Cabinets filled with old china occupied the corners, and grotesque footstools with sprawling legs of acanthus pattern were placed before each chair. Mirrors were greatly in evidence, all handsomely framed, the majority bearing sconces which still contained black sticks of wax. Upon a walnut sideboard a massive candelabrum threw out seven silver arms. Above the fireplace were arranged several bizarre ornaments of Indian make, intermingled with porcelain vases painted with gross designs after Giulio Romano. The pictures, which had evidently been lately rehung after having fallen from their original positions, were numerous, but of little artistic worth. The subjects were generally unpleasant, or suggestive; such as Actaeon watching Diana, the loves of Jupiter and Leda, of Venus and Adonis, of Aaron and Tamora, with coloured copies of Hogarth's Marriage *à la mode*. Upon a Louis Quinze table a fan was sprawling, the scenes of The Harlot's Progress painted upon its mounts, and beside it a box containing patches. The escutcheon of the Hoopers, set into the central window, cast a bar of colour across the rotten carpet. The squire gazed upon his surroundings without any sense of amazement, but with a distinct fascination, until he discovered himself putting up a hand to adjust the periwig which was not there. Both uncle and niece had altogether forgotten their absent host.

"It seems to be getting rather dark," the girl said tremulously.

"The sun has gone behind the trees, and the creepers are thick against the window," replied the squire with extraordinary lightheartedness. "Look here, Flora! A French horn, such as is used upon our coaches. And here a bent sword, twisted I doubt not by our host when in town while defending himself against the Mohawks, and here one of the furred caps which we old men wear while our wigs are with the barber. And now let me hear you draw some music out of this beautiful harpsichord."

The girl laughed, waking echoes in that strange place, and saying lightly, "I will endeavour, my respected relative, to give you the gratification which you desire," drew up a chair, and sat down before the impossible instrument.

"By God! what a place for a dance," cried the reverend squire, cutting a fantastic caper, then bounding after his hat as it rolled across the room. "Look at these boards, where they show through the carpet. All of oak, a foot and more in width, somewhat worm-eaten, but none the worse for that." Holding out his coat-tails, the old gentleman bowed gravely to his niece, and commenced to dance round her.

There came a sound of heels clicking upon the stones of the hall, followed by a rich voice:

"Bravo! bravissimo! That step was worthy of a dancing-master. If I had but a fiddle I would play you a measure which should set you skipping."

A handsome man strolled into the saloon, an open snuff-box between his finger and thumb, attired in laced coat and embroidered waistcoat, silk knee-breeches and stockings, silver-buckled highlows, and a big white wig. A quantity of lace surrounded his throat, and his smiling face was highly powdered and his chin patched.

"Why, Sir John! my dear Sir John!" exclaimed Mr. Price, ceasing from his gambols, and bowing to the new-comer with his toes turned out in most approved style. "This is a very extraordinary and unexpected pleasure, I do assure you, good Sir John."

"Nay, but you are mistaken," came the answer, as the speaker bowed low to the lady at the harpsichord. "The humble personage before you is merely the poor parson of Thorlund parish."

At that the squire of Kingsmore went very red and awkward; and finally blurted out the remarkable statement:

"I am totally at a loss to explain why we are here in these preposterous garments. Flora, my dear, what could your tiring-woman have been thinking of, to send you out with not an atom of powder to your head, nor a patch to your face. And I believe we are expected to drink a dish of tea. Where is our host that I may apologize in a suitable manner?"

"He has been for some hours in a state of drowsiness," Dr. Berry explained, with a careless wave of the snuff-box. "I am unable to understand what has come over him. He is dressed ready to receive you, but I cannot keep him awake. I will, however, inform him that you have arrived. As for your clothes that is a matter which can be easily attended to. There are, in the rooms upstairs, presses filled with apparel for both sexes, secure against dust and moth."

"Pray show me the way," said the squire with old-fashioned urbanity. "My charming niece, shall we accompany the learned doctor and make ourselves presentable?"

The strange characters passed out, making for the stairway and the unexplored regions above. For them the clock of time had been set back, or rather the hands were continuing to move at the point where their progress had been arrested more than a century back. The drama had been suddenly broken into during the eighteenth century; and now that figures had come again upon the scene the drama went on, as though there had been no interval, and those who were present had to take their cue, and assume the parts of those men and women, Hoopers or Branscombes, long since driven off that stage.

After a short interval of silence a sound of singing filled the long saloon. The vocalist was Dr. Berry, who was drawing an accompaniment of broken music from the harpsichord, while Conway lolled sleepily upon a sofa, costumed as a *beau* of a past age. To them entered a lady and an old man, the latter exceedingly quaint and undignified, the former tall and handsome; both attired after the best manner of the time in which they dimly believed they were drawing breath and inspiration.

"It is certainly growing very dark," said the squire of Kingsmore, as he advanced with mincing step into the saloon. "And it is still early in the evening."

"The clouds are coming up thickly," replied the musician. "The windows are also obscured by ivy, and trees surround this peaceful retreat upon every side. Our host continues to be drowsy," he went on, pointing to the sofa and its silk-clad occupant; and having spoken he crossed over, shook the sleeper gently by the shoulder, and called, "Wake, my friend, here are your guests."

Conway opened his eyes. His face was perfectly pallid, but there were lines of laughter drawn about his mouth which gave him a curious resemblance to the mask of comedy, hanging in the room across the hall. He rose slowly, and with perfect breeding, altogether unlike his usual manner, bowed silently to his guests. Then he seated himself again, and became aesthetically engrossed upon a painted vase.

Flora came forward, and asked, "Are you tired, Mr. Conway?"

"I have still a sleepy humour upon me," the owner of the Strath replied, passing as he spoke a hand across his forehead.

Dr. Berry was posing before one of the mirrors.

"Shall we play?" Conway suggested, stretching out his arms and smiling vacantly.

"By all means let us play," assented the old squire, admitting into his nostrils a pinch of dust which had no doubt been choice *rappee* a hundred years before.

A small sane voice whispered to these mummers that they were playing at folly, just as the drunkard may be conscious that he is making a deplorable exhibition of human frailty, although the knowledge in no way aids him to act like a sober being. They set out a table, old-fashioned cards and markers were produced;

and they commenced to play. The silence of the house was only disturbed by a faint moaning of wind in the chimneys.

"Gott in Himmel! as our gracious king would say. I am scarce able to read my cards," cried Mr. Price, after they had played the first hand.

"It is growing damnably dark," muttered Conway, not ashamed to swear before the lady because such was the custom of the time. "Set a light to the candles, doctor. There is a tinder-box upon the mantel. The king," he muttered, turning to Mr. Price, the sane intellect struggling to assert itself. "Who is our king?"

There was a perplexed interval, occupied by a mental conflict between enlightenment and possession, before Mr. Price replied somewhat testily, "Why, George the Second. Though 'tis said he has not long to live. God save our Augustus!"

"Truly the spirit of comedy prevails this evening," observed the sober voice of the doctor, who was lighting the ancient candles with a modern wax vesta.

"Ha!" exclaimed the old squire, picking at the yellow ruffles upon his wrist. "What is that, doctor? Comedy! Why, to be sure, let us laugh and sing. Where are the servants? Let us have a bowl of punch and a few long pipes."

He stumbled in his big shoes towards the bell-rope, tugged it, and the cord came away in his hand.

"I have no servants," said Conway meditatively. "But there is wine in the house. I will bring you some."

He left the saloon, and they could hear him laughing across the hall. Dr. Berry went on lighting the old candles in the sconces, in the ormolu chandelier, and the candelabrum, until the saloon began to glitter. He closed the decayed shutters and drew the torn folds of the crimson curtains, singing a ballad as he worked. The light revealed a painted ceiling, in the centre of which appeared a nymph entwining the stem of an apple-tree with garlands of flowers.

"A forest of lights!" cried Mr. Price, standing before the chimney-glass and lifting his hands in rapture. "The view of this handsome apartment regarded thus is indeed exquisite. The lights dazzle and shine from one mirror to another in an endless vista. Ha! here comes our wine. What elegant glasses, my dear Sir! What a superb piece of workmanship is this salver!"

They drank, to the health of their dying king, to George William Frederick, Prince of Wales, to a lord admiral, and a great duke, all of whom had left the body many generations back. They drank confusion to the French and prosperity to their country. Then the scholar took Flora by the hand, and leading her out into the centre of the saloon danced with her a minuet.

The prosaic figure of a coachman appeared startlingly at the entrance. Having failed to make himself heard, and finding the front door open, he had taken the liberty to enter, and now stood struggling with amazement and some little fear, and yet without finding anything of an incongruous nature in the scene before him.

"Beg pardon, sir," he said, addressing the capering little gentleman whom he recognised as his master. "Do you want the horses to stand, sir, or shall I put them up at the Inn?"

Another wave of sanity passed across Mr. Price's brain. He understood that it was his duty to leave that present company and go into an altogether mysterious world. With many apologies, and much snuff-taking, he approached the master of the house to take his leave.

"I shall see you at Almack's or White's, when we are next in town," he said after a final warm good-night, glibly repeating the words that were forced upon his tongue, although feeling them to be absurd.

There was still daylight upon the village. A couple of labourers, their day's work done, had proceeded towards the iron gates, attracted by the Kingsmore carriage, and had been summoned by the coachman to hold the horses while he went in search of his master. These men stood craning their necks towards the garden, until they saw in the twilight two figures approaching; an old gentleman in a monstrous periwig, handsomely embroidered sack coat, flowing waistcoat, and gleaming silk stockings, assisting the progress of a young and beautiful lady, with protruding panier and powdered head, a fan swinging from her wrist, and a soiled Pamela hat upon her whitened hair.

ENTR'ACTE

An avowal of poverty is a disgrace to no man; but to make no effort to escape from it is certainly disgraceful.—*Thucydides*.

A fortnight had passed since Conway's departure from his rooms in town, and still the profligate gave no sign of his existence. Every morning, when the postman's knock sounded along the street, a weary man crept down a dirty flight of stairs from his attic, praying for a letter which might cheer his heart, but finding none. After a meagre breakfast he would venture out to another house, to inquire if there was anything for Mr. Drayton. The answer was always in the negative.

The hack-writer had been compelled to abandon Conway's rooms, not so much because the place was being subjected to a thorough cleansing, as owing to the fact that the rent was overdue, and the attentions of the agent had become pressing. Drayton had written several letters to his patron, acquainting him with this fact. As these letters were not returned, he concluded they had been received, and yet nothing came from the distant country to prove that Conway was alive. This continued silence was becoming a serious matter for Drayton, who at that time was in a desperate state of poverty. Younger men were jostling him out of the ranks of an overcrowded profession, his one suit of clothes was more than threadbare, and his health had begun to fail for want of sufficient food. He knew that Conway hated country life, and would never separate himself from the pleasures of town unless compelled to do so. Concluding that the missing man was ill, or had met with an accident, Drayton resolved to go down into the country and find his way to the Strath.

This determination came on a morning when he found himself absolutely penniless.

Leaving the wretched lodging-house, he passed into the street where the sun was showering golden favours upon rich and poor alike, let himself into Conway's rooms by means of the key which had been left with him, and searching in a cupboard found to his delight a tin of biscuits and some apples. Having breakfasted, he passed into the bedroom and exploited his patron's wardrobe, remarking as a justification for the act he contemplated, "Conway has always been good-natured, and I don't think he will mind. Anyhow I will play boldly and take the risk."

The impecunious writer believed in being thorough in his methods. Having come to a decision, he discarded his own seedy garments in favour of one of Conway's numerous suits, borrowed a pair of boots, which were not, like his, gaping at the seams, and a change of linen; and presently returned to the sitting-room better dressed than he had ever been in his life. There was a jar of whisky in the cupboard. Drayton helped himself moderately, then sat down to think. As he contemplated a railway journey it was obviously necessary to be provided with cash; and to that end it would be equally necessary to pawn something.

He looked round the room to select a victim. Pictures were too bulky; an inquisitive policeman might meet him at the door and put inconvenient questions. There were, however, numerous small money-bringers, such as a marble clock, a pair of field-glasses, a handsome tantalus, a silver cup, any of which he might very easily hypothecate. He selected the clock, and approaching the chimney-piece had put up his hands to remove it, when the two masks above caught his eye. Straightway his arms dropped at his sides, and his mind became possessed by a new and quaint idea.

Five minutes later he was hurrying down the street towards a familiar pawn-shop, with the pair of grotesque faces wrapped in brown paper beneath his arm. He felt unusually excited, and somewhat conscience-stricken at purloining the heirlooms.

At first sight it seemed as though he was to be sharply disillusioned, for the pawnbroker, who knew Drayton well enough, pushed the parcel back indignantly.

"Having a lark, ain't you?" he satirically demanded, noting the writer's unusually well-dressed appearance, and jumping at the conclusion that he had made some money and had spent an undue portion of it in liquor. "There's a toy-shop round the corner," he went on, endeavouring to repay insult by insult. "Take 'em there. Maybe they'll give you a penny for the pair."

Like many of his profession Drayton was sensitive, and sarcasm hurt him. Muttering an apology, he caught up the masks and slipped out of the shop, hot and awkward, with the idea of returning for the clock that he might convince the pawnbroker of the seriousness of his intentions; but when again upon the street the former influence possessed his mind, and there flashed across his vision the picture of a dusty little shop, a mile westward, beside which he had often lingered, to glance at the fantastic objects exposed for sale, and to wonder how the proprietor made a living, because he had never seen a buyer enter or leave the house. Mechanically he turned his footsteps towards the mean and dirty street, where the little curio-shop survived, while more ornate trading ventures went to the wall.

A swarthy little man advanced from a black recess when the writer entered, and in a guttural voice sought to learn what the gentleman required. Somewhat nervously Drayton explained the object of his visit, and opening his parcel placed the masks side by side upon the counter. The dealer assumed a pair of spectacles, and bent his head to examine the two brown objects; then, with a muttered apology, he lifted the models tenderly and carried them towards the light.

"They are worth very little," he said deliberately, as he looked back. "I will advance you five shillings upon the pair."

"That is no good to me," Drayton replied.

"If you desire to sell I would give you one pound," the little man said, his foreign accent becoming more pronounced.

"I do not wish to sell," said the writer. "I want to borrow five pounds."

The curio-dealer said nothing, but his head inclined slightly. Then he walked away into a back-room and very quickly reappeared, with five sovereigns and a scrap of pasteboard on his little crooked hand. Drayton confessed that he had not a copper on him to pay for the ticket, whereupon the little man gravely gave him change for one of the sovereigns, bowed him out of the shop without a word, and then scurried back into the dark recess, shouting:

"Jacob! Where is that boy? Jacob! Run, my son—run!"

ACT III

Scene I.—HEROIC

All that thou sayest I can bear unmoved; for thou hast a voice bereft of power, like a shadow. Thou canst do nought but talk.—*Euripides*.

It was dusk when Drayton entered the parish of Thorlund, after a wearisome railway journey, and a long tramp of nine miles from the station. He walked straight to the partly-open iron gate, without pausing to seek information from a homeward-bound ploughman, the only being whom he met upon the road. He knew he had reached the Strath. He felt that he had known the place all his life. To one born and brought up in the metropolis, to struggle for daily bread, it was a joy to see that wilderness of flowers, and to breathe the heavy perfume wafted across the grass. The weary man pushed at the gate and passed in. Great stagbeetles were droning across the bushes. He removed his hat reverently, and waded through the tall herbage towards the house.

His eyes were heavy, as though with sleep, when he reached the door and rapped upon it, gently at first, then loudly, and finally with an energy akin to fury.

He had no idea how long an interval elapsed, before an old woman shuffled across the hall, and held up a sharp white face to hear what he had to say. She was short-sighted, deaf, and asthmatic, incapable of deep feeling, untroubled by emotions. This poor creature had been on the eve of being cast out 'broke' from the cottage home of her relatives; and the rector, hearing of it by chance, had rescued her for a time, and secured her poor services for the owner of the Strath. The influence of the house failed with her, perhaps because there was in her so little that was capable of responding to its dramatic power.

"Mr. Conway," she whined sadly. "He is walking in the orchard."

Drayton recrossed the weedy moat and walked away, plucking flowers as he went, pushing them into his button-holes, the brim of his hat, behind his ears, and even into his hair; and when they fell replacing them with others.

A ragged hedge appeared before him, and beyond were apple and pear trees with sparse foliage fluttering and whispering above mossy trunks. Hearing a human voice, Drayton peered through a gate to behold the man whom he had come so far to seek, walking through the long grass among the drooping branches, reading aloud from a book, and smiling as he read. Pausing close beside the hedge which concealed Drayton from his view he recited thoughtfully:

"I profess I know not what to think, but still there are some scruples remaining with me. Is it not certain I see things at a distance? Do we not perceive the stars and moon, for example, to be a great way off? Is not this, I say, manifest to the senses?"

"It is manifest," muttered Drayton, as he tumbled stupidly through the hedge.

Not a sign of surprise crossed Conway's white face, when the apparition fantastically dressed with flowers stood by him in the fading light. He continued his even paces, after motioning to the visitor to keep step at his side; and when Drayton obeyed the two men walked on through the orchard to the music of the evening, regarding one another, if they considered the matter at all, as spiritual beings unnecessarily encumbered with flesh.

"Tell me, my friend," said the late debauchee, who in his former state had hated the sight of books and the thought of philosophy, "what was the cause that impelled the rustic mentioned by Horace to lie on the bank of the stream, waiting until the waters should pass? Have we there ignorance in its most inexplicable form, or a super-normal belief in the wonder working power of faith?"

"Or a passionate longing for a revolution of nature's laws," Drayton added in the same gentle manner. "So often had he watched the flow of the stream that the sight may have wearied him. His wish might have suggested a half-belief that the source had failed, that the waters were actually flowing away, that any moment might witness their final exhaustion. Perhaps again, in monstrous arrogance, the fool believed that he stood beyond the law and at his word the waters would be stayed."

"When the brain has been wrought upon by insanity the sufferer will lift himself to the plane of godship," Conway mused, drawing down a mossy branch and gazing thoughtfully at the little emerald apples. "But our author assumes that his hero is sane."

"Yet we are unable to deduce sanity from his actions," Drayton argued. "There are limits to the imaginings of ignorance. The most insensate mortal knows that the apple, if detached from the bough, will fall to the ground. The observation of countless generations of ancestors has imbued him with so much knowledge. Instinct alone should advise him that the river must flow continually."

"I acknowledge it," Conway murmured. "The sanest philosopher is also the humblest. He who loses his reason holds up giants and examines them through a microscope."

They continued to pace the orchard through the thickening air; and Conway still felt no astonishment at finding Drayton by his side, attired in a suit of his own clothes. As for the latter he had certainly some dim remembrance of a visit to a pawn-shop, of a landlord waiting for the overdue rent, and of a back attic in a noisy street; but such matters were very distant and indistinct. Had he been told he had pawned the masks a decade ago, or even assured he had not pledged them at all, he would have assented.

"Is this happiness?" he inquired of his companion.

"Wonderful happiness," Conway answered. "I sleep much. My head aches a little, but it is no pain. It is a gentle heaviness, which does not cloud my vision. When I am awake I read. After supper I will read to you. The house is full of books."

"Do you hear voices?'"

Conway shook his head with a sleepy smile.

"It is always peaceful here."

"To-morrow I shall write," went on the uneducated man confidently.

They went by slow periods to the house.

The deaf old woman had no culinary skill, therefore the meal awaiting them was of the plainest—thin soup, a piece of mutton, a milk pudding, and a little fruit. Both men were silent, Conway reading from a book beside his plate, Drayton already absorbed upon the first act of a play which he intended to begin at once. When his host rose he also pushed back his chair, and they stood gazing at one another foolishly, until Conway pointed towards the flight of stairs. Side by side they crept up into the darkness.

Passing along the passage they entered a windowless room cumbered with much furniture and mouldy books; a great bed, heavily draped, occupied the centre; the carpet had been eaten away, and the rotten planks crumbled beneath their tread; a sofa and two chairs occupied spaces at the foot of the bed, and between the chairs stood a marble table, and upon the table two candles in bronze candlesticks, which when lighted revealed also a manuscript book in shagreen covers and a floriated cross. On one arm of this cross some long vanished hand had scratched the name of Winifred; on the other Geoffrey in similarly tremulous characters.

Drayton seated himself upon the sofa, and drawing the heavy draperies apart admitted light across the bed. There was nothing to be seen, except a mass of tumbled garments, and a black heap which might once have been a wreath of flowers.

There came a scurrying of rats from beyond the wainscoting, and after that silence.

"What room is this?" asked Drayton, as he permitted the damp curtains to fall and close.

"The bedroom of Winifred Hooper," Conway replied, without raising his eyes from a closely written page, dated along the margin January 14th, 1742. The writing was fine, and perfectly distinct, sloping from left to right, blurred occasionally by the damps of time, or perhaps by tears from the writer's eyes. The master of the house snuffed the candles, and said:

"I found this book to-day, in that cupboard beside the fireplace. It is the journal of one who formerly lived in this house. I will read you a few pages, and if you grow weary, or desire to sleep, put up your hand and I will cease."

Drayton was huddled at the end of the sofa, his arms folded tightly across his breast, his eyes fixed upon the cross. He made a motion of assent, and straightway the host began to read:

"I write to you, my Geoffrey, although I know you may never see these lines, therefore I will not commence with Beloved, or My Love. Such words spring warmly from my heart, but lie as cold as snow upon these pages. Yet I write them. 'Tis but a little happiness.

I am alone in the wind. It is so cold a wind. It howls round the house, and enters this room, to make my candle flicker. Snow has been falling all the day, and the garden lies buried, and the great tombs in the churchyard are covered with white sheets. The dead shall sleep to-night more warmly than I. My father is playing chess with Mr. Blair, the rector of Thorlund, in the saloon. At the end of their game a summons will come for me, and I must go down and sing. They say my voice is beautiful, but that is because I sing to you, and sometimes you seem so near that tears will come into my eyes, and my voice will tell again what it has already told, and would so gladly tell again, until I hear the drunken parson thumping his great shoes upon the floor, and shouting, 'My God! She sings like Farinelli.'

"Let me tell you how I have passed this day. In the morning I walked out. It was so still, and winter fog was lying along the valley. I heard the horses stamping in the stable, and saw the white mist steaming off the moat, while I scattered bread for my hungry sparrows. (Pardon this careful account of my trivial actions, Geoffrey. I could not write if I did not hope that Providence might place this little book into your hands some day, perhaps when you are wedded, and I am in the vault. You will not be false to your wife if you kiss this, because my hand has rested for a cold hour upon it.) Then I walked into the plantation, and beneath the bushes were snowdrops, so pale and white. They seemed to be shivering and to say, 'Why does the sun not shine?' But I knew that it was I who shivered, because the snow flowers are children of the winter, and I am made for the bluebell and the rose. Do you, I wonder, sometimes recall to mind that daffodil I plucked and gave to you last spring? I planted a chestnut beside the bulb, and the tiny tree grows strongly and the daffodil will come up again this spring in just the same spot, and will bear a bloom like that I gave to you, but you will not be here to take it from my hand.

"That same day, while walking with me through the plantation, you stepped upon and crushed a crocus. After you had gone, I went back for the bulb, and planted it in a box which stands beside me now. The divided bulb has sent up two little spikes of bloom, but one is very much stronger than the other. The weak one is mine, the strong is yours. Mine will flower last and fade first. I cannot water mine without watering yours, or I would be selfish and make the spears of equal strength.

"During the afternoon I walked to Queensmore to visit my uncle the vicar, a man I cannot love, because he is so hard, and I fear a miser also. The wheels of the coaches had beaten down the snow, but it was slippery to walk, and once I went down. Had you been there you would have taken me up, and carried me against my will—so I would have declared—down Stone Hill, as you carried me once when my foot gave me pain from the sign-post to the village stocks. A coach passed me, the guard blowing upon his horn as though to warm himself, the passengers very cold and miserable, the poor horses sadly weary. A woman in the basket called, "Good-luck, pretty dear," and I started when I understood the good wish was intended for me. It cheered me on my lonely walk. I am sure the sharp wind had put colour into my face and brightened my eyes. Perhaps I was pretty then. But I am white again now, and the mirror opposite tells me that my prettiness was borrowed after all. It was only for the hour. And, Geoffrey, you were not there to see it.

"The bushes are covered with berries this winter, and I am glad to know that my singing-birds will not starve. But I have found some stiff little bodies upon the road. There is misteltoe in our orchard, but none has been brought into the house. On Christmas night my father was out late, and when he returned drank deep, and would have beaten me, for no fault whatsoever save that I had seen him come home, had I not ran from him and hidden in the lumber-room. No Yule log burnt in this house; no hackin, nor turkey, nor plum-porridge was served at our table; the village mummers did not enter this garden; and when I heard the bells a-ringing I shut myself in my room and tried to be brave. I had seen woodmen hauling the Yule log merrily towards Kingsmore, and Mr. Price himself was sitting atop, with a great branch of holly in his hand, singing a carol with all his might. They are merry folk at Kingsmore. I could hear their drums and fifes on Christmas Eve, and Deborah tells me the whole company gambolled and danced all night, and their boar's head was one of the largest seen, and their masque the most diverting, and their ale the finest ever brewed. Happy that 'tis given to some to spend their lives in giving pleasure to their fellow-men. Deborah tells me also, or will whisper it rather, how that she heard the phantom bells in the long pasture between here and Queensmore.

"But, Geoffrey, I wander. Would you desire to hear of my uncle, whom I found this afternoon in his study, sitting without a fire, a red cloak round him, and stiff white gloves upon his hands? I think you would rather I wrote about myself. I will promise you I am no bigger than when you saw me last, and then you thought me, I fear, somewhat too small a person to contain a heart so big with love. But there, wise sweetheart, you were deceived. My face has not greatly changed. My eyes are just as blue, but as they look back at me from the mirror they do not smile. I would not have them try, because happiness cannot cannot be forced. I see I have written the word cannot twice. I have a little scar upon my wrist, which was not there when you departed. Shall I tell you how it came? But, no! I would not have you think me impatient. I am like the willow tree beside the stream, which yields to every blast, and rises forgetful of the few weak leaves that the wind has taken away.

"I have been to the window in the passage. The snow is deep and smooth, and all the world is silent. What a pitiless thing is this frost, and yet how kindly does it work! It soothes the unprotected into sleep, and draws life away, so painlessly, so gently. How different from cruel man or beast. Yesterday I discovered my cat playing with a poor mouse. I took the little thing from her, but alas, it shivered once and died in my hand. I could have cried for it. I knew!

"My candle is burning out. I would gladly seek warmth in my bed, but dare not while the noise below continues. Where are you, Geoffrey? Oh, my love, I know you will play the man amid the wicked society of our time. I pray you shun the court, the painted faces, the cringing favourites, shun also the gaming-house, and the cockpit. Nay, I mean no harm. My father is shouting for me upon the stairs. Ah, Geoffrey! Come again."

Scene II.—PASTORAL

Let me, neither in adversity, nor in the joys of prosperity, be associated with women.—*Aeschylus*.

After searching diligently Flora discovered a little farm-house some three miles to the west of Kingsmore, which the tenants were glad to let at a weekly rental, sufficient to give them a long awaited opportunity of visiting relations elsewhere. On a set day Maude presented herself with a cartload of baggage; and after spending a night beneath Mr. Price's roof, and horrifying this simple old gentleman exceedingly, went on with her friend in the morning to the retreat on the side of the hill, with which she was graciously pleased to declare herself 'pretty well satisfied on the whole.' During the week that ensued she was occupied, putting the place into her idea of order, and endeavouring to regain the prettiness which she believed London had taken from her by driving abroad in a donkey cart. But before the first week had elapsed she had begun to complain, ungrateful person that she was, of the monotony of country life.

The empty-headed little woman would have been horrified had anyone dared to suggest that she was not a perfectly righteous person. What harm, she would have argued indignantly, had she done in the world? It was true she had married Mr. Juxon for the sake of his money, but then she did not believe people ever married for love. It was certainly too comical to suppose that any woman could possibly fall in love with Herbert, who was short and bald-headed. She had been true to him, she considered, and constancy was all that could reasonably be required from her. It was his duty to go on making money, and when he remained in the city until dark, as he had been doing lately, she did not inquire the cause. She had certainly been surprised when he raised no objection to her proposed jaunt; but it never entered her head to imagine that his affairs might not be going any too prosperously. She would have been vastly astounded could she have heard the remark which he made when he watched her train depart. He had given a sigh of relief, and said, "It will be better for her not to know."

"I have nothing but trouble, my dear," said the ungrateful person, who had been a penniless little nobody before the stockbroker married her, to Flora, as they sat together on a tiny lawn under a dwarfed tree in front of the bijou residence. "I have lately suspected that Herbert drinks. Men who stay late in the city, as he has been doing, cannot be at work, because as everyone knows there is no work done after four o'clock. They meet together in some horrid low place, drink brandy and swear, and make bets on horse-races."

Flora trailed her handkerchief along the grass for the delectation of a fat kitten, and made no reply.

"It is disgusting," went on the little lady. "Drunkenness is so vulgar and costermongery. I had a letter this morning," she added in aggrieved tones. "He wants to come here from Saturday to Monday, and I have written to say that I have not got the house in order yet, and he is not to come. I am here for privacy," she concluded pathetically.

"Pretty people must not expect to have privacy. Especially when they have husbands," said Flora.

Maude Juxon laughed delightedly. Flora could say what she liked, so long as she wrapped the sting of her truth in a sheath of flattery. The kitten jumped across the lawn sideways, its tail like a lamp-brush, flung a mad somersault, and dashed into a briar-bush, bringing down a shower of petals.

"When are you going to take me to that remarkable house in Thorlund?" asked the beauty.

Flora turned grave at once, and answered shortly, "Never."

"That's jealousy," murmured Mrs. Juxon. "I want to see the house."

"You can tell that to Mr. Conway. He is coming to Kingsmore on Thursday, that is if he can remember the engagement," said Flora. "I am not going with you to that house."

"Is that clever delightful poet coming too?" cried Maude, sincerely interested at last. "That nice, handsome, doctor clergyman?"

"He never goes into society," said Flora. "I suppose he's afraid of meeting fascinating little women like you. Do you really think him handsome?"

"Oh yes, superb. His head is like one of those pictures you see, somewhere or other. And that beautiful silvered hair, and smooth grave face, and great grey eyes—why, Flora, there isn't an actor in London half as handsome. I'm sure he looks a saint."

"He neglects his parish fearfully," said the girl.

"Well, you can't expect him to take any interest in those stupid labouring people," said Maude with some asperity. "I shall intercept him in one of his walks, and tell him he's to come to Kingsmore on Thursday. Now do say something, and don't leave all the talking to me," she went on fretfully. "You have become such a silent person lately. Tell me all about Mr. Conway. Does he like you? Has he money? Do you think we could persuade him to give a dance in his wonderful house?"

Flora was troubled. She had been given reason to suppose that Conway did 'like her,' when at a distance from the Strath. She supposed him to be fairly well off; he gave the idea of a man who had never done a day's work in his life. As for a dance at the Strath, she found herself smiling at the suggestion, then began to wonder why the idea should appear incongruous.

Neither she nor her uncle could recall what had taken place during their visit to the Strath. When upon the road they had discovered themselves costumed after the fashion of a by-gone day; but memory had given them no answer when they asked why those old habits were upon them, or what had been their actions inside the house. Soberly and silently they had returned to reassume their modern garments, and Mr. Price had since avoided any reference to that afternoon.

The same with Conway, Drayton, and, in a lesser degree, with Dr. Berry. Inside the Strath they were puppets; outside they resumed—although there were exceptions to this rule—their normal selves. The time spent among the antique furniture, or along the tangled walks, left no more memory than a night of sleep. They discovered a subtle influence drawing them back, as opium will recall its victims to their dreams. They knew that the sleep induced by the Strath was delightful, that happiness was given there; but former experience told them nothing concerning the nature of that sleep, or the substance of that happiness.

Outside the garden Conway fell beneath Flora's spell, and

would decide to settle every pressing affair in London by letter upon his return; Dr. Berry continued his work on Aeolian poetry, and vaguely remembered that he had a flock. Inside the garden the world went away from them, and they were mimes, speaking the words put into their mouths, and playing the parts which had been assigned to them. All that their minds were capable of producing was brought out there. So long as they did not attempt to oppose their will against that of the controller of the masque, as Henry Reed had done, all went well.

"Of course the place is haunted," said Maude with a dainty shiver, when her friend had told her all that she knew. "I don't think I want to go there after all. But I should like to see the china. You say there is lovely china in the drawing-room?"

"Beautiful," said Flora. "Uncle says there was a rage for china during Queen Anne's reign."

"No atrocities? No horrible wool-work, or samplers, or antimacassars? No wax-flowers, or leather fruit, or horsehair sofas?" went on the little lady, confusing her periods.

"I saw none," said Flora. "I only remember the china, and some pictures which wouldn't be allowed nowadays, and a quantity of mirrors and candles."

"I am glad there is nothing vulgar," said Maude. "I almost think I could go there, if there were plenty of people with me. If the house is haunted I expect it will all be done in a proper and genteel fashion. When I went to see Hamlet I was quite prepared to be frightened when the ghost came on, but I wasn't, not in the least. He was such a gentle and aristocratic ghost. I expect the bogey of the Strath would be just like that."

The stars in their courses were propitious to Maude. Towards evening on the following day she encountered the rector of Thorlund, after driving over to the hamlet in a gig drawn by a tandem of donkeys, and placing herself in ambush so to speak along his usual walk. She had been introduced to the scholar by Mr. Price in his off-hand fashion upon the day of her arrival, chancing upon him as they drove from the station towards Kingsmore. Directly she espied the scholar, she abandoned gig and donkeys and fluttered along the field road, pretending to be busily engaged in gathering a handful of marguerites and ragged-robins.

He, poor man, was fully occupied with the problem of Sappho's morality, mentally weighing the evidence in her favour, sifting the chaff of legend from the grains of fact as best he might. He did not perceive Madame Papillon until he heard her salutation; and then he started and stared up into the golden mist which the sun was trailing across the side of the hill.

Maude was pretty—just then wonderfully so, because she was anxious to please—somewhat doll-like perhaps, but beautifully made, and scented, and bravely tricked out in *batiste* and lace and flowers and innocent infant hat. Her throat was as white and soft as the petal of a lily, and her little nose as dainty as a rosebud. She was frothing over with life and health, and her feet in toy white shoes were as light as bird's wings. Perhaps it was unfortunate for the scholar that his mind should have been occupied by thoughts of Sappho, whom he admired and loved academically as the world's one poetess. Some Greek escaped his lips involuntarily; he was no pedant, but the sweet Ionic words were as familiar as his own tongue, and better expressed his thoughts.

"How funny I should have met you!" cried lady frivolous. "Because I was wondering whether I could summon up enough courage to go all by myself to the rectory and leave a message. I don't believe you recognise me. The sun is dazzling, isn't it?"

"Ah," said the scholar. "Yes, the sun blinds me." He took off his hat, and the light glinted across the silver of his hair and made it live.

He did not question himself as to whether this divinity was maid, wife, or widow; he only knew that the apparition was very good to gaze upon, and he found himself hoping that it would not vanish suddenly.

"I hope your carriage is safe," he murmured.

"My carriage!" exclaimed Maude with ringing laughter. "Why, it's only a wobbly gig, drawn by two of the most ridiculous donkeys. Do come and look at them. They have ears as long as—as—"

"King Midas after his transformation," suggested the scholar.

"That's it," said Maude, who had no idea what he meant. "But they are champion trotters. Come into the cart and I'll drive you home. We shall be packed tight, but I'm small."

There was something here which made lyric poetry doubly

sweet to the scholar's mind. A life of dreams, of fingers on pen, and eyes in books, had fallowed his heart unconsciously for the reception of a seed which had been with him nothing but a name. His eyes were sleepy as he approached the cart, and the lines about his mouth showed weakness, and there was irresolution in all his actions. This was not Dr. Berry of the study and the Strath. It was Dr. Berry who was learning that he was a man.

"Get in," said Maude.

The scholar obeyed, and the dainty creature followed. The cart was, as she had said, very small. They filled it, as they sat facing one another, Maude's scented frills trailing upon the scholar's feet, her breath coming to him when she spoke, her hat brushing his forehead when she turned with some sudden motion. For the first time in his life Dr. Berry cast down his eyes and was ashamed. He did not know that the little beauty was a butterfly: but he began to understand why Leander swam across the Hellespont and why Sappho flung herself from the Leucadian rock.

The birds were singing in the beech-wood as they had never sung before.

"The country is beautiful," Maude was saying. "Oh, Dr. Berry, I could live here always, just to walk, sleep, and dream in the sun. But there would be winter. How I wish we could have summer every day!"

Maude meant nothing that she said. She knew how pretty she looked in furs. She was a rattle, not understanding her own noise; but the scholar hung upon her words, and believed them inspired, and did not know they were murmurings from a shell.

"You have a message for me?" he said, without perception of a labourer, who passed, and grinned as he touched his hat, at the strange conjunction of the stately poet with that tiny cart and the donkeys and the pretty lady.

"Yes," said Maude, flicking at the flies with her toy whip. "You are to be at Kingsmore on Thursday. Flora commands your presence, and so do I. It is impossible for you to refuse."

"You will be there?" mused the thinker.

"Of course. And I'll see that you have a comfortable chair in the rosiest corner of the lawn, and if you feel a sudden desire to write you shall have pen and ink, and if you are lazy you can talk to me.

But you must not be too clever. I shall tell Flora you are coming. How do you go to Kingsmore?"

"I seldom leave my home," the poet answered. "I am not able to fit myself into society."

"It's easy," said Maude.

"I always walk," he went on.

"But that must be tiring, especially when the sun is hot. Suppose," said Maude, "suppose you found this little cart on the top of the hill outside Thorlund at half-past-three on Thursday afternoon, and suppose I drove you in triumph across to Kingsmore—wouldn't that save you a lot of trouble, and mightn't it be rather an inducement for you to keep your promise?"

Dr. Berry could not remember how he answered, whether indeed he spoke at all. He looked towards the hill which rose above his valley, and saw the white road bending away in the far distance. "Would it not be cruel upon these little animals?" he said, with a more confident smile.

"Not a bit," replied Maude. "They are full of oats, and they shall eat all Thursday morning to prepare themselves for the honour of drawing wisdom and—"

"Beauty," added the scholar, sincerely. Folly he should have said, but Maude was well masked.

One low thatched roof peeped from its green bower, and the mossy spire of the church pointed reproachfully upward. The poet did not look there. His eyes were upon the things of earth. A pink rose at Maude's throat shed its petals when the cart jolted across a ridge, and the dainty fragments rained upon his hands. He began to gather them up one by one, storing them unconsciously in the warm hollow of his hand. Maude's eyes were dancing with satisfaction. He had called her beautiful and she was happy.

The day dedicated to Thor arrived. Down in the valley the sun scorched, but a gentle breeze was playing across the hills when Dr. Berry reach the summit and seated himself upon a hummock of short grass. He had done nothing all the morning, except pace study and garden, wondering at the tenderness with which he was able to criticise the self-dedicatory odes of comparatively obscure singers. So it was passion that called out what was best in mortals. Had Archilochus not loved Neobule he would have passed into the cloud of oblivion. Had Sappho been cold and chaste that magnificent ode to the Goddess of Love could never have been given to the world. The heart, mused the scholar, not the mind, strikes into being the living fire.

He saw nothing of a frivolous nature in the donkey tandem. He walked down to meet the cart as it ascended the hill, and Maude greeted him warmly and began to chat vigorously. She had never spoken agreeably to her husband, but, as she would have argued, it was absurd to fascinate a man who belonged to her. She was a child, playing with fire, and not to be warned of danger until the fire burnt her.

"God bless my soul!" exclaimed Mr. Price with more than his usual fervour, when the gig came jingling up the avenue. Flora contented herself with smiling, while Mrs. Neill, a fragile lady filled with inaccuracies of speech, put up her glasses and made her customary statement, *apropos* of nothing in particular, that social customs had changed very much for the worse since that age of respectability when her dear brother and herself attended school.

The hill country was very sparsely populated with gentry. There were not more than a dozen guests, of whom the majority had covered a considerable distance and were on that account leaving early. Everyone knew the recluse of Thorlund, either by name or reputation, and upon him were showered the honours of the afternoon. Dr. Berry found himself in a new element which was not so distasteful as he had supposed.

"Maudie, how did you manage?" Flora whispered.

"I circumvented him, and told him he was to come," explained the little lady. "And here he is."

"But you drove him!"

"Why not? He brought himself down to my level beautifully."

Flora slipped away to attend to her guests, giving thanks because she believed she was more righteous than her friend.

A bald-headed clergyman annexed the scholar, and was leading him apart with inaccurate historical chatter, when Maude intervened, routed the bald-headed clergyman, and installed Dr. Berry into the comfortable chair which she had promised him. Then she brought tea and little cakes and strawberries, and soothed him with empty talk, which seemed to him more worthy of attention than words of wisdom. This man, who had shunned women all his life, not from any innate dislike for the sex, but simply because no inclination had drawn him on, found his tongue loosened by the fascinations of the butterfly. Presently he began to speak of himself, his aspirations, and his work, Maude leading him on with skilful flattery.

"How I would like to see your wonderful book," she sighed.

"It is not finished," he said. "There is still much to be done and I work slowly. I have a conviction that my translations are, not only more accurate, but more artistic and powerful than any which have preceded them. I think if I could read you some of those early lyrics—"

"I should cry," interrupted Maude pathetically. "I'm certain I should. Poetry, or music, or sad pieces at the theatre, always make me cry. I went to a dreadful pathetic play last winter, and I cried all down a pretty new frock and spoilt it."

"Yours is indeed the true poetic temperament," said the scholar earnestly. "What a rare and precious gift it is! You, more than anyone, can understand me when I say that my work has engrossed my life. Many in their ignorance sneer at the classics, but your mind can respond with mine to the true message of art. Being yourself beautiful you are able more readily to appreciate the pure beauty of those poetic jewels with which the human intellect has enriched the world."

This last remark was balm and honey to the silly soul of his listener.

"When the book comes out I shall buy it," she declared. "And you must write something nice and original upon the front, and I shall read it again and again. Will it be out soon? I know a book doesn't take long, because I met an author once, and he told me it took him three weeks to write one of his."

"I have been fifteen years over my work, and I expect it will take me another five to complete," said Dr. Berry.

"Oh, but I can't wait all that time," cried Maude. "I shall be old by then."

"'Age cannot wither her, nor custom stale her infinite variety,'" quoted the scholar with unmistakable sincerity.

"How lovely!" said smiling Maude.

He could not see through the pretence of that outward show to the empty soul within. He never doubted her sincerity; her beauty was apparent; and he thought her clever and a poetess at heart.

"I will tell you what you must do," Maude rattled on brilliantly. "You must read me some of your beautiful poems. Pick out the very best, and come over to my farm-house on Sunday—no, that's your work-day—on Monday, and I will give you a cup of tea. I shall look forward to it immensely. You won't forget? I shall expect you on Monday."

"Would you like to hear my verses?" said the delighted scholar. "You shall hear them. We will discuss their merits. You will be able to help me by suggestion and advice. Two minds are better than one. Two kindred minds strike sparks."

"And I will make you a nice rice cake," said the little lady, irrelevantly, but as she thought very happily.

At that point Mrs. Neill interposed, to claim her share of the lion. She had met him upon previous visits to her brother's house, and was desirous of showing him the hidden beauties of the garden; and obtaining at the same time a full account of the means and position of the young man who had been lavishing some polite attentions upon Flora, to-wit Conway, who had been expected that afternoon, but had failed to appear.

"Maude, you selfish child, I have come for your gentleman," she announced. "I want to take you down the garden, Dr. Berry, and show you a pretty little corpse quite covered with fly-orchids."

The good lady had meant to say copse. Maude shrieked with laughter, and corrected her rudely, because she was indignant at being deprived of her property; and, having revenged herself, she tripped away across the lawn in a pink froth of frills, with one innocent blue-eyed glance behind.

"She is very beautiful," murmured Dr. Berry. "And as clever and good as she is beautiful."

Scene III.—EXTRAVAGANZA

Human nature is so constituted as to be incapable of lonely satisfaction; man, like those plants which are formed to embrace others, is led by an instinctive impulse to recline on his species.—*Cicero*.

To account for Conway's non-appearance at Kingsmore vicarage it will be necessary to revert to the day of Dr. Berry's meeting with Maude upon the upland, because that encounter was in the main responsible, although indirectly, for the young man's absence. The scholar walked back to the rectory, but did not open his books that evening. Outpourings from the intellects of the immortals would not content him then. In a heat he cast off an original poem and proceeded with it into the garden of the Strath; and there he came upon Conway who was confused by struggling memories and a present anxiety. Money had been required of him for the settlement of accounts. Being unable to comprehend the meaning of that demand he had taken his trouble to Drayton; but the writer, who was entirely engrossed upon his historical play, gave him little satisfaction. "If the woman asks for money, give it her," he said, and straightway had returned to his work.

Dr. Berry's understanding was less obscured. After listening to Conway's complaint, he advised him to leave the garden, and walk out of the valley. "You will then perceive what should be done," he added. "If you require to write letters, go into my study, and write them there."

Conway did as he was directed, that is to say he left the garden; but he did not enter the rectory. He walked out of the valley, and when darkness came upon the country he was still walking, with his face set towards the town. Night fell upon the Strath, but the master was absent. The next day Drayton noticed that he was alone, but his mind had no desire to learn the cause. Another day went, but Conway remained absent. The next morning a letter came to Drayton, and the dazed writer found himself charged with various heinous offences. It appeared that the profligate's furniture had been seized for non-payment of rent, and among the articles on the inventory made by the agent the two masks did not appear. Therefore, the writer argued, Drayton had most perfidiously stolen them. The shaky epistle concluded with the statement that the writer was about to return to Thorlund for the sole purpose of dragging the 'ungrateful, sponging, thievish brute,' Drayton to-wit, out of his house by the ears.

"A strange document," murmured the gentle scribe. "Interesting also as illustrating a phase of the human mind. Penned, I should determine, by a dissolute character, somewhat under the influence of *aqua-fortis*."

As the letter was not of sufficient interest to be subjected to any more critical analysis, he set it aside, and went into the orchard to think of other things. Late in the evening Conway returned; but so soon as he entered upon his property, shame took the place of anger. He became dimly conscious that he had degraded himself during the past three days. Very soon the determination, which he had made that morning, to offer the Strath for sale, and to resume his former manner of living, became forgotten. As he made towards the house, feeling sleep settling again about his eyes, he encountered the perfidious Drayton; but, instead of seizing the thief by the ears, he passed his arm within that of the writer, and asked, "Have you finished the translation of that ode of Horace, the song in which he deals with woman's love?"

Drayton put a hand to his forehead, and presently replied, "I have forgotten. I will make you the English rendering to-night. Have you not been out a long time?" he added.

"Yes," said Conway absently. "I have been troubled with bad dreams of late." This was Conway's first and final effort to break from the influence of the Strath; and after failure his mind, like that of his companion, succumbed entirely.

There came a day when rain soaked the moss-grown garden and the trunks of the trees were black with moisture. Mists were exhaled from the stagnant moat to form into shapes about the house. The spell-bound wanderers, hovering between the seen and unseen, found the Strath altered. It remained peaceful in its decay; there was neither fluttering of tapestries nor whisper of misery; but over all brooded an indefinable sensation of calamity impending.

In that room where Winifred Hooper had slept and written, Conway sat alone, with her journal between his hands. The influence impelled him to reason concerning himself. "What was he?" A card, engraved with a mere name, lay on the table, but the words Charles Conway brought no answer to his question. Perhaps he was a product of that damp old house, an ephemeral growth like the mosses and lichens upon its walls, or a passing shadow, with a name to distinguish it from other shadows. One touch of sunlight might cause him to vanish into vapour. Or again a little spark roving like Jack o' lanthorn through space, seeking another spark with which to unite and strike the wondrous flame called life. He saw a face in the time-stained mirror. Was it that of Flora Neill, or of Winifred Hooper, or of Lone Nance of the hills? The spark which was himself became blown into fire, and waved to and fro. . . . The place became a museum, and he a dry and dusty exhibit, catalogued Charles Conway, and numbered 31. He was a curiosity, genuine and of some practical use once, but now out of fashion. What had he done in his foolish life? Walked out with his hair in papers, inhaling snuff through the pepper-pot head of a clouded cane; sauntered at auctions, or in the Mall; spent one quarter of the day in dressing, another in dining, a third at the coffee-house, a fourth at play; half the night in drawing-rooms, the other half in sleep. What noise had he made in the world, beyond piping on the French horn, or springing the rattle of a drunken watchman? If there had been work to his hand he had closed his eyes. Work! Why should a man work? What was the reward for a life devoted to tilling the ground, to fighting the French, to ministering to the sick, to sitting at the king's council? The finest machine must break down some day, and rust, and become old framework. Work! What about Southey, poet laureate, sweating heart and brain, and confessing at the end that it had not been possible for him to lay by anything for old age? What about old learned Johnson, putting off his threadbare clothes upon his birthday, and muttering bitterly, "I can now look back upon threescore and four years, in which little has been done, and little has been enjoyed; a life diversified by misery, spent part in the sluggishness of penury, and part under the violence of pain, in gloomy discontent or importunate distress?" What about Lamb, thanking for nothing a great minister who brought the reward of labour as the hand of death dragged him off the scene?

The Strath was in a morbid mood. Drayton was pacing the saloon, crying like a woman. The deaf crone prepared food in the kitchen, working out her time indifferent to the drama. The rain poured heavily flooding the worm-eaten boards of the upper rooms. Conway raised his hands, which held the book in shagreen covers, brought the yellow pages nearer to his eyes, and read aloud:

"To-day the wind is warm, and the birds sing merrily. For it is spring, the gladdest time in all the year. Were this a letter to you, my love, as I would cheer myself by believing, I might tell you much that would bring you pleasure, and much that would not be true. I might describe to you the beauty of the country. I might tell you how happy I am to breathe the odours of the young larches, and to feel the warmth of the sun. I might assure you how I laugh in the mornings, and sometimes sing the songs you taught me, and how I watch the roads with a light heart, sure that you are upon your way. And I might promise you, praying God the same moment to forgive the lie, that I know no trouble. But, alas, this is my journal, and here I may not cheat myself.

"Spring will never come again, unless it brings you, Geoffrey. All day I have sat beside a downstairs window, listening to the joyful sounds of life, watching the little leaves unfolding, and the first yellow butterfly playing across the lawn. Everything in nature has something to do, and I alone am idle. I can only sit, with my hands together, wondering that there should be joy upon earth for the brown sparrow, and none for me. Yet the sparrow might pine and cease her twitter, perchance give up her little ghost, were she to be imprisoned in a cage. Even so there might be happiness for her. She might see her mate, and sometimes hear his song.

"Last night my father threw at me a log of wood, which struck my ankle, and to-day I cannot bear my shoe. Ah, Geoffrey, could you but see my poor swollen foot! I dwell upon the happy thought that you are nursing it in your dear hands, and looking up into my face with your tender eyes. Would you not come through fire and water to save me? But I know all now. The light of life has gone, and each morning and evening the message of curfew comes, ringing, "No more! No more!"

"My father has admitted much over his wine. Your messengers have never reached this valley. Perhaps they have been killed upon the highway, for my father's men are instructed to watch the roads, and he has lost all scruples. I cannot warn you, Geoffrey. I am not able to bid you keep away from me. Would I, if I could? I do not know. I have become selfish. You might meet Sir John, and he is stronger than you. Were they to carry you dead into this house . . . well, we should be together at last, for I would throw away my chance of heaven in the hope that my soul might pass with yours through space. If you killed my father I would yet receive you with the same love. I am unnatural indeed, but he has beaten me with a cane when in his cruel mood, and has pulled me to the ground by my hair, and closed his hand round my arm, tighter and tighter like a vice, until I have satisfied his cruelty by fainting.

"I know that my father is a highwayman and the most daring of them all. It is when I am so unfortunate as to see him returning from some expedition that he is more than usual pitiless. I have seen Thomas Reed, his trusted man, leading the chestnut mare—the swiftest horse in the country, they say—sweating to her stable at midnight, and I have seen his masks, his pistols, and his sword. He will have this Reed into the saloon to drink with him. I have heard them fighting but Reed is a strong-willed fellow, and I know my father cannot break with him, lest he should turn informer. I know the vileness of their lives; but God also must know, and if there be justice above—which sometimes I am wicked enough to doubt—an end must come, and soon.

"Placing before me the beloved face which I hold in my heart, I painted your portrait, and finished it last Saturday at sunset. It was a happy sorrow to kiss those cold lips, to touch and retouch that fair hair, only one shade darker than my own, and to bring into being your own dear smile. During that night the portrait seemed to me to have taken life, and through the hours of darkness—for I sleep but little—I thought you were protecting me, and I felt the warmth of your eyes, and heard your breathing, and your soft whisper, "Winifred," just as you whispered it—ah, so long ago—with your lips against my hair. It was so like you, Geoffrey. Even that tiny spot, where you were cut as a child above your left eyebrow, was there in all the beauty of its blemish. On Sunday

I went to church, not indeed to listen to Mr. Blair's hypocrisies, but to pray with all my soul for you and for myself; and returning hurried to your portrait to tell it how I love you. But it had been cut into pieces, and the pieces were strewed about the floor.

"I did not shed any tears. Indeed it is seldom that I cry now, not because I am stronger, but perhaps I have shed them all. I began to sing, and put a flower into my hair, and laughed and talked to you, so that I might forget how I was shivering. I am made of tough stuff, though I am small and white, and as for my heart is it not yours, and did you not replace my loss with the gift of your own? It is your strength that holds me up. But it was a good portrait, Geoffrey, else my father had not recognised it.

"That night I saw a strong light pouring through the keyhole and the chinks in the wood. While I looked the door came open, and there was old Deborah, standing in her nightdress, with a candle in her hand, and the passage round her was filled with light and a fragrant odour. She made me a sign that I should not be afraid and said, 'There is a stranger waiting for you below.' So I got up, and wrapped a cloak round me, and went down. There was light everywhere, but I could not see whence it came. Standing in the hall I saw an old man, clad in white, with hair flowing upon his shoulders, and holding a great pitcher between his hands. He came to me, when I stopped in fear, and spoke in a low sweet voice, 'I am bidden to return you these. They are your tears.' But when I held out my hands to take the pitcher it dropped and I found myself standing among pearls, and it was dark, and the old man was gone. Then I awoke and discovered that I had been walking in my sleep.

"Do you not dream, dear, in your London home? Do you never see me, bending low, drawing my hair across your face? Do you not hear me calling? Cannot you feel my lips near yours in sleep? Am I never with you? Oh, my love, I am there. Look, and you shall see me. Call, and I will answer. Put out your hand, and I will touch it. What has space to do with love? There is nothing between us, but the will of God. I am yours, beloved, and you are mine until these shadows pass away."

There the book fell, and it seemed to Conway that an invisible hand had struck it out of his. He rose, leaving the journal lying open as it had fallen, and hurried from the room. A gloom filled the passage and the house was full of horror, resounding with the sufferings of its past inhabitants, and dripping with their tears. His hand closed upon the damp balustrade, and the rotten wood exuded moisture like a sponge. A minute later the owner, but not the master, of the Strath was speeding through the garden, his being reaching out to find an affinity, as embryonic life must grope into the darkness for its promised soul.

The deluge had ceased. Milk rivulets bubbled down the chalk road and dark clouds scudded across the hills, while Conway hastened in the direction of Kingsmore, with Winifred Hooper's piteous voice still sounding in his ears. When he came near the grass-filled road which led to Queensmore he thought he saw her. She reached scarcely to his shoulder, the pretty pale maid, and over her white forehead the fair hair clustered and tumbled into tendrils round her ears and neck. There was a scar upon her delicate wrist, and she limped slightly as she walked from the sign-post downwards. Her voice was exceedingly plaintive, and the words caught in her throat with the sound of a sob. Her eyes were large and blue, like two cornflowers upon white satin, and her features were small and very frail. They quivered when the wind met them.

On the far side of the hills a more serious dreamer was at that moment shaking out his umbrella in the porch of a little farmhouse, while its dainty bedecked mistress implored him to wait until the rain had passed, and insisted upon retaining a precious bundle of manuscript—of which she could understand no single word—that she might study it alone. And the handsome dreamer remained yet another hour, until the watery sun broke through the clouds and tinged the mist with red, and when he departed the manuscript which he left behind was not so precious as it had been.

At Kingsmore the sun was shining through the rain. A bow was bending across the sky, one end of its span over the ruins of Queensmore, the other filling a chalk-pit with coloured vapour. Mr. Price assumed one of his shameful overcoats, a slouch hat, and long boots, and went out upon the farm to poke about in ditches and free obstructed drain-pipes. Mrs. Neill was upstairs, writing ungrammatical letters. Flora roamed aimlessly about the house, yawning for dulness, and well able to appreciate the saying of Chilo the sage, that one of the three most difficult things in life is to make a profitable use of leisure time.

Finally she wandered into the study, a room forbidden to her sex, therefore the more attractive, and stood aghast at its untidiness. Mr. Price was the most unmethodical man incarnate. Upon his writing-desk were farming-reports, parish-magazines, bundles of twine, sermons, cigarettes, horse-shoes, theological works, and samples of wool. More books were piled upon a central table, novels, bibles, philosophical works, and agricultural digests, thrown together with bags of grain, much of which was scattered over the carpet, and eggs dated in blue pencil. The fireplace was filled with rubbish, an old saddle, and a broken reaping-hook. The single armchair was piled with horse-cloths. The pictures on the walls, chiefly framed photographs of horses and landscapes, were hanging awry and begrimed with dust. An open work of Josephus was covered with cartridges, and a brace of pigeons, shot in the early morning, were staining the right reverend bishop's latest charge. The remaining chairs were occupied with a jumble of tools, coats, and hats. Boots and guns were lying about the carpet. A bust of Shakspere supported a leather shooting-cap; and a little oak desk of ecclesiastical design held a couple of soiled collars, an incomplete copy of a book of common prayer tied together with string, a flask half filled with sherry, some candle-ends, and a half-dozen unanswered letters.

"No one would imagine uncle was well off," Flora murmured, moving through the confusion, with her skirts gathered round her. "I wonder how much he loses every year on this stupid farm. It would be much more sensible if he put by the money for me to spend later on."

She approached the window and pushed it open; but while shaking some rain-drops off the back of her hand footsteps became audible upon the wet gravel. She knew it was not her uncle's tread, and looking out saw Conway, his garments splashed with chalky mud, and his face flushed by the wind.

She was at the door before he could ring. He came up, and said quickly, but solemnly, as though it were a matter of the last importance, seizing her hand and looking into her eyes, "There is a change to-day."

The girl flushed, because she saw a crisis impending. Conway was altogether different; younger, fresher, better-looking. There was not a trace of nervousness in his manner.

"Won't you come in?" she said. "How wet you are! Uncle is out, but will be back soon, and then we will have tea. You are right about the change. But we agricultural people wanted this rain."

"It is the Strath," he exclaimed. "The change is there."

Flora looked round, with a very uncomfortable feeling. There was not a sound in the house, except the ticking of a big clock in the hall.

"Come in," she repeated.

"I cannot quite remember what has happened," Conway went on rapidly, his eyes fixed stupidly upon her. "I want you to come back with me. The rain has stopped. I want to show you a room in my house, a room with a blocked up window. I think you will recognise it."

"Mr. Conway," Flora exclaimed. "Do you know what you are talking about?"

"I have something to show you there. I have made a discovery, and I must share it with you. Is it not Cicero who says, 'Were a man to be carried up to Heaven, he would receive little pleasure from the scene, if there were none to whom he might relate his experience?' "

"I cannot talk to you while you are in this state," said Flora.

"Then will you come with me to Queensmore? We can cross by Deadman's Hill. I can tell you everything there, but here I cannot remember things."

"If you have anything to say to me I can hear it here," Flora replied. "Mother is in the house," she added. "But, if you are going to stay—come in."

"You want to sit down?" said Conway. "Your ankle pains you still?"

The strong-minded girl looked at the speaker in dismay. This was sheer madness.

"I have not hurt my ankle," she said.

"It must have been some time ago," he muttered.

"Mr. Conway, if you will take my advice you will live no longer in the Strath," Flora said strongly. "Remember what happened to your uncle there. They have never been able to discover who killed him. No stranger could have entered Thorlund without being observed. It is a horrible place."

Conway shook his head, perplexed at her argument. The Strath was to him a Paradise.

"That is only because you are not there," he answered. "Hooper is dead now, and the house is yours. The Reeds were always interlopers. I want you to take possession of the Strath at once."

"You want me to have the Strath?" exclaimed Flora with a laugh.

"It waits for you," he replied.

"And its master?" she said.

"There is no master. I am its servant, and yours."

"You have made a quaint proposal, Mr. Conway," the girl said flippantly. "If the Strath were mine I would take uncle's advice and have it down; and if you were my servant—well, I might perhaps want to give you notice and engage another. I think you had better not stay," she went on. "You are not yourself. I am sure you do not know what you have been saying."

"I cannot enjoy life alone," cried Conway.

"Is Mr. Drayton so unsociable? Give up the Strath, Mr. Conway. Take my advice—and another house, before it is too late."

Then, as Conway still evinced no inclination either to enter the house or to move away, Flora unsympathetically shut him out.

Scene IV.—SENTIMENTAL COMEDY

Praise undeserved is satire in disguise.—*Broadhurst.*

Implicit faith had never become rooted in Dr. Berry's mind. He had sought ordination because "out of these Convertites there is much matter to be heard and learned," and the disposition of his mind towards retirement seemed to him a call sufficient. He believed that it was necessary to pay tribute for the delights of Nature, the flowers, the trees, and the sight of the sun. This was a debt which might be discharged by accommodating the will to that of the higher influences, and by living in tune with the unseen.

The scholar was gentle, charitable, and forgiving. He would have emptied his pockets to benefit an unworthy beggar, and have travelled far out of his way to relieve suffering, and yet in many things he remained more ignorant than a child.

During the past twenty years he had changed, both outwardly and inwardly. The greater part of his time had been spent in the imaginative world within the influence of the Strath, until the day had come when he could not clearly distinguish between shadow and substance. Gradually the tension between mind and body had relaxed while the light across the past had become correlatively stronger. He could not give up the Strath, nor was he able to understand the dangers which threatened him there.

His friendship with Maude had introduced another change into his strange existence. He had been very near the borderland when she had come to signal him back to the material world. He had however passed too far away ever to return as a rational being. He could only look back. And she could not advance to him, because she was made of stuff which would not float across the gulf which spread between them. He was deceived, and she was dazzled. He knew that he wanted to be near her, and listen to the silly prattle, which by process of filtration through his brain became wisdom. Her mind throbbed in response to his; she, he believed, was filled with the divine fire of poetry; they met, he assured himself, upon common ground.

"But that's not real," she exclaimed, breaking in upon his reading; and he paused to set a query against that line.

"And that jingles."

He pencilled upon the margin the words, "More dignity required."

"That's heavenly!"

And happily he marked the verse "Good."

Maude was only speaking whatever came into her head, lolling among cushions, eating chocolate, twisting her pretty hair round slender pink-tipped fingers, and thinking how handsome he looked with the sunlight upon his head.

When she informed him that her husband was coming down on Saturday, she was a little disappointed when he absently remarked, "Indeed." She would have been astounded had she known that he did not even consider the affinity she had so plainly suggested. Husband to him was a word, such as man or woman. Had Mr. Juxon entered that room, the scholar would have greeted the financier with his invariable courtliness, and have proceeded to a appropriate Maude to himself as before.

"I'm coming to Church on Sunday," said Maude triumphantly, as though the idea appeared to her worthy of a reward for originality.

"I will, in that case, select a sermon which I am sure will interest you," came the grave reply. "A careful inquiry into the nature of the Bacchanalian Mysteries."

"It sounds nice," said she dubiously.

"I will have cushions placed for you in the front seat underneath the pulpit."

"And I'll wear my new hat," she rattled joyously. "How about the donkeys? Where shall I put them up?"

"There is a small stable at the rectory. I will tell the sexton to wait for you by the lich-gate."

"The what gate?" said Lady Ignorant.

"The gate of the churchyard. We still call it by the Anglo-Saxon name."

"Oh yes," said Maude, reaching towards the bell. "Now we will have supper. You will stop for supper."

Sunday morning there was a jingling of silver bells in Thorlund valley, and Maude made her entry in a pink and white hat and a radiant costume. A stout man was packed into the cart with her, he who provided for her luxuries, and received in return upon that particular day the assurance that he was crushing her dress, added to instructions that he should make himself as small as nature would permit. Mr. Juxon had pointed out the propriety of accompanying his wife to church.

The stockbroker had few natural advantages. He was neither elegant nor learned; but he was very true to his wife and sincere in his love for her. Indeed she was everything to him. He had made the mistake of giving way to her always, and at the outset had failed to show her that without his purse she could do nothing. Juxon was not a saint; he did not object to a certain amount of chicanery in the transaction of business; but in private life he was thoroughly upright. He had caught Psyche in his hand, and when she struggled he let her go, lest he should damage the beauty of her wings.

Dr. Berry came down to the porch and entered with them, retaining Maude's hand in his affectionate manner, and grasping the arm of her husband as he walked between them to their cushioned pew. The stockbroker's eyes were upon him, but the rector did not feel them. Both men were perfectly honest in their different ways. The scholar made no secret of his admiration for Maude. The husband was mistrustful, but when Dr. Berry left them, after an invitation to luncheon, his suspicions gave way to wonder. Either this learned man was the simplest soul incarnate or a consummate knave. The latter supposition was reduced to an absurdity by one glance at the pale face uplifted in the pulpit. Then the unpleasant thought occurred that fault, if fault there was, lay entirely with his wife. He looked at her. The sunlight was slanting across the little church, and in the midst of a dusty beam sat Maude, a vision of innocence in pink, her head tilted back, her lips apart, her ears filled with the music of Dr. Berry's rich tones. There was no colour in the stained windows to be compared with hers; there was no cherub weeping, or flambeau-waving, over the recumbent effigies of the Hoopers more modest or free from guile.

The rector's sermon was paganism from beginning to end. It was an account of the birth and early history of the drama. He began by remarking upon the prevalence of mankind to bow down before the works of their own hands; to worship the seen, in preference to the unseen. He pointed out that the drama in its original form was the direct result of idol-worship; and not only the drama, but all the arts—sculpture, painting, poetry, and architecture—came into existence, and were inspired, by the worship of false gods.

Being unable to form any clear notion of divinity, men endeavoured to represent the subjects of their thoughts under the human form.

The divinity would need a dwelling-place among them; therefore they built temples.

He would require their gratitude and worship; and so poetry came into being, also the music and dance which accompanied it.

A hymn accompanied by music was the first state of the dramatic performance.

Such exhibitions were invariably connected with the celebration of religious duties; and the theatre in which they were performed was a temple dedicated to Bacchus. In the earliest times it was the custom for the entire population of a city to meet together in some public place, and praise the gods with songs and dances. These songs were martial, but tinged with religious feeling; and the god to whom they were usually offered was Apollo. They were accompanied by the lyre, because Apollo was not only the god of the sun, but the god of music also. Later this religion became slightly altered, and moon-worship was introduced into Greece, very possibly from Egypt. Then Bacchus, or Dionysus, was adopted as the sun-god, in place of Apollo, and Demeter his sister became the moon-goddess. It was a natural transition in a wine-producing country. The sun ripened the grapes, and Bacchus was the god of wine. Demeter was the earth which grew the vine. So the Bacchic festivals in honour of the wine-god came into being; the lesser festival, accompanied by the song and dance, and procession of the fig-wood phallus, was held to celebrate the vintage; the greater festival was held in the spring, when Bacchus was worshipped as the Deliverer, because he had brought the people safely through the winter. The former was a country festival, and from it comedy originated; the latter was held in the city, and it was the beginning of tragedy.

As the god of wine, light, and procreation, the festivals of Bacchus were accompanied by liveliness and mirth. The sun-god was supposed to be attended by certain grotesque creatures; the Sileni, represented as old men generally intoxicated, who were not very appropriately regarded as the deities presiding over running streams; and the Satyrs, half-men and half-goats, who were not divinities, but merely representatives of the original worshippers, who were goat-herds, and during the festival assumed the skins of the goats which they had sacrificed as an offering to the god of wine.

The earliest state of the drama was therefore a hymn to Bacchus, which was called the Dithyramb; who invented the hymn is not known, nor is the precise meaning of the name. It was danced in a wild fashion by a chorus around a fiery altar, and accompanied by the flute. The poet Arion introduced many striking changes into the Dithyramb, the most important of which was a tragic style of declamation. He substituted the soft lyre for the shrill flute, and decency and order in place of irregularity and licentiousness. The name of Bacchus was dropped, and the deeds of semi-divine heroes were exploited in the hymn; there were no actors; it remained a chorus, but of a mimetic nature, and led by the exarchus—the forerunner of the principal character—who was the best dancer and mimic. The others took their cue from him. Thus, in the course of lamentation, when the exarchus struck himself as a sign of grief the rest of the chorus would imitate his example.

While the feast of Bacchus was thus developing another cause contributed to the birth of the drama. This was the recitation of Homer's poetry by wandering minstrels. These men carried a staff as the symbol of their business, and chanted the national poetry with musical accompaniment. As these recitations increased in popularity many of the living poets became themselves minstrels in order to make their own works known; every kind of poetry was recited; and the musical accompaniment was dropped. Minstrelsy became a profitable trade. On great occasions, when a large number of the rhapsodes, as they were called, came together, different parts would be assigned, which were recited alternately; making the first approach towards a theatrical dialogue. The next step was to unite the methods of the minstrels with the Bacchanalian goat-song; and it was that blending which brought the drama into life.

The man who accomplished this was Thespis, but his action was probably the result of an accident. He discovered that the Bacchanalian chorus became tired of singing in the course of the festival, and so he introduced a minstrel, or an actor, to rest them. This actor was himself. He disguised his face with pigments, and prepared a mask in order that he might be able to sustain more than one character. He addressed himself to the chorus, which stood near the thymele or altar of Bacchus, and that the singers might have no difficulty in hearing him he stood upon a table, which was the origin of the stage.

Thus tragedy became established; but after a time the lower

classes grew discontented with the serious performances, and missed the buffoonery of the Satyrs, which was the principal feature of the vintage festival. They considered also that Bacchus was not sufficiently honoured by performances which dealt with heroes and other gods. To remove their discontent the Satyrical drama was introduced, that is to say plays in which the chorus was composed of Satyrs. In the meantime comedy, which at the outset was nothing more than a Bacchanalian orgy, was gaining ground. At the festival of the vintage the countryfolk went about from one village to another in carts, or on foot, making jesting and abusive speeches and singing licentious songs. Such a song was called Comus. The same word signified also a night revel. Young men would go into the streets after supper with torches, and sing to the flute and lyre. Such a party was called a Comus. Thus the Bacchic reveller was known as a Comodus or comus-singer, just as the singer of the Dithyramb was known as a Tragodus or wearer of a goat-skin.

The orgies of the vintage were still confined to the country and the lower classes. They were unspeakably coarse, and consisted largely in the abuse of public characters. For that reason comedy was subsequently introduced to the city. One political party in Athens desired to attack its opponents, and could think of no better method than the introduction of the lower order of country-folk, to repeat their performance in the town, and to speak the words which were put into their mouths. This led to the recognition and establishment of comedy, which in its then form was little more than the scurrilous abuse of some unpopular demagogue; the aim of comedy being to exhibit individuals in a ridiculous light, and worse than they were; while tragedy showed them as sublime, and better than man could be.

The preacher went on to consider the subject of representation, pointing out that the performances, which it was the duty of every citizen to attend, were of a religious character; the actors wore the festal robes used in the Bacchanalian processions; the theatre was the temple of the god; and its central point was the smoking altar. He went on to trace the connection between religion and art; and concluded his strange sermon, which interested nobody, except the only one who understood it and that was himself, with a discussion upon the scenic accessories and the dramatic incidents connected with public worship, both in pagan temples and Christian churches, from the earliest times to the present day.

Service over—neither Conway nor Drayton attended, because the Strath was no observer of the first day in the week—the rector joined the Juxons in the churchyard, and escorted them to the rectory, talking with unusual brightness. He demanded Maude's opinion upon his sermon, and she replied that it had been too long. At that Juxon interposed with a few quiet words of praise, but the rector maintained that Maude was right. There was much extraneous matter which should have been removed. He ought to have remembered that his sermon was to be heard by a gifted critic. He feared that long association with rustics had dulled the edge of his intellect. The stockbroker listened with increasing amazement.

Whatever doubts he might still have entertained regarding Dr. Berry's attitude towards his wife were to be set at rest that afternoon. After luncheon they sat upon the lawn, and the stockbroker politely introduced the subject of Greece, although he knew little about the country, beyond the fact that its bonds were not easily negotiable; and the conversation naturally passed to the poet's special period and the great work of his life.

"You should read some of Dr. Berry's poems," remarked Maude, who was beginning to feel neglected.

From that moment she had no cause for complaint upon that score.

"Mine is not the intellect," said the scholar. "I am little more than a translator. It has been my effort to express in our own tongue the thoughts of the ancient singers." Again he placed his hand upon Juxon's arm. "In my recent endeavours this lady has been an inspiration. Before she came into my life I worked in a groove, which I can now perceive was leading me towards the dangers of commonplace. I lacked tenderness; the softer qualities were altogether lacking. I was neither sufficiently broad-minded nor sympathetic. But she has shown me my faults."

Maude became scarlet. She cast an agonised glance upon her husband, but his head was down.

"Upon the occasion of our first meeting she expressed great interest in my work," went on the musical voice. "She was good enough to invite me to her house. I confess I hesitated. It may seem strange to you, but throughout my previous life I had refrained from female society. To my shame be it said I could not believe that the analytical faculty could be found highly developed within any beautiful woman. Fortunately for me I went to this lady's house, and she convinced me I was wrong. I found appreciation, a tender listener, a sympathetic critic, an affectionate adviser. Such a help-meet was the one thing wanting in my life, though I had not known it."

"Yes," said Juxon.

Maude was digging her sun-shade into the turf. It was horrible to know she could say nothing in self-defence. She was painfully conscious how often she had told her husband she could not tolerate being read to, she absolutely never had an opinion to give, she hated reading, and thought all learning a bore. Now she was being extolled before her husband as an efficient critic upon one of the most brain-vexing periods of history.

"I went again and again to this lady's house," Dr. Berry continued, lifting his hat reverently and gazing into the sky. "Not content with rendering me very much valuable assistance, she showered upon me her hospitality also. The welcome I have always received from her has made a very deep impression upon my heart. Quite recently we spent a memorable evening together, I in reading my translations—for I find she has not as yet made herself thoroughly conversant with the earlier Greek—she in suggesting alterations and improvements, dealing chiefly with the necessity for introducing more natural tenderness of feeling. Afterwards we had supper, and her conversation I remember was beautiful and inspiring."

"I am glad my wife has been of such service to you," said Juxon.

"She has been a guiding star," said Dr. Berry, putting out his white hand and touching Maude's fingers tenderly. "And I trust she will ever remain so. I have become a changed man of late. My studious interests have redoubled. Formerly I was working for myself alone. Now I have her approbation to secure. Through the light of her mind I am enabled to see many truths which formerly were hidden from my eyes. I have been callous; but she has quickened me with new life. I have to thank her for my present insight into the tender mysteries of devotional love."

"Herbert," Maude cried with a gasp. "I think we ought to be going."

"I hope," said the scholar, closing his fingers affectionately round Juxon's fat hand, "that you also have realised this happiness. I understand now that there is help for every man in this world, when he has been led to that one of his species whose being throbs in unison with his own. Our most secret ambition may be realised through the mind of a faithful friend."

Juxon rose. He looked at his wife, and their eyes met. He was not angry with her then. He was sorry for himself. She had won the heart of a far more intellectual man than himself, and he had given her nothing beyond that which he now believed her soul despised. He had given her liberty to move about the world, a certain position, the very clothes she stood in. He compared his flabby features and half-bald head with the grave handsome face, the sensitive mouth, and silvered hair of his dreamy host, and the mystery became solved. He understood that women require something besides luxuries and freedom; and he had neither fascination nor charm of tongue to offer.

Again the silver bells jingled through Thorlund and the donkeys presently stopped their trot, to walk the long hill. Maude was indignant because she felt she had been made ridiculous. She had not a word to say, until the cart reached the grass-grown road which led to Queensmore, then she lashed her diminutive team spitefully, and exclaimed, "I suppose Dr. Berry is mad."

"I thought him original," answered her husband quietly, "but remarkably sane."

"That is just the sort of exasperating remark I might have expected," said Maude angrily. "He made a perfect idiot of me. Why didn't you change the subject?"

"He regards you as a saint. It was not for me to disagree with him," her husband answered. "I must own I was astonished to find you held up as an art critic," he added with a gentle, and perfectly legitimate, touch of irony.

"It was all utterly idiotic," said Maude. "And I will never ask him to the cottage again. I am not going home, I want to go and see Flora."

The following morning Juxon returned to his business, which

just then was engrossing all the attention which he was able to bestow; and after his solitary dinner he sat down and wrote a long letter to Maude. For a man of his temperament it was easier to write than to speak.

When Flora came over on Tuesday morning she found her friend simmering with indignation and a sense of injury.

"I have had a ridiculous letter from Herbert," she began at once, "He talks of my duty to him and to our child. I'm sure Peggy is much happier with a nurse than she could ever be with me. Besides it makes one feel old and ugly to have a growing child hanging to one's skirts and crumpling them. He says, as I am so fond of the country, he will take a house within easy reach of London, and go backwards and forwards. That is altogether absurd. If the weather happened to be bad he would stop at home whole days and ruin his business. And I don't want to be planted down. I like to go about. And he says he knows I mean nothing, but I ought not to encourage Dr. Berry's visits and this poetry reading. What rubbish, Flora! Dr. Berry's voice is so soothing, and I like to watch his face. Do you know he said all sorts of nice things about me on Sunday—called me his guiding star, and—and angel of inspiration, and Herbert was there and had to listen! Sit down, and I'll tell you all about it."

Thereupon the little weathercock favoured her friend with an account of the scene in the rectory garden, adding her own airy touches of imagination to what she could remember of the scholar's actual utterances.

"I always thought you were a wicked person, and now I am sure of it," said Flora, when the pink lady had done bubbling. "You had much better make the best of your husband and be good. As for Dr. Berry, I should advise you to leave him severely alone. You know you are just a little bit fascinated, and he might become dangerous, and you might be stupid, and Mr. Juxon would hear of it—and then, where would Miss Maudie be then, poor thing?" she concluded flippantly.

"You are always preaching," said her friend pettishly. "You have changed altogether, and I don't like you now."

"Givers of advice are often unpopular," Miss Neill admitted. "But you are right about my preaching. I have been lecturing uncle on the condition of his study, and advising Mr. Conway to destroy that house. By the way he has been trying, in a weird sort of way, to approach."

"What! Proposing?" cried Maude, forgetting her own tribulations.

"Something rather like it. You will please remember I am still a line moving through space, and Mr. Conway has chosen to establish himself as my curve for the time being. It is the duty of the curve to remain motionless, but he has forgotten propriety and jumped out to meet me."

"With the result that you jumped back?"

Flora nodded.

"The idea of calling me wicked!" exclaimed Mrs. Juxon indignantly. "A married woman has certain flirting privileges, but an unmarried girl has none. You will play your game too long, and some day you will wake up and find yourself growing old and ugly, and then you may whistle as much as you like but no one will come to you. I have a heart, Flora, and yours is just a horrid cold lump of stone. You will become a nasty old crabbed spinster, sitting at a window, knitting socks for missionaries, keeping cats and canaries, and saying atrocious things about your neighbours."

"You may threaten," said the fair-haired girl loftily. "Remember what I said to you at home. The sympathies will not be forbidden. If you are married without love, some state of the soul will assert itself."

"Rubbish," said the little lady. "Go into the garden, while I write no-thank-you to Herbert, and pick me some roses."

"You know I cannot touch roses."

"Then do, for goodness sake, take a piece of string and play with the kitten."

So Flora went on her way, Maude Juxon on hers; and the Strath waited for them both.

Scene V.—PAGEANT

> Toss fortune back her tinsel and her plume,
> And drop this mask of flesh behind the scene.—*Young*.

The two dwellers in the Strath went on dreaming. Drayton had reserved a small antechamber leading out from the saloon for his work-room. Here the escutcheon of the mask was endlessly repeated in wood, plaster, and copper; a pinched tragic face was represented, crest-like, upon the picture frames, and along the cornice. And it was here that the tragic influence of the house was felt more strongly than elsewhere.

The day was grey. The sun had shone little of late; and a moist wind carried restlessly through the garden. The playwright sat nursing a volume which served him for a desk. He appeared in good health, although his eyes had a trick of roving, and at times he would shudder as though with cold. He believed that he had never been so well in his life, and this opinion was shared by Conway, who was lying in the saloon, listening to his friend. The journal that he loved was lying open upon a cushion before him. The draperies which divided the two rooms were fastened back, and when the enraptured voice came louder to his ears Conway put back his head and laughed in sheer happiness as he heard the noisy sophistry of the writer:

"I cannot conceive a Deity who finds pleasure in tragedy. The Creator must understand and appreciate comedy. If there be the divine frown, there must be also the divine laughter. I am assured that the Sublime would rather see a wine-skin dressed out in child's clothes than the lion-hide and the club; and rather hear the quack of the frog-souls against the Acherusian lake than those anguished cries in the grove of the Eumenides. If that be so, let us have no more tragedy. Let us grow wings and fly to Cloudcuckootown, and take a bird's eye view across mortality."

"Before you attempt to fly, be sure that your wings will bear you," called Conway, also speaking in the spirit of ancient comedy.

"The nearer the sun the greater the effort; and if you fall there may be no Icarian sea to receive you."

"Give me a theme, and I will set to work upon it," cried the enraptured Drayton.

"Listen then," said Conway, picking up the journal. "Take a well known theme. In old fields we gather fresh flowers, and new learning may be found in the oldest tales." Then he went on thus to read:

"Can there be anything more bitter than solitude? This morning I was driven out by my aching tongue to speak to nature. I called to the flowers, and they were silent. I cried to the birds, and they chattered, but not to me. I whispered to the stream, and it murmured, but not to me. The eyes I saw in that water were not those you have in your memory, my fair-haired love. I spoke to the trees, to the wind, to the clouds, and despairingly to God. The trees whispered, and the wind murmured, but not for me; the clouds drifted on; and God remained more silent than any of the wonders He has made.

"The prisoner in the Fleet has consolations which I may not share. He may wrangle with his turnkey concerning fees, or argue with his fellows in misfortune. I have nothing, but memory and faith. There is a place for me in this world, and I may not fill it; a love, and I may not have it; a life, and I may not enter into it; one voice above all others, and I may not hear it. This is to be in prison indeed.

"You will wonder, Geoffrey, should this little book in time to come be brought into your hands, why I did not escape from this misery, before death, like some kindly nurse, snatched me from my play-things and put me to my bed. Let me answer you. The roads are watched, not only against your coming, but against my going. I know that silent men follow me. Were I to enter a coach, I should be dragged down. Were I to steal forth some night, I should be seized, brought back by violence, and beaten for my effort.

"Sir John fears me, because I know too much concerning his two-faced life. Yet for my freedom I would promise anything, nay, I have promised, but 'tis of no avail. He knows that the caged bird is secure, but let that bird fly, and it will be seen no more. There is also another, more bitter reason. That it is which now tears out my heart. My uncle, miser and parson of Queensmore, told me, with a grin and a screwing up of his pig-like eyes, that you were lately taken by the press. That pitiless and cunning wolf my father set the plot to be rid of you. May God alone forgive him.

"Is it true? While I write these words are you far upon the seas, shamefully degraded and abused? You could not have kept from me a whole year. You would have found a way, for love laughs at swords, and knows no fear, and has no sense of bodily pain. You have gone far from me, and I am left with a sad last hope that someone will be found to tell you I was true. My final breath shall be in prayer that you may be brought some day into Thorlund, to stand upon a cold stone marking the spot where I shall be in silence. Do not be afraid, Geoffrey, even though it be night and a wild wind beating; for your mind shall not be troubled and you shall see no ghostly sight. You will know I did myself no harm.

"Would that I might leave you something, a ribbon, a lock of hair, a ring. Why, so I will. None but old Deborah shall handle this small white body when I am wrung out of it, and she will do my bidding yet. Our vault lies beneath the chancel. You have but to shut yourself in the church during the night, raise the great stone beside the wall—'tis graven with the Hooper arms, surmounted by a cross fimbriated—and descend the stone steps. Beloved, do not be afraid. I shall be loving you still, and I may be nearer than you think. If a light breath passes, call it not night wind. Upon my body you shall find the ring you gave me, and the lock of hair which now lies upon my forehead. Yet I have forgotten. My brain is wandering. How shall you discover this poor record of my daily life?

"The trees are white with dust, and the flowers wither. No rain has fallen for long, and the people who dwell upon the hills are hard put to it for water, and much sickness is, I hear, abroad. Mr. Blair takes his customary ease, smokes his long pipe, makes fishing-lines, and turns a deaf ear to the calls of the cottage folk. His duty begins and ends with his Sunday sermons, and these he is too idle or too ignorant to write himself. What a little charity there is in this great world! I can do nothing for the poor. I may not visit them, nor send one bottle of my father's wine. Reed, who is the master of this house, keeps a sharp eye upon the household, and nothing goes out without his knowledge. 'Tis strange that my father should trust him, and none besides, but villainy acquaints a man with vile partners.

"To-day I met with Poor John, one who has lost his wits and roams about the country making verses. I see him often, at evening trapping sparrows in the ivy, at morning whistling beneath the elms, and at noon lying beside the stream to laugh at the image of his white face. He asked me for apples, as his custom is, but I could only tell him that all last year's apples were done. Then he gave me a whistle, which he had made, and directed me to go into the woods and blow upon it, when I would immediately set all the birds a-singing. And so he left me grinning. Poor John do they call him? Why, he is far happier than I. I could envy this gentle madman. He views his surroundings through a weird atmosphere of imagination, and regards sane suffering men and women as underlings, and passes them in the belief that he is nature's king, never knowing what a misshapen oaf he seems to them.

"It is exceeding hot. My brain aches and my eyes burn. This is my twentieth summer. I have lived a long time. You have been given and taken away; I mourn the loss and forget to be thankful for the gift. My books tell me nothing is left for a woman when the time of her love-making is passed. The man may still have his ambitions. He may attempt to follow in the steps of Mr. Pope, Mr. Garrick, Mr. Hogarth, or Mr. Fielding. He may serve his country, or aid the Pretender, winning scars and fame, as you may be doing while I write, my Geoffrey. But Miss Hooper, sad, and white, and shivering—what may she do? Nothing but sigh, and wait, and hope; and sighing kills, waiting maddens, and as for hope—why, hope is a fading flower. Oh, Geoffrey, cannot you send some small message through all this darkness, something to tell me that you live? Cannot you make a sign? I listen in the night for the movement of your spirit, or the echo of your mind. Ought I not to feel your heart longing for me? I hear only the night throbbing, the insects murmuring, the house creaking, and beyond there is cold pitiless space half-lit by stars. The daffodils were glorious this year, Geoffrey. They filled the plantation with a light of gold, and yours was there, and I stood by it alone."

The reader stopped, and a gentle movement came from the ante-room.

"There was a time when every living creature saw the bright side of things," said the voice of Drayton. "Even when the human emotions were first represented upon the stage, it was believed that happiness ruled the world, until the philosophers discovered that whereas one play aroused the laughter of the audience another excited their compassion and their tears. Thereupon the drama became divided into its two great heads, known as the goat-song and the wine-song, the goat being the prize for tragedy, the wine for comedy. Comedy is the beginning of the story; tragedy is the end; there is only the difference of a letter between them. That which you have read seems to me to contain the germ of tragedy. When my modern drama, dealing with the life and death of George the Third, is completed I will give the world that story. The emotions are there," he went on noisily. "I see light there, and it must be the phosphorescence of the dead which produces it."

Conway joined the speaker. His face was pale, and his eyes shone with a mad light as he cried, "Let us remain here and work together. Let us discover the origin of love, and find the cause of its unhappy ending. Why does the glamour of life end when love has been satisfied?"

"Because of that satisfaction," said the other character.

"That could never be so here."

"There is a vast region outside," said Drayton. "Love is here a religion; there a passion. Here desire becomes etherealised by possession, and consummation leads to higher things; there ambition, rivalries, and all the petty wedges of worldliness are driven in to love's destruction. It ends in a tragedy there. It must end so, because of that finality. For every thing that knows an end is a tragedy."

All the little tragic masks frowned at the spell-bound men, in copper and wood and plaster.

"There is no such thing as comedy at all."

"Call the drama a knot," said Drayton. "Call the gradual unloosening of that knot comedy, the complete unfastening tragedy. The one deals with human beings, the other with actions. The light which falls upon the stage is constant, if difficult to discern. That light is not shed by religion, for religion is a superstition, and superstition is a flickering lamp which requires to be often recharged and changed. We live in the faintly glimmering region which lies outside, where there is no terror and no suffering, because we are spiritual. This state cannot be tragic, because it knows no ending."

"Our minds demand an ending," the other urged.

"When the body ceases to be material the mind will be unable to realise an ending," said the man, who but a few weeks back had with difficulty made a living by writing snippets of nonsense for people of no intellect. "We are living in the half-light under these present conditions. It is the finest state we are capable of attaining while encumbered with the body."

He leaned forward, parted the creepers, and holding them apart continued: "I perceive a woman walking in the garden. She is looking into the lilies beyond the topiary hedge. Her hair is dark, and her face tanned by exposure to the weather. Now she turns to me. There is a poetic gloom in her dark eyes."

Before Drayton had done speaking he was alone. Conway had stepped into the garden. The creepers fell back across the window, the scribe's fingers closed round the pencil, and he resumed his automatic labours.

It was Lone Nance who stood in the garden. She was often there, but the dreamers had not sighted her before, because she had hidden herself when she saw them coming. They had heard a singing voice during the still evenings, but had given it no heed. What was it to them if the nightingale sang old ballads, and the blackcap madrigals, so long as the songs were in tune with the influence?

He, who was called the master of the Strath, reached the yew hedge, and discovered the girl scraping moss from a long low stone. She looked up at him fearlessly with large eyes lightly blurred with tears.

"Why do you kneel beside that stone?" Conway muttered, not venturing to remove his eyes lest the vision should disappear. "And why are there tears in your eyes?"

The girl put out her hand and held up the speckled and stiffened body of a thrush, which had been smitten by some hawk and had tumbled into the garden to die in the dust.

"The birds come to the Strath to die," she said. "I will not bury it, for there may still be life in its little brain. I will let it lie upon the stems of this long grass, where the wind shall rock it up and down, and the sun shall warm it, until the little body may forget that it is dead."

"Why are you scraping the moss off that stone?" he urged.

"I was running on the hills when a voice stopped me and called me into the valley," she answered.

"I did not hear it," he said.

"At sunset there is always a voice, like music melting in the air," she said. "You must make no sound, or you will not hear it. He hears it." She nodded in the direction of the rectory.

"What is that stone? Why is it broken across the middle?"

"This stone cries out, and the house answers it," went on the girl in a low voice. "Lives and hearts have been broken here. He was young and he was beautiful. As they carried him past the gates into the garden he sighed once and that was all. They buried the body here that night, and covered the grave with a great stone taken from the stable-yard. But in the morning the stone was broken. The spirit had escaped in spite of them."

"What was his name?" Conway asked.

"I do not know. His hair was fair, and his eyes were blue. I have seen him walking with the lady of the white lilies."

She stroked the stone. Her hand was a deep brown, bearing marks of bramble scratches, and the fingers were delicate. Her head was small. There were white seeds of grass held in its thick dark hair. She was strong and healthy, this wild girl.

"I have never been in there," she said, pointing towards the house.

"Come with me," said Conway. Holding the girl's hand, he led her through the garden, across the moat, into his home, and left her at length beside the door of what had been Miss Hooper's room. "This is your place," he said quietly. "You will find here all that you can require."

But there still existed a gross world of evil-thinking outside the influence, and there was materialism even within the Strath. Early in the afternoon the crone of the kitchen accosted the master, as he walked in a state of innocence, and stated her intention of quitting the place forthwith. The influence had left her absolutely untouched; she had no laughter to give, nor shudder to spend. But she could not tolerate the presence of Lone Nance; and if the girl were to remain she, the speaker, would go, and that immediately, even to the work house and her pauper's coffin.

Conway could not understand, nor was he able to reason with the rachitic dame, who insisted upon dragging the custom of another world into his paradise. Why this turmoil because another character had been added to the drama? He did not know why she should seek to disturb his state of peace. There were the iron gates in all visibility; she might so easily walk off the stage. The birds did not first come to him, and scold noisily, if they intended to fly away.

"Human nature has many phases," observed the philosophic Drayton, when the respectable dame came and appealed to him. "One well-defined trait is a longing after change." Then he gravely handed her the Ethics of Aristotle, and bade her study the pages for her soul's good.

Finally the poor muddy-minded creature became appeased, not through the wisdom of Aristotle, nor yet by the indifference of her masters, but owing to the natural passing of her indignation after the noisy assertion of her wrongs. She returned to the kitchen, after a manner mollified, to grope grumbling among the pots, and to prepare the evening meal which differed not from day to day.

That same evening rumour went rustling into Kingsmore, where the relations of Lone Nance lived, and charges were brought against Conway, as gross as they were false, while wiseacres nodded heads of clay and recalled predictions made by them aforetime. They had seen the squire of Thorlund at the fair, and had written him down a fellow of the baser sort. They exhorted the lone girl's guardians to take immediate action; but these practical folk merely realised that there was no longer a superfluous mouth to feed and an irresponsible spirit to suppress. Only one old man was sage enough to say, "No harm will come to her if she is at the Strath." To those who reminded him of Henry Reed's fate the grandfather replied, "He set himself against the place."

When Dr. Berry came into the garden at his accustomed time he discovered a young woman, dressed in the mode of the eighteenth century, selecting blooms from the rose-bushes. He bent his head courteously and passed without a word.

The night fell, close, humid, and dark. There was not a breath of wind to move the heavy clouds which obliterated space and its starlight. Through a mist hanging about the garden beamed the light of a single candle, set beside the stone under the topiary hedge. The long yellow flame rose like an ear of wheat, and only flickered when a moth darted into it. There was a sound of music in the house, and presently the chorus reached the garden, and loomed into the misty radiance of the candlelight. First came Nance, grave and self-possessed, her head bare, her hands full of white roses; then Drayton and Conway; and finally Dr. Berry. They were holding sprigs of rosemary gathered from the herb-garden.

They took their stand about the stone, and when the girl had covered it with her robes the exarchus recited the office of the dead. The garden was steeped in silence outside the halo of light. The window of the saloon could be seen faintly glowing in the distance, but the outlines of the house were lost.

The Dithyramb was sung and the chorus marched away, leaving the solemn candle to burn itself away among the blooms. The Bacchanalians sat down to eat and to drink, but there was no sound of laughter, nor any careless word. The mind of the house was grim.

The procession made its way out the second time, Dr. Berry leading. Behind him came Conway and Drayton carrying iron bars and chisels. They passed the gate leading into the churchyard. Beneath a drip-stone terminating in a diabolic face, at the west end of the building, the scholar left them and went to his house for the key. The atmosphere continued to be dense; not a sound was heard, except the squeaking of bats, and the cry of a nightjar.

When the heavily clamped door had been opened, the three men passed into the mouldy interior. The rector locked the door, lighted one of the chancel lamps, and indicated a long stone let into the tiles, beneath the north wall of the building; and, when the others hesitated, he snatched the bar from Conway's nervous hands and forced its point into the mortar which crumbled in the crevice.

A canopied memorial, adorned by miniature fluted columns and capitals of spiral volutes, acanthus-leaf bosses, brackets of decorated foliage, grape pendants, and crotchets terminating in mitrehead finials, had been let into the chancel wall, where a marble slab lyingly recited virtues of dead and gone Hoopers. There was no mention of Sir John, nor of his wife Edith, nor of his daughter Winifred; and the parish registers dealing with their period had been destroyed by carelessness and by fire. The baronet, as was well known, had been buried in unconsecrated ground. The stone which closed the entry to the vault was soft and much chipped. The cement crumbled at a touch. Conway, who had joined the work in fearful expectancy, felt the slab heave. Another moment it came up, and they could hear the hollow sound made by fragments of mortar falling into the vault below.

A step appeared, dry and dusty, and when a candle was brought and lowered they discerned a narrow flight leading into the silent space. Dr. Berry was the first to descend, and Conway the last. A brick arch sloped over them, and on either side appeared stout shelves, supporting narrow berths where the bodies of the extinct family had been put aside like old garments in a press.

"This is the one," the scholar whispered, raising the candle above his head, and tapping a worm-eaten plank which gave forth a hollow echo.

"Died December 12th, aged 20," muttered Conway.

"Let us see whether her lover came to her," the scholar murmured.

There was nothing terrible about those swathed remains. Only a lock of fair hair, which had escaped from its bonds somehow, glistened when the candlelight entered the coffin. What had been little white hands were folded; and between them Conway perceived a tiny packet, bound with white ribbon, and inscribed with one word "Geoffrey." He put out his hand, but shrank, afraid to rob the dead.

"It was never meant for me," he whispered.

"Nevertheless take it," urged the rector. "She does not need it now."

Conway put out his arm, but again the effort failed. The packet was retained jealously, and the grave-breaker had neither the courage nor the inclination to use force. He turned away quickly, and sought the steps, muttering as he escaped, "She will not let it go."

"I wished to bury it beneath the stone where her lover lies," murmured Dr. Berry, as he also turned away. "But she knows what is best."

As they replaced the stone, the light went out. Velvety darkness, heavy as cobwebs, closed down, submerging them, leaving them standing as it were upon the bottom of the sea of space. Then Drayton spoke:

"A current of cold air passed me. It was going from east to west."

"It passed me also," said the rector. "And I could see its outline and its eyes."

Scene VI.—MELODRAMA

And the Voices of the Dialogue would be Strong and Manly,
And the Ditty High and Tragicall; Not nice or Dainty.—*Bacon*.

Drinkers of tea in Kingsmore continued to talk scandal concerning Conway and Nancy Reed; but when the evil practice extended beyond the farm-houses and reached the untidy Vicarage, Mr. Price considered the time had come for him to act. The breath of ill-report was poison to the simple squire. Having drunk his customary four cups of tea, he roundly lectured his sister and niece; and when he had finished his sermon he went out to the stable-yard, saddled a cob with his own hands, then jogged across the hills to Thorlund, to acquaint himself personally with the facts relating to his peccant parishioner Lone Nance.

The squire remained a very short time at the Strath; yet it was long enough to satisfy him. He trotted back contented, although ignorant that he had regarded his neighbour's domestic affairs through the spectacles which the spirit of the place had thought good to push before his eyes. Reaching home, he fell in with Flora, and after removing himself slowly from the saddle thus expressed his mind:

"The only way of punishing scandal-mongers is to disgrace them publicly. Our ancestors had the sense to know that. When gossips made a nuisance of themselves they had their heads harnessed in an iron cage. I could name a few chattering people who would be none the worse for a dose of old English penalties. Give me the stocks again, and let me see the public nuisances with their ankles picketed, and a beadle handy to encourage honest folk to jeer at them—"

"I suppose you have been to the Strath?" broke in Flora, who knew by experience that when her uncle was mounted upon a hobby his speech was liable to flow.

"Where I discovered the truth," the vicar snapped. "Mr. Conway finds that old woman totally inadequate, and I'm sure I don't wonder. It appears that Nancy Reed came and offered her services and he accepted them. It is all quite respectable and right. But the extraordinary part of it is the girl appears to be perfectly sane."

"Did you go into the house?" Flora asked, with meaning.

"I stood in the hall for about five minutes, and enjoyed a very interesting conversation with Mr. Drayton. A most well-informed man, my dear, and as clear-headed as anyone could be. I have asked him to come and visit us. Really I found the Strath quite fascinating. After all I should be sorry to see it pulled down."

"Did you interview this young woman?" Flora pursued.

"What?" said her uncle, somewhat blankly. "Well, I cannot remember that I did," he went on crossly. "I was perfectly satisfied. Anyhow it's not a subject for you to discuss, and I do not wish to hear any more questions."

The squire was walking beside the girl, who was tall enough to look down upon him. As they came near the house he turned to her, and asked sharply, for he was not in a good humour that evening, how many men it had pleased her to refuse to marry.

"Four at present," replied Flora carelessly.

"Ah!" exclaimed her uncle. "It is evident you are incapable of selecting a husband for yourself. When is your reply going to be in the affirmative?"

"Probably never. I don't want to marry, and I don't want to talk about it," returned Flora.

"Bless my soul! A good-looking girl not want to talk about matrimony!" said the astounded squire. "I want to see you settled," he went on seriously. "I am an old man, and I should like to have the pleasure of uniting you to some suitable partner before I take my departure."

"You have someone in your mind," she suggested. "Is it Mr. Conway?"

"You might do worse, I suppose," said the vicar, stroking his chin, and glancing at her out of the corners of his eyes.

"And live at the Strath?" she went on.

"You might improve it."

"Not very long ago you told me Mr. Conway was not a gentleman," Flora reminded him. "You remarked that he was connected with the Reeds of this village. You called the Strath a haunted house. Do you know what has caused your mind to change so completely?"

The vicar stared her in amazement.

"It is the house," she said. "You have just come from there, and I believe its influence is still upon you. You were not expressing your own opinions just now. They are not your opinions."

"Flora," the old gentleman exclaimed angrily, "I may be over seventy, but I am not a fool, and I am not to be told by a young girl that I do not know what I am talking about. I want you to marry, and of course I hope you will choose a worthy gentleman. In my young days girls were not allowed to have opinions of their own, and it was very much better for them. I did not ask your poor dear aunt if she would marry me. I went to her father, who, I believe, was far more capable of judging a man than she could ever have been and told him I wanted his daughter. That is the way marriages ought to be arranged. If any man asks me for you, and I think him desirable, I shall take it upon myself to answer for you, and if you refuse to accept him I shall leave my money elsewhere. I have an idea you have behaved disgracefully."

With that the squire led his horse off to the stable; while Flora, very white and angry, mounted her bicycle and rode across country to seek consolation from Maude.

The little lady was not at home. A man of general uselessness, who was rolling the lawn without energy, volunteered the information that his mistress had driven off in her donkey-cart half an hour earlier. Flora returned to the road, and tempted by a long declivity ran down into Thorlund.

She saw no one in the hamlet; not a living thing appeared upon the road; only a subdued hammering issued from the smithy on the side of the hill. The Strath never appeared more alluring than when flooded in evening sunlight. It seemed to be breathing softly, reaching a dreamy influence over church, fields, and hills, hushing nature into silence. Flora walked to the gate in the churchyard, responding to a summons which would accept no denial; and for the second time found herself in the garden with the eyes of the house upon her soul.

The mood had changed; on her former visit the house had transferred her into a light-hearted mummer. Then it suggested solemn truths, responsibilities which might not be avoided, and the necessary sorrows of existence. It suggested that a thin veil separated knowledge from belief; creatures of a day could not afford to dally; the mind which faces the whirlwind must bend or be broken; women who will not obey the call of destiny must die, even as Henry Reed had died; tragedy arises from self-will; obedience is the road to happiness. Through this atmosphere Flora wandered, with an indefinite longing for a guide, beginning to comprehend that she could no more struggle against destiny than the butterfly against the storm.

A rebellious desire came over her to defy those influences, and in that moment it seemed to her that the light darkened. She experienced the stunning sensation of walking out to execution before a howling mob; there was the ancient tragic wail, "Alas, my sister!" and she saw a stage with curtain descending slowly before a dying body. Here then was the end of those who opposed themselves to destiny. So she resigned herself, and immediately the light became clear, and her mind was at rest. She was told contemptuously that she was human, therefore ignorant, and fated to stumble. She was like a foolish moth coming out of darkness, burning its beauty, and returning into darkness.

Life must be something more than a glimmering meteor. It is a flame burning well, or flickering feebly, according to the supply of soul. A life might light the world, and continue burning. Far back in the morning mists of time a fair woman had struck the lyre. It still vibrated. Four thousand men had held at bay three millions of foes, falling at last, envied, their tomb an altar; and a general in command of a few heroes had faced the fighting force of the world, and hurled it back, with death in the front, destruction in the rear. The light shed by such lives might never be extinguished.

Flora had sought originality. She had longed to render herself conspicuous by a line of action contrary to the laws of the drama. It was for the Strath to open her eyes, and point out, what should have been obvious, namely that she was a very ordinary woman. Originality does not consist in doing uncommon things, but in doing common things in an uncommon way. Thousands of men had fought and fallen, before Miltiades occupied the plain of Marathon, or Leonidas led his handful to the pass of the Hot Springs. Hundreds of singers had lifted up their voices, before Sappho's throat melted with its music. They were immortal, because they had played the fine old parts as well as it was possible to play them. But let a man or woman create a fresh part which was contrary to the laws of the drama—then would come failure, dishonour, and the hisses of the audience.

The voice of warning was clear. Away from the Strath the girl might assume her part of attracting men with no idea of union; but there at least she was bound by the custom of ages. She stirred among strange forces. The dramatic fingers of destiny indicated the well-worn paths along which she must walk, through pain and difficulties by performing a woman's duty, to attain present happiness and rest at last. The influence suggested, moreover, that she might not turn into that beaten track without a punishment for having gone astray.

The lessons of the Strath were those of the didactic drama, which teaches that mortals must submit to unchanging laws. The battle of free-will against destiny was its theme when serious, but under the teaching there lurked undoubtedly the sting of malevolence, of hatred for the actors upon its stage, and a desire to destroy them if it might. It had no phantasm to show, nor could it terrify by any sound; it could only shape minds for good or evil, causing the puppets to act and speak in comic or in tragic mood, showing them that life is not a small thing, the world no passing scene, but rather a permanent stage, upon which actors pass and repass, each playing many characters, with the same passions in them, and the same destiny always behind.

Unmindful of time or place Flora walked on until she reached the orchard. And there other voices came to her ears, and looking out she saw Conway and Nance walking beneath the mossy branches.

She stood aloof, watching those dream-like figures crossing the bright green orchard, her ears filled with the drowsy hum of their voices, until the knowledge came that she was jealous of the brown village girl who trailed across the grass the long discarded garments of Winifred Hooper, and rested a hand, half hidden in lace ruffles, upon the arm of her new-found friend.

Flora swayed to and fro beside the hedge, and endeavoured to reason with her sane self, but the Strath held her fast. Could this wild Medea-like passion be love, or was it hatred? There was hatred in her heart, but it was for Nance, and her eyes had never seen the girl before that day. A breath of wind shivered through the trees, and strong-minded Flora bent beneath the tragic influence of the place.

She ran to the house and entered the hall, which was filled with dust-flecked sunbeams. Then into the saloon, where Drayton was lying asleep with a smile upon his white face. A mask of tragedy stared from the wall with pitiful blank eyes. Flora smiled wildly at the emblem; then, catching the reflection of her own face in one of the mirrors, shrank because of its tragic similarity. She caught up the rusty sword, which her uncle had handled upon their former visit, and passed again through the garden with the day upon one side, and the night upon the other.

The man and the girl were still walking within the orchard. Flora felt no sense of nervousness, when they approached her hiding-place. She could see the lone girl's face, idealised in that atmosphere, its large eyes roaming restfully across the sun-mists. She could hear the long grass brushing against their garments. A few more steps and they would have passed; but the opposing influence had already issued its warning, and Nance stopped a few paces from the hedge, and lifting her hand pointed towards the exact spot where Flora stood concealed.

"What is that?" she said to her companion.

"It is a holly bush," Conway answered.

"A flash of light passed through it," the girl said.

"It was the sun. See how it flashes through the apple-trees."

"There is a dark shadow round the holly bush, and the light that I saw was cold," Nance went on. "This morning a robin was singing there. It has flown away, and now the sun has gone too. Let us follow them. I hear the robin singing beside the stream."

They turned and went away, Nance casting back glances at the deep green bush, until they came into a jungle of roses, leading towards a little stream which murmured evermore among its weeds. Here the girl paused and pushed Conway into the sunlight. "Go to the holly bush," she said. "There is an enemy in the garden."

He regarded her with calm astonishment.

"There is danger there, and it is to me," she went on. "You are safe. I will sit here, and watch the water until you come."

Her wild eyes aroused him and he returned, smiling in perplexity, wading through masses of scented herbs, and tangled brakes of briars, scattering rose petals all over the slope; and so advanced, forgetful of his mission, until he saw Flora walking to meet him with the bent sword hanging from her hand.

He remembered her dimly as one who had scorned him once, but the thought that she was out of place in that garden did not occur, until another breath of wind came from the house and set the leaves in motion; and then there came a suggestion of treachery and the memory of bodily death.

"So you would have killed her," he said quietly, as they stopped face to face.

Flora was deathly pale. After that wave of passion a spirit of cunning had entered into her. She was following her enemy, hoping to find her alone; but now that she was confronted by the man of her desires resolution began to ebb and the deeper self came uppermost.

"I would only have frightened her," she said glibly. "She has no right to be here—in my place."

"This is not your place," he answered. "Nor is it mine. I was brought here to learn, but I am on probation. One who was here before me rebelled against the master of the house, and he was punished."

"Have you always acted according to the dictates of your master's mind?" she asked.

"I dare not do otherwise."

"Neither do I," she cried. "My enemy is here, and I was told to hide in the holly-bush and kill her as she passed."

"She has done you no wrong."

"She is winning your love. She is drawing you away from me. She walks by your side, with her hand upon yours, and looks into your eyes, and you return her words of affection, and give her smile for smile. I was watching while you walked together in the orchard. I heard your flatteries—"

"You are lying," the male actor interposed. "She is as clean as the light. I gave her no word of flattery. She has a place in this garden. You have none. I do not know you, and I do not desire to see you again. Put down that sword, and go."

The wind was blowing steadily from the house.

"Do not speak so cruelly," she prayed. "Do not look at me with those hard eyes. It is my love which has driven me to this. I will go if you bid me, or come if you call, or kill myself if you would be rid of me. Have pity upon me. Let me walk with you. Come into the orchard, and talk to me as you talked to her, and let me rest my hand upon your arm."

Conway stepped from her to an open spot, and faced the wind.

"I believe there is no sincerity in you," he said. "I have had dreams of a woman like you, one who would lead men on by smiles, and later spurn them. You are tall and you are beautiful, but I do not trust you. I am told you are incapable of love, and this one thing I feel—it is dangerous for you to be here. Give me that sword."

She put out her arm and gave it him.

"Come with me."

"Give me something to carry away with me," she prayed.

He plucked a white rose and handed it to her. She touched it, and screamed. That environment, which had caused her to forget the world and to act a strange part, had not removed her natural antipathies. The bloom was dashed to pieces between them. She allowed herself to be hurried on, through the deepening shadows and that cold scrutinising wind, in silence and hopelessness, towards the ivy-covered wall and the gate which stood ajar as she had left it. Conway fell back from her, as she fled through and escaped.

At the sight of the grass road, and blue hills beyond, the girl's normal conditions were established. But as she passed out there was a feeling in her body, as though some vital essence, which had abandoned her temporarily, was then restored, and with it came a dull pain throbbing above her eyes.

Conway stumbled stupidly back to the side of the stream, where he found Nance singing to the water and making boats of buttercups. He gave her the old sword without a word of explanation, and she as silently received and flung it into the water, where the long tresses of weeds closed over and hid it from their sight.

Then she sang him an old sad song.

Mr. Price had just returned from the farm, and was standing on his lawn drawing long white hairs meditatively off the arm of his overcoat. Seeing his niece he hurried to her, smiling in his genial fashion, because he had been afraid she might have taken his late lecture too much to heart, and it was not in his nature to play the part of stern guardian for long.

"Been taking the air?" he cried. "Your mother was wondering where you had gone to. Why, child, your face is as white as chalk."

"I have a horrible headache," said Flora sulkily. "I am going to lie down. I actually went into the Strath and met Mr. Conway, and I believe I had a row with him about something or other, but I really cannot remember, because my head is so bad. It was an extraordinary thing my going there at all."

Scene VII.—IDYLL

> Now fast beside the pathway stood
> A ruin'd village, shagg'd with wood,
> A melancholy place.—*William Stewart Ross.*

Maude Juxon had failed to materialize at the time of Flora's visit, because she was on the other side of the great chalky billows, enjoying life after her usual manner, that is to say by wasting it in vain pursuits. Had Flora dropped into the Thorlund valley earlier, she would certainly have seen the notorious little tandem of asses in front of the rectory. So glorious was the evening that Maude determined to give herself the gratification of calling upon Dr. Berry, to offer him a drive through the serene and poetic atmosphere.

The spoilt beauty had soon forgiven the scholar for that indiscreet praise of herself before her husband. Indeed she liked him the better for his panegyric, which at least convinced her of the thorough genuineness of his nature. She knew that he liked her; it flattered her that he should think her clever. She had been indeed so impressed by this fact that she spent two terrible days struggling to compose an equal number of original lines of poetry; and when the effort brought forth, after much ruffling of silken hair and puckering of pretty brows, nothing but a silly series of ragged syllables, she shamelessly copied Sir Nicholas Breton's 'Farewell to the World' from an old book of English poetry which she discovered in the house, and this inky forgery was crumpled in her pocket when she jumped into the cart.

The rector was in the church, said the housekeeper, and thither Maude repaired, to discover him unpoetically engaged in discussing the condition of the roof with a pair of ruddy sheep-farmers. Some mossy tiles had been worked awry by wind and weather, and in time of rain a puddle would occur symbolically in the vicinity of the font. As Maude's bright colours illuminated the porch, the first bucolic was expressing his conviction that a certain handy labourer in his employ would experience no difficulty in resettling the recalcitrant tiles: the second bucolic indifferently suggested that the repairer should be summoned forthwith; the rector dreamily concurred, and the meeting was adjourned.

"Now you are coming for a drive," said Maude, when the farmers had clamped away, side by side like twin brethren. "I am sure you deserve it, after being shut up with those things. What funny voices they have, and the red on their cheeks is just like blobs of paint! Why is it that big men squeak, and little men bellow? How can you talk to them? I shouldn't know what to say after I had exhausted the weather."

"With these men, fortunately, that subject cannot be exhausted," said the poet. "It is very kind of you to invite me to drive with you on this magnificent evening, but I always find you kind and good," he went on, gazing into the marvellous flora of her hat with his calm thought-filled eyes. "I have not seen you for three days, and in that time have made, I am ashamed to say, no appreciable progress with my work. I dream too much. Even when I sit beside my table I am unable to control my thoughts. I am carried away beyond the border, and there wander at will between truths and half-truths. And there I am lost, and when I awake it is late, and nothing has been recorded."

"Oh!" exclaimed Maude. "I hope you don't talk like that to the sheep-men and the cow-men?"

"I speak upon such matters to you only," he replied tenderly. "Because I know you understand."

He dropped the church key among the weeds on the gravel walk, and did not appear to notice his loss until Maude stooped and picked it up for him.

"Look at my cart!" she exclaimed, with childish pleasure. "Doesn't it shine? I have just had it varnished, and those pink lines painted round it. May I have some of your poppies?"

"Let me gather them for you," said the scholar, as she hovered about the border. "You will soil your gloves."

Immediately he began to decollate all manner of poppies, scarlet, white, and variegated, great sleep-scented globes of blossom, ragged, and fluffy, and seed-capped, until Maude arrested his hand with a scream of laughter.

"No, no! What could I do with those things—as big as cabbages? It is the pink Shirley ones I want."

Laughing and chattering, she selected half-a-dozen of the prettiest, and fastened them into her dress; while the abashed scholar strewed the flowers of his own selection about the turf.

"Don't waste them," cried Maude. "Go and stick them about the heads of my donkeys."

The poet did so, but as he bent his silvered head over the long ears of the little steeds, a voice out of the breeze from the garden of the Strath sardonically whispered, "Oh, scholar, scholar! How has your wisdom served you? Has it fitted you for nothing better than to deck a donkey's head with poppies? Reason and infatuation, to say truth, keep little company together."

"You too must wear a flower," said Maude, approaching him. "Here is a pink rose for you." She lifted her dainty self on tip-toe, and fastened the bloom into his coat with perfumed white-gloved fingers, rattling on, "We must preserve the scheme of colour. I like every thing on me and near me pink. When I die I should like to be carried away on one of those delicious pink clouds we see at sunset."

"A beautiful thought," he said reverently, touching her hand lightly as it brushed a petal from his coat. "And beautifully expressed by a true poetic mind."

"I am clever?" cried Maude eagerly. "I really am a little clever?"

He smiled upon her, as he replied devoutly, "Cleverness is a small thing. It is an attribute we allow even to the lower animals. You are inspired."

Then he submitted to be packed into the little cart and driven from the valley.

At the sign-post Maude whipped her leader round to the right, and they descended the slope which ended among the ruins of Queensmore. The little lady had been silent for some minutes. That copied poem made itself uncomfortable in her pocket. She knew that her companion was widely read. He might recognise it, and she would be shamefully unmasked. She did not so much mind his discovering her shallowness, because it was somewhat of a strain to maintain the part; but what she did fear was lest a forced acknowledgement of her sheer ignorance might also deprive her of beauty in his eyes. She did not want to lose her present hold upon him. She liked him, she told herself, immensely, because he was handsome and dignified, so immeasurably, if unconsciously, superior to all the men she had known. She had seen her husband standing by his side. She could never have believed it possible for two men to be so widely different; the one had seemingly all the gifts Nature had to bestow; the other had—mere money.

She refused to consider Herbert Juxon's healthy mind and honest heart, and resolutely turned her eyes from his excessive forbearance. She had received a letter from him that morning. Somehow his kindly utterances always irritated her. He was coming to her on Saturday; he wished he could take her upon the Continent for a time, but business was holding him closely to the city; he intended to look out for a house in the country, which he hoped might suit her health; it was his ambition to make her happy. But his kindly words and thoughts were merely hailstones upon this butterfly.

The wheels jolted round a bend in the grass-grown road, and the entrance to what had been the village appeared before them. On a dark winter's day the scene would have inspired with melancholy; then, mellowed with sunshine and enriched by flowering grasses, lush reeds and lichens, it made a gratifying picture for the artist. Ruin and decay were all around; here, brambles choked the bleak foundation of a former ale-house, the bricks and woodwork of which had been carted away; there, a roofless cottage gaped with doorless mouth and stared with empty window sockets.

The church had been a low thatched building with a shingled spire. The remains were tottering upon a slight eminence beside a gigantic yew. The thatch sagged heavily, loaded with moist mosses of an emerald green, and the rotten rafters snagged inward like broken ribs. The interior was stripped bare. Its bell miles away was used for calling children to school; its encaustic tiles and fittings had been distributed abroad; its font and brasses had passed into the hands of collectors of antiques; even the burying place had been rifled, and the old grave stones taken to fill gaps in walls or to floor pig-sties.

A portion of the parsonage stood gaunt and spectral, its windows gloomy gaps fringed with ivy, its garden a pasture ground for straying cattle and adventurous sheep. The roof was golden with lichen, and the gutter-line broken picturesquely into a dog-tooth pattern by tiles, jutting off, awaiting removal by October winds. Swallows were darting in and out of the space once occupied by the door, where old parson Hooper had often entered in ragged red-lined coat and stiff gloves eager to count his gold. The village green beyond, where a rust-red pump leaned far out of the perpendicular, was a mere field, lined geometrically by four cart-tracks. White butterflies were swarming, and fruit-trees grew unpruned, and all the old gardens writhed with caterpillars; the grass and reeds fluttered lazily; a gentle sound issued through the vacant windows that were left.

Maude tried to be solemn as they drove through this desolation. She quickly found herself incapable of sustaining the effort, and dropping the reins demanded from her companion accurate information as to whether *asinus vulgaris* really delighted in consuming herbaceous plants of a spiny character.

"By refusing to do so the animal would destroy a long cherished belief," the scholar replied.

"Then their little hearts shall rejoice," said Maude. "There are enough thistles here to feed a hundred donkeys for a year. I will tie one of the reins round this pump, and the beasts may eat prickles while we explore."

When the tethering process had been accomplished they roamed through the village of the past, and presently entered the churchyard. A low tomb beneath a cypress offered a shady resting-place which met with Maude's approval, and thither she led the scholar, who was prepared to indulge her smallest whim. Seating themselves upon the sunken masonry, they watched the drops of sunlight filtering through the leaves, and making satin-like patches upon the mouldering and mossy stones which sealed down the bodies of those who long ago had taken the mystic road, which, in the words of a wise Greek, is not of difficult passage, nor uneven, nor full of windings, but all very straight and downhill, and can be gone along with shut eyes.

"It is heavenly," said Maude with a sigh, firmly believing she was perfectly happy, and fortunately ignorant of the saying of another Greek, that a woman knows only two happy days, that of her marriage, and that of her funeral.

Dr. Berry was leaning forward, his beautifully shaped hands clasped between his knees, his eyes fixed upon an inscription still faintly legible beside a laurel, "Here innocence and beauty lie." A beautiful woman was close beside him and in her soul, he believed, innocence was personified. The gently rounded summit of Deadman's Hill rose in the distance. Clearly outlined against the rosy sky stood the tall rugged post which marked the spot of the gallows where former villains had been compelled to submit to fate. The gallows had long ago been swept away. The post, which stood as its representative, cast a long narrow shadow across the ruins.

"Say something," urged the pink idol.

"I shall remember this," he answered dreamily.

Maude flushed a little. She did not like to be reminded of the future, when her dainty bloom must ripen off and the wrinkle assert its tyranny. "Ruins always make people sad," she said a little crossly. "The only ruins which could deject me would be those of my prettiness," she went on in a lower voice.

"Dear lady," murmured the poet, taking her hand impulsively. "Beauty will never leave you. It is the soul gazing from your eyes that gives you loveliness, and the soul does not age. Fifty years hence there may be snow upon your head and lines along your brow, but the beauty that is within can defy the years."

Maude conceived that moment profitable for the production of her borrowed master-piece. Releasing her hand, she burrowed into her pocket and brought forth an inky ball of manuscript, which she unrolled with blushes and smoothed modestly upon her knee, saying in a small faltering voice:

"You've never asked if I have written anything, but I—I've listened to you so often I want you to—to hear what I have done. Will you let me read you a little poem of my own?"

Her heart began to thump.

"My sister! My dear sister!" the scholar cried. "This is indeed a privilege. How selfish I have been! Completely engrossed in my own work, I had forgotten yours. Let me put myself in the disciple's place and learn."

He stretched himself upon the grass by her feet, and in that posture of humility put back his uncovered head, that he might behold her pretty features, and the brilliant curls fluttering beneath the brim of her hat.

"I am ready," he murmured.

"It is sad," said Maude warningly.

"We poets love the sorrowful theme. The sweetest music is also the saddest. But read! I am impatient to hear."

"It is called Farewell to the World," she murmured, with shy deprecation, and then hurriedly, "I believe you don't want to hear it. I'm sure you'll think it stupid."

"I shall feel only admiration, with perhaps some little envy," he answered. "But why are you so diffident? Am not I a poor weaver of fancies, like yourself?"

His encouragement was so kindly and sincere that Maude gained courage. With increasing colour she began to read:

"Go! Bid, the world, with all its trash, farewell."

"Slower," he entreated with upraised hand. "The music is lost when the time gallops."

Maude's fear began to be dissipated when the title and opening line passed unchallenged. She continued with more confidence, until her dainty voice sounded disdainfully the last of the stanza, "Leave it, I say, and bid the world farewell."

A few moments of silence intervened before the poet spoke:

"For freshness of conception, strength of imagery, and purity of line, that verse is only to be surpassed by the best work of the Elizabethan poets. It recalls indeed to my mind Sir Nicholas Breton's—"

"Oh!" Maude interrupted, dreadfully pale. "You don't think I—" And there she stopped in dire confusion.

"Indeed the similarity is but upon the surface," he continued. "We all have our models. The Elizabethan, to whom I have just referred, had neither your originality nor your strength of metaphor. To draw from the model is one thing; to improve upon it is another. Talent may copy, but genius will improve."

Maude breathed again and, after resolutely repelling the idea that she was acting with shameless wickedness, read the second stanza with boldness, the third and last with impudence, and sat, joyous in her sins, awaiting the verdict.

"That verse again," he prayed.

When she had complied with this request, he repeated the first line in a resonant voice, with his eyes fixed upon the ruined church:

"Then let us lie as dead, till there we live."

Silence fell again, intensified by the ticking of the insects in the grass and the wings of the swallows cutting through the air. Dr. Berry turned abruptly and seizing Maude's right hand pressed it passionately to his lips. He was paying his tribute then, not to face and figure, nor to dainty garments, but to a beautiful soul which was not there at all.

"I am a mere clerk," he said in a thrilling voice. "A poor transcriber of the ideas of others, while you soar through the clouds, and drink out of the golden cup of the gods. How hollow must my poor lines have sounded upon your ears! Yet you listened patiently, and approved, condescending to stoop and lift me upon your pinions and point out to me the path to the stars. My feeble song is but a piping of pan-pipes. Yours is a trumpet blast, stirring the depths."

"I'm so glad you like it," said Maude, blushing deeply, and delighted by his praise.

"What is your inspiration?" he continued, gazing up into her flushed face. "Tell me what stirs your soul. It is not true, as men have said, and will still affirm, that wisdom lies latent in the mind. We are the inspired media of an influence, that influence emanating from the minds which have preceded us. One great poet of the past heard a gentle fluttering of wings above his head. Another thought he could see a butterfly quivering about his pen. I, if I may mention my unworthy self, have a strange nervousness, the sense of a presence, a quickened heart, and a pricking sensation round my forehead. When the inspiration passes I am depressed and weak."

"I don't know," quavered Maude. "Oh yes! I like to smell roses."

"It is fitting," he said reverently. "Daintiness and sweetness make appropriate food for the divine soul. I see now that I have been misled. I have always refused to admit that the poetess, if born into this present age, would be able to break the bonds of social and domestic life, and fly upward with her song. Tell me," he added in a low and pleading tone, "confide in me, dear sister. Only the heart which has been wrung, and the mind which has cried, 'The hand of God has touched me,' could have controlled the brain to fashion such sorrowful truths as those you have recited. You have already passed through tribulation?"

A robin darted into the cypress, and his beautiful little body throbbed with song.

"Indeed I have," said Maude pathetically. "I have had dreadful troubles, but have never told anyone."

Honestly she believed what she said. She did not know that her silly life had been a mere ramble through a pleasance. Never having seen suffering, she did not know what it was. But she had a husband whom she did not care for, ambitions which had not been realised, clothes which had not come up to her expectations, and friends whom she knew had scoffed at her idle ways. So she had passed indeed through the valley of tribulation.

"We do not talk of these things," the scholar gently answered. "Like the Laconian, we hold the fox to our bosom, and though it may gnaw, and we may wince and faint, we still declare the creature is not there. We clutch the rose tightly, and aver there are no thorns. But those who love us know, and we are glad that they should know, because we need sympathy even as the flowers need dew. I have not known suffering, and while thankful for the privilege, I confess my work lacks that refining touch which suffering alone can give. Dear sister, put your hands for one moment upon mine."

The little lady quivering slightly, permitted him to take her hands. Her eyes were hidden by her hat, and waves of pink chased one another across her face and throat.

"Our souls are here united," he cried triumphantly. "Beautiful and inspired poetess! Did you not feel that restful sense of approaching union when first we met? We have grown together, during these blissful days, like two blooms upon one stem. Our ideals are the same. Together we may succeed in realising them. I have perhaps—pardon the presumption—more learning, but you have far clearer sight, a more perfect mind, and a soul quickened into fire by the suffering you have undergone. We will bring these forces together. How perfectly destiny works! She brought you to me at the time when I needed you most. And I have served you a little. You were neglecting your gifts. The fires were smouldering ineffectually. I flatter myself that, if we had failed to meet, that magnificent lyric I have just heard would never have been penned by this white hand."

"It wouldn't," Maude quavered.

"Then I have served you, but the debt upon my side remains still large. What a mysterious thing is this union! You have often seen a climbing plant reaching out for support, and when it finds a stem to which it may cling it grows into full perfection; but if it cannot establish the union it must wither. The same with our souls. But destiny is so kind she would not see us wither. You and I have been languishing, but now we shall grow—together and undivided."

He pressed her hands together, and bent his head over them.

INCIDENTAL

All things are changing; and thou thyself art perpetually altering and, so to speak, wasting away always.—*Marcus Antoninus*.

The time of ripened fruit had come, and the grass was yellow and sere. Change was upon the face of the country, the prospect was mantled in mists, and the shortened evenings were dark with rain-clouds. The note of Nature's song had altered. Autumn had taken the lyre out of summer's reluctant hand, and as she struck her fiercer notes the foliage turned from green to gold, and the migratory birds went away.

The spirit of change had settled upon the Bethel of Thorlund. The interior was in better order than formerly. The spider had been routed, and the mouse discomfited; the strong coarse flowers of autumn glimmered dimly at the east, where the old hangings had been replaced by new; the brass-work shone, and the damp altar itself awoke one day from a long lethargy to find itself resplendent in a new green mantle. The sleep which hung so long upon the rector's eyes had been in some part dissipated. Foolish Maude was the murderess of that slumber. Through her trivial and wholly terrestrial mind Dr. Berry perceived that one side of his environment lacked the beauty which was requisite for his bodily peace. Hitherto his mind had been so fully occupied in its strange flights that his charge the church had been but lightly included. But, subsequent to that memorable evening in the churchyard of ruined Queensmore, his lower self noted, with a distinct uneasiness, a certain lack of harmony between dreamland and the earthly vision. His manner of life had made stains which he would willingly have seen eliminated. The neglected church was one of these blots. He opened his eyes, and removed this reproach, in order that his poetic soul might no longer receive offence. This partial awakening was not spiritual, because at the same time he attended more carefully to his own appearance. His hair was more thoughtfully arranged, and his shoes were more elegant. Selfishness was the root, pride the stem, and vanity the bloom of this sudden growth, which had been raised into being and propagated as a pastime by Maude.

Change had come also over the spirit of the influence. It was stronger, more assertive, and more binding. It was at the same time more sinister. Conway and Drayton had become drifting particles controlled by the house, the instruments of its will, like electrons imprisoned within the atom. They roamed the garden in a perpetual state of dreams, responding to every breath from the hidden chamber, where the heart of the Strath was beating. Had Drayton been able to remind his companion of those past days of profligacy, Conway might have shaken his head with a perplexed smile. Had the older man been told of his former struggles to keep oil in the lamp of life, he would probably have replied, "I am thankful such misfortunes have never occurred to me."

As for Lone Nance she was noisy no longer. The Strath supplied what had been wanting in her. Had she wandered again into the country, she would doubtless have been seized by the former wildness, and claimed by the old evils; the borrowed reason would have left her; she would have sunk again to the level of the animals. Conway would often sit and gaze upon her face. Though she was brown and tanned, she brought back for him fair-haired Winifred, walking sadly through the orchard in glimmering white, her small pale face set towards the road, watching the night for the lover who did not come.

Flora too had changed since that evening when her soul had been stripped bare. She had the feeling that youth was departing from her, and that her woman's pride of beauty was beginning to wane. Mr. Price regarded her with apprehension, believing her to be ill. But she was not ill. She was only undergoing her punishment for having defied the first principles of the drama. She had come to regard her former opinions with a sort of loathing akin to fear. She confessed that she was an unnatural woman, after all her boastings of having made a step in advance of the remainder of her sex. What had actually occurred during her visit to the house of the drama she did not know; but she carried away a dream that evening which became a cloud darkening her life.

Upon a cheerless afternoon when a mass of grey vapour spread across the sky dropping warm rain at intervals, Conway brought his fellow-dreamer to Kingsmore vicarage.

Flora flushed when the leading character of the Strath entered. She had never been backward in speaking to any man, but then she was afraid. She knew that she desired to attract Conway, that she would still draw back if she could make him approach, but the knowledge came to her that power was wanting. She had lost the old art. At a glance she understood that he had no real affection for her. Could she have come to the Strath with a pure mind, as a humble heroine seeking development, as one anxious to discharge the high, if seemingly commonplace, functions of a woman, even as Nancy Reed had unwittingly approached the house, it might have been otherwise.

Mr. Price sought possession of Drayton, and Flora stood in the garden with the man whom she desired to shrink from, but could not. The rain had ceased, but the grass was mantled with film, and all the trees dripped moisture. The girl was cold; she was wearing white, which did not suit her. She might have recalled to him Winifred, as she had done once before, because she too was fair-haired, but she did not. Conway appeared to have forgotten that she was near. Once Flora would have been enraged at being thus slighted, but now she was pitying herself. A cluster rose, still showing a few blooms, wreathed an old-fashioned archway, and Flora in passing brushed against one of the flowers, and shivered when it became immediately resolved into a number of wet petals about their feet.

"I have changed a little lately," she said with a new timidity. "I can touch a rose now."

Conway stopped when she spoke, and looked fixedly into the mist.

"Could you never hold a rose?" he said. "That is unnatural."

It was the cruellest word he could have uttered. She shrank from him again, but gathered courage to say, as they moved on, "It is not easy to conquer any antipathy. Last summer I would faint, if I came into a room where roses were. Next year, perhaps, I shall be able to wear them."

Nancy wore roses in her hair. Indeed she was always fragrant with flowers. Conway had been sorry to see the grass flaked all over with shell-like petals; but Nance assured him that at the Strath roses bloomed all the year round. When Flora confessed that the fragrance of the queen of blossoms had caused her to faint the gulf between them became wider.

"There is a rose-bush at Queensmore, close beside the ruins of the church," he went on, in the abstracted manner which had been his of late. "I walked there early in the summer, when the flowers were at their best. It was close upon evening, and as I looked through the trees I thought I saw a woman, clothed in white, leaning over a tomb. When I came nearer I saw it was this bush covered with blooms. I went back and tried to make out the white woman again, but could not."

"I drove through Queensmore once by moonlight," said Flora.

"The ruins show us what a small thing life is," Conway answered sagely. "They teach us that no trouble is worth taking very much to heart, because suffering, like our time here, does not last for long. You know my house?" he added sharply.

"I have been inside it once," the girl faltered.

"Why is not that a ruin? Queensmore flourished for years after my house was abandoned, but the village has fallen, and the Strath stands. It has defied wind and weather. Its foundations are secure, and its walls sound, although creepers were rotting the bricks before any man now living was born. Do you know the secret of its strength?"

"They built for eternity in those days," said Flora more lightly.

"It is because the house has a soul," went on Conway, as though she had not answered. "Because it lives and breathes, and has its moods like us. If it were to die it would crumble in a day. You would understand if you lived there. The Strath resembles you and me, in that it contains a spirit, which, while it remains, preserves the fabric from corruption."

Flora was about to reply, as pleasantly as she dared, when to her great relief little bells sounded through the damp air, and Maude Juxon came to join the party, as pink and fresh as ever, although her curls were limp, and her hat saddened by raindrops. She tripped to her friend and embraced her daintily with sympathetic comments upon her appearance.

"You are white, and thin, and ghostly," she declared. "My dear, you should do as I tell you and take a glass of warm milk, with an egg beaten up in it, every morning directly you wake up. I have been quarrelling with myself all day," she ran on, "because I was dull; and now I'm damp and cold. Mr. Conway, say something to make me laugh."

"I am no comedian," said the owner of the house, which was just then very far removed from the fantastic mood. "I live, you must remember, in a valley, and it is the inhabitants of the mountains who laugh and sing."

"But now you are out of your valley you might laugh and sing," suggested the beauty. "Well, I shall go into the house and search diligently for a fire. It is shivery out here. Come along, Flora. How is your mother's cold? It is so stupid to catch colds. I never do, but then I take care of myself. A cold is so unbecoming, but of course when one is old that doesn't matter."

Frivolous Maude rendered her society one service. It was not easy to be depressed in her presence, and her pretty face, always laughing at nothing, quickly changed the atmosphere of any room which had been dark and dull before her arrival. When all that could be said against her had been urged, the fact remained that she was always full of life and sound, like a shallow stream bubbling with bright waters unceasingly.

Her husband came frequently on the Saturday evening, leaving early on the Monday. He too had changed; he had stopped "worrying," to use Maude's expression, and talked no longer of a house in the country. The careless wife would possibly have laughed as usual, had anyone suggested to her that she was spending more money than her husband could afford. When he gave up persuading her to return, she believed he had accepted his defeat. As a matter of truth Juxon was hard hit; he was in a tight corner; he had ceased begging his wife to come back because there was no longer a home to offer her. His lease had run out, and he could not afford to renew it; and while Maude fared luxuriously in her farm-house, the husband lived and slept in his office, where there would be a light showing until the small hours of morning.

He had been hard pressed before to meet his obligations on settling day, but had escaped, and made the running as strongly as ever, and he trusted that energy and ingenuity would pull him through again. He was made of tough material, this stout little stockbroker. His only fear was lest Maude might stumble across the truth. When he found it impossible to allow her all the money she asked for, he stinted himself and did his best; while she sulked and called him stingy, and told him to his face that he did not deserve her. He only smiled in his quiet way, instead of shaking her as she deserved; and refreshed by the hill breezes, went back to work, pouring all his energies into a final struggle which should decide whether he was fitted to survive, or fated to go to the wall. His work would have been less arduous, had he married a wife who would have shared his burden, and assisted him with sympathy.

That very day Maude had received a message which, stated concisely, ran thus: "Could you obtain a more inexpensive cottage? I have suffered an unexpected reverse. Nothing to worry about, but clients have been more dilatory than usual in paying purchase price of their investments and differences owing on speculations. And when they are behindhand I must find the money." The little lady had driven into Kingsmore to send a telegram in reply. A telegram was so much less troublesome than a letter. On this occasion she was not extravagant, so all she had to say in response to her husband's note was the single word, "Nonsense." It was very inconsiderate of Herbert, she thought. She had told him so often that she did not want to be troubled with business matters. As for that reverse, if it was of no importance, as he implied, why on earth did he want to mention it to her? She was most distinctly an injured person and a long-suffering wife.

The influence of the Strath extended even to Kingsmore vicarage. Conway and Drayton had brought it with them, and the heartless little lady was no doubt its object. So far Maude had escaped. She had come, as she thought, to visit her friend that day by mere chance, not knowing that she had been led to that place by the destiny which was then weaving her idle phrases into a net through the meshes of which she would not escape until she had learnt to know herself.

It was natural, she thought, that she should speak to Conway concerning the house of which she had heard so much. She longed to behold for herself its china and pictures. The garden, she owned, did not interest her in the least, because she liked order as represented by carpet-bedding and level lawns. Then she knew that Drayton was a writer. Dr. Berry had spoken kindly of him.

"I can criticise," Maude declared, with wicked confidence. "I must see your work and give you my opinion, Mr. Drayton."

The scribe muttered something which sounded complimentary, but he did not display any of Dr. Berry's enthusiasm. He was not in the least a clever man, but his eyes were open, and he was well aware that Maude was sounding brass and a tinkling cymbal.

"Is it true you have a stone floor in the hall?" went on the lady frivolous, turning to Conway.

"And the floor of what you call the saloon is of real solid oak," she went on, when he had replied.

"It is not solid now," he said.

"Marvellously preserved," interpolated Mr. Price, swamping his saucer by adding to the contents of his tea-cup his customary three lumps of sugar.

"And there are mirrors round the walls, and candlesticks—what do you call those things with a lot of branches?—and old pictures, and windows with those quaint diamond panes of yellow glass," Maude cried. "Oh, Mr. Conway, you shall give a dance. Just a little dance for us."

"Don't, Maude," said Flora.

"Be quiet, Flora. Mr. Conway, it would be perfect, and we will wear fancy costumes and masks, and believe we are those wicked people of the eighteenth century one reads about—yes, a masked ball, and I will help you with the supper."

"My dear lady, the place would frighten you to death," said Mr. Price.

"Of course I know the house is haunted," said Maude flippantly. "But these gentlemen have not been frightened to death, and I don't mind groans and rattling of chains and all that sort of thing, so long as I don't see real ghosts in white sheets. Besides we shall be making such a noise the ghosts won't be given a chance. I shan't be frightened. Why, with people all round me I believe I might endure one glimpse at the wicked baronet himself."

"The Strath is not haunted," said Drayton stolidly.

"Then we must have that dance," cried Maude. "Yes, Mr.

Conway, you have promised. No outsiders. Just us, and Dr. Berry, of course."

"Certainly we might have a dance," agreed Conway with some spirit.

"At the end of the month," cried Maude. "You need not worry, Mr. Conway. Flora and I will attend to all the preliminaries, and I know we shall have a lovely time."

"I do not see the use of wearing masks," objected the squarson. "As there are to be so few of us it will be impossible to conceal our identity."

"Masks will be appropriate," said Drayton almost sharply; and his voice settled the matter.

When the two men who were bound for Thorlund left the vicarage rain was again falling. On this return journey they talked incessantly; but it was not until they reached the summit of the hill, and saw the ivied roof of the Strath among the wet trees, that the thought of the proposed masquerade recurred to their minds. It was Conway who touched upon the subject by remarking:

"Do you imagine that a dance would give offence?"

Drayton understood and answered, as he inclined his head towards the dreamy hollow, "Not if the suggestion came from there."

ACT IV

Scene I.—PUPPENSPIELE

To have a wife, and to be father of children, bring many troubles into life.—*Menander*.

While rain was falling upon just and unjust, Herbert Juxon sat in his gas-lit office up a gloomy court, struggling to conquer the London which roared around him. A clock indicated half-past-three. The stockbroker was working excitedly, because he believed that the combination which might restore him much that he had lost was nearly made.

Without lifting his eyes from the file of letters and the pencilled notes before him, he held out his hand to take a message from his clerk; and at that moment the door opened noisily, and a man hurried in, hatless and unannounced. He was a lawyer, well-known in the city, and one of Juxon's friends. The son of parchment bent over the desk, and making himself on this occasion a man of few words, whispered into the stockbroker's ear. Juxon's face went white for a moment, then he recovered, and jerked out a nervous laugh.

"It is impossible," he muttered. "The business is a small one, but it has been established for so long. I have heard rumours. They did not come from a reliable source, and I could not trust them. I had no time to think of them. But my little nest-egg is there."

"Get it out. You have just time—if it is not already too late," whispered the counsellor; and then he left, as hurriedly as he had entered.

Juxon pounced upon his cheque-book, filled a form, then, glancing up at the clock, caught at his hat and raced from his office and the court. He dodged breathlessly along the crowded streets, until he came to a dark lane, which he entered at the double, and turned in at the door of a private bank where his money was deposited. He had always banked there, having no suspicion regarding its stability, and the manager was a personal friend of long standing, who, he firmly believed, would have given him a word of warning had any crisis been impending. He noticed, as he passed the threshold, a group of men discussing in low tones.

The cashier himself received Juxon's cheque, but he did not say a word; nor did he once raise his eyes, after a nervous word of greeting and one hasty glance upon the stockbroker's heated face. His own face twitched, in spite of himself, when he glanced at the figures on the slip of paper. He flung open a drawer and produced a handful of gold, which he swept towards the client, so fiercely that some of the coins rolled away along the floor; and then he rushed round to the door, locked and bolted it. There was a crash of broken glass, followed by an outcry and an uproar at the head of the lane. It was twelve minutes to four; and the little bank had failed.

Juxon received the blow with the patience which was part of his nature. He said nothing, but slipped clear of the crowd assembling rapidly before the bankrupt premises, and escaped into the comparative silence of his office. He believed in being quiet under affliction. He was not religious in the accepted sense of the word; but he was strong and upright, for his mind was unobscured by any perplexing creed; just as the faith of the savage, who kneels beneath the sun, amid the wonders of nature, may be at least as pure as that of the priest, standing before an altar, bound and tied by superstitions of man's creation. Had Juxon been a scholar, he would probably have uttered the consoling words of Philemon the dramatist, "If thou couldst only know the evils which others suffer, thou wouldst gladly submit to thine own."

Four hours later Juxon was hurrying from a suburban station, between parallel rows of lamp-posts, along numerous streets, past endless red villas exasperatingly alike. In a street, which differed from others only in name, he drew up before a house which was made dissimilar to its neighbours by the possession of a distinctive number. He knocked, waited impatiently, and knocked again; and then an elderly woman, attired in the uniform of a nurse, admitted him to the little house, and ushered him into a tiny room, where a pretty four-year-old child was sitting up in her cot playing with a doll's house.

"Daddy!" cried the child in an ecstasy, holding out two pink arms.

"Here he is again," laughed the stockbroker. "Like a bad old battered shilling."

The tiny lady, who was already wonderfully like Maude in appearance, received his caresses, returned them with interest, and straightway demanded with odd severity:

"Where's Mummy?"

"Far away in the country, little Peggy," said the father. "Only Daddy left. Are you glad to see him, sweetheart?"

"Vewy," lisped the dainty miss. "Here's a wose-bud for you." She collected a white rose, somewhat the worse for ill-treatment, from the quilt, and lifted it laughing to his lips. "Put it in you coat. Here's one for Mummy, a pwettier one, but Mummy won't have it. You shall have it instead, Daddy. My Mummy is pwettier than my Daddy," she announced generally to a family of small dolls. "But I love my Daddy most, 'cause he comes to see me, and my Mummy don't. Oh, Daddy!"

Thereupon a pair of cherubic lips parted, and a chocolate disappeared between two rows of pretty teeth. "But you must have one too—the greatest one," came from the little mouth in action.

"I was afraid you would be asleep, my Daisy," said the father. "How you are growing, miss! You are getting quite a giantess. Do you know what a giantess is, darling?"

The fair curls were shaken violently.

"Well, a giantess is a great tall lady, who has to stoop whenever she comes into a house, lest she should knock the roof off. If you go on growing so fast, you will be like that some day, Miss Peggy, and you will look down, and pat me on the head, and say, 'Poor old Daddy, what a long way down you are.' Now, Daisy, shut your eyes, and open your mouth just as wide as ever you can."

"Don't tell Nursie," adjured the smallest of the transgressors.

"Of course not. It would never do to be caught by Nurse, or she might slap us both. What were you doing before I came, sweetheart?"

"Talking to my dollies," said Peggy, munching busily and pointing to the doll's house. "You was answering me lots, but Mummy wouldn't speak. Naughty Mummy!" She picked up a little pink doll, with flaxen hair and scarlet cheeks, and scolded it scrupulously. "And Mummy don't stand up nice a bit."

"Why can't she stand up, Peggy?" asked the father.

"I stooded her up and down she went—so! It is silly of her, isn't it? P'raps she ain't vewy stwong, poor Mummy! I'll put her on the sofa. She looks pwetty on the sofa, doing nothing, 'cept laugh. This is you, Daddy. You're so drefful busy you ain't got time to talk much, and when you laugh it's quick—so! And then you go on working."

"That is quite true, Peggy. You see I have you and Mummy to work for, so I mustn't be idle. And now I must run off again, and work, and work."

There were protestations and tearful blue eyes, but the former were checked by the promise of a visit the very next evening, and the latter were kissed bright again. But before the stockbroker left his little daughter, he bent over her, and said in a whisper, "When I am gone, Daisy, say over and over again until you go to sleep, 'God help Mummy'."

"God help dear Daddy and Mummy," a small voice amended.

The honest man caught his treasure in his arms and kissed her many times.

"Good-night, sweet Daisy."

"Come again vewy quick, Daddy."

When in the street again there was an elasticity in Juxon's step which had not been apparent earlier in the evening. There were heavy odds facing him. Many men would have shrunk from the difficult task of restoring the ruined fabric. A few cowards might even have sought the easiest way out; but quiet Mr. Juxon was prepared to go on playing the game. Although outwardly commonplace, and lacking in originality, he was not an ordinary man. His character could not be better revealed than by the statement that he did not entertain a single bitter thought towards his absent wife.

He did not intend that she should hear the truth, and he was resolved that she should not want even the least of those luxuries which she had hitherto enjoyed. He argued that she had a right to look to him for these things, and because he was true of heart he determined she should have them, if only he could avert that imminent and final disaster by hard work.

He reached his lonely office in the deserted city, leaving far behind the voices of paper-vendors screaming in malicious enjoyment the news of the bank failure. He turned up the gas, removed his coat, and wrapped a moistened handkerchief round his forehead. He smiled at the excessive plainness of his careworn face when it met his eyes in the glass. Was it possible that any woman could care for him, if he were poor? That smile was still upon his lips when he sat down to his desk. "There is still a chance," he muttered. "The veriest loophole, but I may struggle through yet. I can fight, and I will fight, and I will go down, if that be my destiny, fighting all the time."

It was close upon midnight when Juxon pushed aside his business books and papers, and began the composition of a letter to a client who was encumbered with wealth in very much the same proportion as Egypt was once troubled with flies. Upon this letter much depended, as without financial assistance he would have to declare himself a defaulter. All the securities which he had to offer were hidden in his safe. They were not so valuable as he could have wished, but he believed they might prove sufficient for his purpose. He wrote quickly, the pen held loosely in his tired fingers, winking his eyes often to dispel the black spots which rose persistently between his face and the sheet of paper.

The clocks chimed over the city of Mammon, which was empty, but not silent. Wind was howling along the deserted streets, and a heavy rain lashed the window. The noise of business was not there, but while men slept Nature awoke to traffic in storm and tempest. Instead of the rolling of carts came the rush of rain water, and the cries of the wind arose in the stead of the voices of men. Round the corners, where by day traffic crushed, nature in wet garments shouted and bustled; and in that one room, which made an eye of light in the solitude of buildings, Juxon went on writing.

How exhausted he was he did not know, until the knowledge came that he had lost control over his pen, which for some moments had scratched upon the paper without any apparent resistance from his hand. There was a coldness in his arm. He dropped the pen and rose, opening and closing his stiffened fingers. Then he brought the paper up to his tired eyes and read what he he had written.

It was an ordinary business letter. There was nothing remarkable about it until he came to the last sentence; and there the writer must have lost control over his pen for a few moments. He was very tired. He had hardly known whether he was writing sense or nonsense. Certainly he had not the slightest idea that he had concluded his letter with the extraordinary sentence, "Go to the Strath." These four words however were staring at him from the paper. There was no sense in them. He did not know what they meant. He had no memory of having written them. He only knew that they were there in his own crabbed handwriting.

"I must be careful," Juxon whispered. "This sort of thing won't do. This is what some people might call insanity. I have been working too much."

He went into the corner of the office, dipped the hot handkerchief which had been around his forehead into cold water, wrung it out, and replaced it. Then he said:—

"My wife is living in the country, and in the neighbourhood stands a house about which strange things are said. That house is called the Strath."

Scene II.—LYRICAL DITHYRAMB

It often happens that those who try to avoid their fate run directly upon it.—*Titus Livius*.

The day of Maude's introduction to the Strath arrived. The careless little lady, to whom the future state was a terrible black cloud, had taken it upon herself to fix a date for their festivities within that house; and as the day was near she deemed it necessary to attend in person and make arrangements upon the spot. Accordingly she decked herself out in a vesture of pink wrought about with divers laces, drove into Thorlund in usual state, and requisitioned the services of Dr. Berry as companion and guide.

The scholar was in a silent mood that calm sunless afternoon. His sleep had been much broken of late, and fear had crept about his bed. He was exceedingly sensitive to every outside influence, and thus had foreseen evil impending, but its nature was not revealed. The thought occurred to the rector that he had wasted his life in selfish pursuits, that punishment was in store; and therefore he was afraid.

Maude prattled joyously as she walked towards the wall, having, as she firmly believed, no sins to be sorry for. It was true she trembled when she set foot inside the garden, and caught at her companion's arm; but Flora had told her strange stories concerning that haunted ground, and for at least the first minute she had a right to be nervous. It was natural weakness, she assured herself, but she was relieved when the sensation passed, as it did suddenly; and to show her relief she laughed, boldly and defiantly, the first foolish laugh that had sounded in that garden for many more years than any living man could look back upon.

There was a dead tree lying within the shadow of the house, its trunk mantled with moss, its few remaining branches smothered in the mud of the moat.

There Conway was seated. He looked with vacant eyes when the visitors approached, and invited them to sit beside him and listen while he read; and when Maude demurred, after a glance at the heavy moss, he removed his cloak, a quaint blue garment lined with scarlet cloth, and spread it across the trunk. Then the little lady condescended to take her ease, and looked about with disapproval and disappointment.

"What a dirty tumbling-down old place!" she observed. "I think you ought to have the garden put into some sort of order; and as for the house it must be full of rats and spiders. I suppose it looks all right when it is lighted up, but by daylight—"

"If you please you must not say these things," Conway interrupted.

"What!" Maude laughed. "Why, what nonsense!"

"You must remember, my friend," said the scholar gently, "this lady has a mind superior to ours. The perfect beauty in art alone appeals to her. She finds her present environment unusual, not having been here before, but time will bring appreciation. What book is that you are holding?"

Conway held out the journal, its pages tinted lightly with ink as yellow as dead grass, and replied, "I will read to you if you will."

"I want to see the house," said Maude.

"Listen a few minutes to a voice from the past," Conway entreated.

Maude, who was accustomed to having her own way, was about to reply indignantly, when she heard a rustling against the side of the house, and turning beheld Drayton gazing at her from between the creepers. The expression on his face silenced her, and the colour began to leave her cheeks. Before she was able to assert herself, the master of the Strath bent his head over the pages which contained the sad record of Winifred Hooper's short life, and his voice came into her ears, ringing sad echoes of the past:

"I have been ill, and have not written in my book for days. I have been lying on my bed, listening to the wind in the trees, and seeing by the light of the harvest-moon forms and faces in the mirror opposite. I am well again now, and wondering why I was so foolish as to spend so long a time out of the air and sunshine, for indeed nothing ailed me except sorrow. Already it seems a long time since I went out, in a white dress, with a thick shawl about me, and my hair hanging down because I was too sick at heart to bind it, and yet it was scarce a week ago. Now we are in autumn, cold and blustering, but is it not always cold when one is sorrowing?

"How true was Mr. Spencer when he wrote, 'for every dram of honey found in love a pound of gall doth over it redound.' I could almost be sorry that I love you, Geoffrey. Love has visited me of late with dreams, when I would find myself struggling with my heart up a steep mountain, knowing that if I might reach the summit I should gain happiness. But at a certain point my strength would always fail. I have read that love requited gives perfect rest, but is it so? Wise Sophocles has better described it as a storm in the heart, which all must endure, even the gods. This written page can only speak. It conveys no feeling. I may write down 'sorrow,' but what can the word convey? A lacerated finger, a pain in the head—no more; and I may so easily, if I will, run my pen through the word, and write instead 'love,' and still nothing is conveyed. Love requited becomes a restless pain when the loved one is far away. How shall lovers when separated express their feelings? It is the presence that speaks, not the tongue. One look is more eloquent than a life of letters.

"My dog has placed his paws upon my knee and looks up with

soft brown eyes. He loves me, and yet speaks only with his eyes. I have seen so little of the world, and my reading of its doings come but rarely, but 'tis enough to humiliate me into a half-belief that the purest love is not in us, but in the animals. Have you watched a mother thrush feeding her fluffy chicks? Or an owl fighting a cotter for the sake of her offspring? Or a dog dying broken-hearted upon his dead master's coat? Are we exceptions, Geoffrey, you and I? Do we love too much, and is it for that cause we are separated, least we should be too happy and thus anticipate the joys of Heaven?

"These are wandering and foolish thoughts. I should turn my mind towards the white hills and the woods, and note the beauty of the changing leaves; but, when I strive to do so, I see the wind whirling the dry foliage down the slopes and around the tombs of the old churchyard. Even when I look across the scenery it is upon the cypress and yew that my eyes are fixed. And yet so strange a creature am I that I would rather suffer than forego the privilege of having won your love.

"I keep this journal in a secret place where my father would not think to look. I must hide it now more securely than ever before, because I have done a dangerous and fearful thing. I have given information against my own father. It is horrible. It is unnatural. It may even happen that he shall be hanged through me. I shall thank Heaven for giving me liberty. I shall go forth to seek you, Geoffrey, and to find you, even if you be in the land of fables known as India. Yesterday I chanced upon Mr. Price along the highway where the road branches to Queensmore village; and when he stopped and spoke to me I was unable to contain my tongue, and before I knew had told him concerning those dark midnight rides. He heard me with amazement, and when I had done placed his hand upon the hilt of his sword, and said, 'Very well indeed. We will see to this. A most notorious highwayman has long been the terror of these roads. To-morrow I will myself ride to town and place this information before the Sheriff, and I promise that the Strath shall be soon more closely watched than you are now. Do not forget, child, that Kingsmore house stands open to give you shelter whensoever you may require it.'

"I supposed that I had passed secure from observation during that interview with worthy Mr. Price, but I was mistaken. Late last night a step came upon my passage, the door gave, and the man Reed advanced one step into my room. He was half-drunken, but I dared not order him out, menial though he be, for he is master here. He told me that my father had given orders I was to be confined in the garden, and if I ventured to disobey I would be brought back and locked within my chamber. I would not shame myself by showing weakness before him, but when I was again alone my silly heart seemed to break, and I fell upon my bed and wept a long hour. No more wanderings upon the solitary hills. My home is now my prison and my grave.

"I have not spoken to my father for more than a week. Last night, after Reed left me, I heard loud oaths and the sounds of fighting; and Deborah to-day told me she saw the squire standing in the hall, very drunk, with blood dripping from his head. There will be violent death in this house if these brawlings endure. Pray God I shall not see it. Even the sight of a mouse's body sets me a-shivering. And so, Geoffrey, I have taken my last walk into the woods. There is a kind of wild pleasure in even that thought. When I go forth again, if I do go forth, you will be at my side, and there will be no winter any more, but I will be your summer, and you shall be my spring, and we will stand together once again where the daffodils grow.

"If it be folly to write so, it is a joy to think it. There is a book already written for each one, with the future set forth. Mine is indeed a small record, a few pages of love, and then a tomb; but yours, I like to think, is a long and noble tale, containing very much that is glorious: victories, rewards, and honours on each page, and then a sweet home and a loving wife—be very good to her for my sake—and smiling old age such as Mr. Addison has portrayed. That is how I read your future, beloved, without the aid of stars or omens. I desire for you a full and perfect life, flowing steadily on gathering strength and nobleness, like the river increasing as it nears the sea. Mine is a little impress upon the sands, which the rising tide smooths silently away."

Dr. Berry moved suddenly forward, sweeping the book out of Conway's hand. Maude had fainted.

Unaided the scholar carried her into the house. He placed his burden upon a sofa and fanned the white face, until a sigh escaped its lips, and the eyelids quivered. Another moment and Maude rose stiffly like a sleep-walker, stared about her with wild eyes, and said in a cold hard voice, as though in continuation of a tragic conversation which had been interrupted by her loss of consciousness, "Then there is nothing left, and I must drown myself."

He tried to hold her, but she shook him off with a tragic gesture and moaned, "I see my fate before me. I must go to it. Do not touch me. Keep away from me. You do not know what I have done."

She covered her face with her hands, and screamed, "I feel the eyes of the dead."

"Dear lady," the scholar interjected. "We are indeed surrounded by the dead, but they are invisible. Let me lead you into the garden."

He took her hand, which was cold and lifeless, and she went with him into the open air; and there sank down in the long grass, shuddering and afraid, shrinking from his consoling touch.

"I have a right to share your suffering," he said.

"You!" she exclaimed, beating her hands together. "What have you done? I can only sink into the stream, and die, and be forgotten. Leave me to myself. Why do you follow me? Why do you touch me? Look at your hands and see how I have soiled them."

"Beloved sister," spoke the tragedian. "I will never forsake you. Remember how our souls were united at the birth of song. You and I, poetess and poet, are joined together for all time by the double bond of art and of love. Your sin is mine also. If punishment must fall, let it fall on us together. It is happiness to suffer with those we love."

"Let me show you," she gasped, with a laugh, as unlike her own empty sound of mirth as the storm wind differs from the whirring of a wing. "Listen! I had a child, and a husband. One night I went into my daughter's room. The child slept, one little hand reaching out towards me, her bright hair tumbling over the pillow, her little bosom rising and falling gently. I seized the pillow, and pressed it over the innocent face, and—and I stood looking down upon a little waxen face which never moved again."

The choregus bent over her, and returned the philosophic answer which the laws of the drama required:

"It was the madness of jealousy. Under somewhat similar circumstances Medea murdered her children. It is as destiny appoints. Nature is exceedingly cruel. You were merely the instrument called upon to remove the child."

"Hear me out," she screamed. "I passed from that room to my husband's side. He was a good man, noble, unselfish, and kind, having one fault only and that his love for me. I discovered him at work. He was always working, that he might provide me with those luxuries which my soul coveted. When I came near, he looked up and said, 'Is our little girl asleep?' And I smiled at him and said, 'I have just come from her, and she is asleep.'"

"For a parallel—" the spell-bound listener interposed; but before he could say more she drowned his voice.

"Then my husband said, 'I have been working all night, and my head pains me.' So I took a handkerchief, and tied it round his head, and went and brought him a cup of wine. He drank it, pressing my hand, and I watched his head fall forward, and his hands shaking, and his strength going from him. And then I helped him to his room and left him, and in the night I heard him call me, but I put my fingers in my ears and turned away, and left him to die of the poison which I had given him."

"Surely," said the actor, "these things happened long ago. The poisoned cup and the suffocation of a sleeper are suggested to us again and again as orthodox punishments of an enemy."

"I myself am guilty," she raved. "With these hands I killed my husband and my child. Look at them, and see how the shadow lies upon them. The sun has not warmed them since."

He took her hands which she had frantically extended. He lifted them and pressed first one and then the other to his lips with the adoration of a monk for holy relics. She was staring above the trees to where the vapoury hills were outlined. This was no longer the silent country dividing two lonely hamlets, but the resounding hills of despair rising above the hell of classical belief, and the autumnal fog was steam escaping from the crater beneath.

"Knowledge of the past comes without study," the scholar proclaimed. "Who teaches the new-born child its prehensile grip? We arrive in this world well equipped. Mind is brought back from beyond, stored with knowledge. The young see visions, but as time passes, and the cares of the world enter, memory weakens, and finally there is nothing left but a craving to learn the future. Yet the past speaks in us all our lives. We return by the same way that we came. Could we look back we should understand all things; but, lest we should grow too wise, we are made to look forward, and so belief declines through half-belief and superstition to unbelief, and we return less learned than when we came. The deeds of others live on in us, and their sins are visited upon our heads."

"You do not speak of hope," she muttered. "You dare not."

"Even while you speak in despair I see the light of hope dawning in your eyes," he answered. "The husband and the child, for whom, in the tenderness of your heart, you mourn, met their death a very great time ago by other hands than these, perhaps in lofty Corinth, or amid the sands of Heliopolis, or beside the stubborn walls of Troy. Can you believe that to you alone appear these visions? There are sins upon the souls of all, there are sins upon my soul, the sins of long ago. I will speak of one. I was then, as now, a priest. It was my duty to interpret signs, and the inspired words which proceeded from the mouths of seers; but not as now to instruct the people respecting the nature of religion. Religion then consisted in the performance of certain mysteries, the secret of which was handed on from father to son, and guarded jealously from the people. The ground allotted to me was small, but beyond was a beautiful garden, wherein I would often wander to weave poetic fancies. For many years this ground was mine, but one day I came upon one who told me it was his, and that it was his intention to cultivate the ground, tear up the flowers, and remove the arbors. He was a rough unlearned man. When he closed the garden against me I hated him, and planned how I might destroy him. Night and day I pondered beside the oracle, watching the incense smoke. At length I went forth. Moonlight was upon the garden. I saw my enemy and crept upon him. I seized his neck, and strangled him. The garden was mine again. Shall I suffer for this memory? Not so. These hands are not guilty. My soul, less sentient than yours, is also less capable of suffering."

"My friend," she moaned. "Are you indeed my friend?"

"Your more than friend," he rapturously replied.

"Then you will obey me. Leave me here."

"It is my duty to watch over you. Alone you may do yourself some harm."

"You may watch me. I will go beneath the trees."

As the poet followed out her bidding he recited the second antistrophe of the second stasimon of the Agamemnon, that magnificent song concerning dreams and destiny in the house. Maude heard and trembled when the new understanding interpreted for her the meaning of those words. Genuine suffering was hers at last. She believed that her husband and child were dead, murdered as she had described. She saw in that enchanted atmosphere the lines of her fate written across the sky in letters of fire, even as Alcephron had read his warning in the flaming gardens of Osiris. No ray of hope lighted the way, and all that came was the dark assurance of the implacable nature of that destiny she had fought against. And the advice suggested by the sinister influence was that she should destroy herself.

Yet, in the very act of punishment, the didactic force brought out all the moral strength and latent good which might be enshrined within its victim. Thus Maude, when compelled to fight, manifested powers the existence of which she had never suspected. She resolutely refused to take the path of cowardice. She longed to live for better things. Instead of a hindrance she would become a help. But whom should she help? At that self-set question she shuddered again, knowing the resolution to have come too late, because those who had loved her were gone. Yet there were others who needed assistance, who might be led on by one so worthless as herself. She would seek them out. She would cover her pink dress with the sister's robes of white and black, and dispense charity for her soul's sake. So comedy and tragedy went on fighting over Maude; and the scholar looked on, chanting his lyric Greek.

Could she awake and find that horror only a dream, her husband and child yet living, what a world of happiness might still be hers. How joyously would she tread, though it were on the path of poverty, towards the life which seeks no recompense beyond a smile. Could it be that the choregus yonder had spoken the truth? Had the double crime which wrenched her heart been committed in a past age, by hands long vanished into earth?

As such questions as these quivered like meteoric flashes across her brain the heavily-charged atmosphere lifted, the mists dissolved, and through a golden fissure in a fast-floating cloud a ray of sunlight darted down the hills. A breath of wind followed, and as the influence withdrew Maude beheld Drayton standing in the grass, throwing up an apple, and catching it as it fell. It was the turn of the dramatic tide. Burlesque was laughing down the tragic frown.

SCENE-SHIFTING

Time, that sees everything, and hears everything, brings all things to light.—*Sophocles*.

The following letter, written by the proprietor of a curiosity shop in central London, was handed in at the toy-shop of one Emmanuel Falk in a by-way of the city of Nuremberg, and perused by the light of a yellow candle:—

"Dear Mr. Falk. I have pleasure in informing you that copies of the masks which belonged to the Biron family have come as pledges into my hands. They are genuine I have no doubt, because I find the name Joseph Falk engraved upon their backs. Permit me to state the incidents connected with this discovery.

"Yesterday a middle-aged Englishman, well-dressed, but apparently pressed for money, entered my shop and requested me to make him an advance, offering as security the pair of masks. Let me tell you he was well aware of their value. He asked for £5 and when I had handed him that amount he left hurriedly. I called my boy Jacob, pointed the man out, and bade him follow. Jacob went after the Englishman to his home. Very soon the man came out with a bag, which Jacob was permitted to carry for some coppers to the underground station. Jacob accompanied the man to Paddington, and standing close behind heard him ask for a ticket to a small town some distance from the metropolis. Not having sufficient money upon him to follow the man to his destination, Jacob returned. In the afternoon I called at the house, which the Englishman had entered after leaving my shop, told the woman who answered my ring that I was a tax-collector, and so managed to discover the name of the man who pawned the masks.

"You know where Mr. Biron can be found. Will you then write to him, letting him know of my discovery, and telling him that I will grant further information if he will communicate with me? The masks cannot leave my shop, as I may be ordered to give them up any day, but if he can visit me I will produce them for his inspection. I presume that the reward which he has offered for so long still holds good, if the information I am able to give may lead to the discovery of the originals? If you will forward this letter I will pay you five per cent upon the transaction, should the affair be brought to a satisfactory conclusion, and to this effect I enclose my commission note duly signed and stamped. If you are not content with my offer, remember, I can certainly discover Mr. Biron through advertisements in the Italian papers; but this would require time, and the masks may be redeemed to-morrow. I must not fail to produce them, because the English law is severe.

"I am, my dear sir, your most obedient, humble servant,

Francesco Cerutti."

The old toy-maker spluttered through his beard until the candle guttered.

"The thief! the rogue!" he shouted. "The son of a dog to offer me his five per cent. I will not help him. Not for twenty. Let him give me my fifty per cent, and I will do business. The vampire! How he would suck my blood. The toad! the fox! Would that I might put him in the Iron Virgin. Would that I might poison the Pegnitz and make him drink of the water."

The candlelight fell with weird effect among stacks of toys, striking a thousand glassy eyes into a semblance of life. There were legions of dolls stuffed with mechanism; there were animals, birds, and realistic reptiles, quivering and mouthing at their long-bearded Frankenstein. Their eyes were so many points of light glinting all colours, tawny-red, yellow, black, winking and leering and grinning. These eyes appeared to the toy-maker to expand during the night and to contract by day. When the sun entered the shop the eyes were small and yellow, having each one a narrow line of black for pupil. Towards evening these pupils were enlarged, and by night became round and far-seeing. Here was a doll whose eyes by the candlelight were unduly large; they might have been disfigured by the use of drugs. Here was another with optic nerves shuddering; and there another with eyes distorted, as it were by some external influence, the refracting surfaces being marred by a shadow cast across the retina. Emmanuel Falk loved those glinting glassy eyes. He felt a creator when he looked at them. He settled himself between the candle and the eyes, and indited a letter to Signore Eugene Biron, at the Strada Nuova di Poggio Reale, Napoli.

A fortnight passed without bringing any reply. A month followed, during which time the Italian Jew and the citizen of Nuremberg exchanged letters, which were impatient on the one side, and indignant on the other. But one day a very thin man entered the crooked street, stopped at the gabled toy-shop, and confronted the proprietor with the intelligence that his name was Eugene Biron.

The toy-maker thought at first that the Lord of all the Dolls had taken life and come to haunt him. Mr. Biron did not appear to darken the doorway as he entered, so hopelessly devoid was he of flesh. He was so thin that the perfect outline of his skull could be traced distinctly. For all that his face was pleasant, because it happened to possess two singularly kind eyes. His head was as bald as an apple. He had neither eyebrows nor beard. He might have been thirty, or he might have been seventy.

"By Gott!" whispered the toy-maker. "What a model! I will make a doll like him by San. Nicholas' Day. He will make the children scream."

Then he welcomed the visitor, and brought him into the sanctity of the work-shop where the toy marvels were planned and composed. Bringing forward a chair, which with a sweep of the hand he cleared of dolls in embryo, he begged his guest to be seated, and floundering to a cupboard produced a bottle of thin wine and two beautiful Venetian glasses chased in blue.

"I have been travelling lately, and while in this neighbourhood happened to write to Italy for my letters," the visitor explained in fluent German. "Having just received your communication, I take the earliest opportunity of visiting you, on the chance of your having some information to add to that which your letter gave."

"But I have nothing," wailed Emmanuel. "That Jew in London did write last week and say that the masks were still in bond. I have used already many postage-stamps upon the man. I did only meet him once, and then he talked me into an arrangement by which I did lose and he did gain—may Gott confound him! He calls himself my humble and obedient servant every time, and next time I write I will sign myself his lofty and unyielding master, by Gott I will. I will be even with that Jew. I would give one hundred of my best dolls to choke him in the Schöne Brunnen. I drink now to your long life, Mr. Biron, and to the increased prosperity of the toy business."

"If you have nothing more to tell me I shall start for England to-night," said the man of no nationality. "I have been searching all my life for these masks, and I may be now on the point of succeeding. Your great-grandfather made, I believe, several copies from the originals—"

"And he did die of it," interrupted the toy-maker excitedly. "Gott in Heaven! They did kill him. Come up these stairs, and I will show you at the top of the house a great iron hook where he did hang himself and die."

"I am afraid the masks may have killed others besides old Joseph Falk," said the visitor solemnly. "That is why I want to discover them."

The bearded toy-maker stared at his hairless guest with open mouth and eyes like two full moons behind his glasses. "And then what you do with them?" he demanded.

"Cremate them," came the reply. "Or give them Christian burial."

"Give to them Christian burial. Mine holy Gott!"

"Surely you know their history?"

"But I do not know," shouted the toy-maker, snatching up a doll and screwing off its head, unmindful of the sawdust which snowed upon his slippers. "I know how Joseph Falk lost his brains and thought himself an actor, and would stand on these stairs reciting poetry. I know this old house was once the terror of all the strasse, and those who came here would sometimes stand and laugh as though the very devil of comedy was in them, and sometimes they would stamp and frown like Faustus at the opera. When Joseph Falk hanged himself Mr. Biron came and took the masks away. I know nothing more, except that these things happened more than a hundred years ago. Bah! they could not make my dolls in those days."

"Falk begged for the masks to be returned to him after he had sold them," said Biron slowly. "I believe he was compelled by his extraordinary nature to love them. He must have been a remarkable man. He called himself a toy-maker, but his toys were the products of a diseased and morbid imagination. He made a clock which, instead of ticking, groaned the seconds, and a candle with machinery attached which caused the flame to burn blue at midnight. Finally he made the masks."

"And they did kill him," muttered the great-grandson. "But he did sell them first to Mr. Biron."

"To my great-grandfather, a man whose mind had suffered through intercourse with Joseph Falk. But is it possible that you, the present head of the family, do not know how the masks were made?"

"By Gott, I do know," cried Emmanuel. "They were made of the skin of animals, treated with human blood. Bah! I will not talk about it. The thought gives me cold feelings here." The toy-maker clapped his hand upon his spine.

"You are wrong," said Biron. "They were made of skin certainly, but not the skin of animals. We will not go closely into details, because, as I have said, Joseph Falk's mind was not a healthy one; but it was the skin of human beings that was used in the making of the masks."

"That is one big lie," roared the toy-maker; and as he uttered these words all the clocks in the establishment, above, around, and below, struck the hour together solemnly.

"I am sorry to say it is true," said Biron quietly. "My great-grandfather's notes leave no doubt on the matter. I will give you a few details concerning the composition of the masks. The idea was suggested to Joseph Falk one night at the opera. He was exceedingly fond of the stage, and his visits were as frequent as business would permit. One night he was attracted by a representation of the masks of Tragedy and Comedy modelled upon the proscenium; and straightway the idea entered his mind of creating two such masks, which should be influential types of the respective branches of the drama which they are supposed to represent. You know that he succeeded in carrying out this project; and you shall now hear how he did so."

"Then he, my great-grandfather, was a devil," cried the toy-maker. "I will forget him. He is not worthy to lie within a stone's cast of the great Dürer. Bah! I will never again pray for him upon All Souls' Day, and I will go no more to the cemetery of St. John to put immortelles upon his grave."

"This is a story of the eighteenth century," went on the visitor. "One of the institutions of this city was the College of Surgeons, which was placed hard by the prison, and distinguished from the buildings surrounding it by a gilded globe which satirists were fond of calling a globule—the only form of medicine which physicians of that day could, or would, dispense. Superstition ruled the art of healing to such an extraordinary extent that astrology was one of the important subjects for examination, and even barbers were required to pass in surgery before being licensed to shave chins. Anyone could be a surgeon in those days. It was in fact as easy as enlisting in the army, or, as a wit has said, as difficult to avoid as the press-gang; and knowing this you will not be surprised to hear that Joseph Falk became enrolled a member of the College, not because he wished to acquire the art of the physicians, but because his membership entitled him to a place in the dissecting-theatre, which was kept well supplied with material by the adjacent prison where executions were frequent."

"Is it not true what I say, that this Joseph Falk prostituted the noble art of toy-making?" cried the great-grandson appealingly to his creations.

"Had he turned his talents in the right direction it is certain he would have produced many useful models of mechanism," Biron went on. "Unfortunately his mind was bent towards the horrible. It happened that fortune favoured him. I do not suppose you have heard of the criminal Cagliari, who perpetrated his villainies in this and many another country during the last half of the eighteenth century; but according to my great-grandfather's notes he seems to have been the most inhuman murderer that has ever troubled the world. This man made a living by decoying youths and young women into secret places, and killing them for the sake of what money and jewellery they possessed. It is said that he despatched some twenty victims in this manner, burying the bodies in a lonely wood which he named the Cagliari Cemetery. Strangely enough he was a well-educated man, of good appearance and address, although entirely lacking in all moral sense. It was however argued at the autopsy that the development of his head showed that he was not a natural creature. Being at last convicted and executed, his body was brought in due course to the dissecting-hall of the College of Surgeons. Joseph Falk managed to secure the malefactor's abnormal head."

"Mine Gott, I do not yet understand these things," muttered the toy-maker.

"From that head he extracted the materials for compounding his mask of Tragedy."

The listener's jaw dropped, and his tongue protruded, but no sound proceeded therefrom. He stared along the vista of glass-eyed dolls, and the orbs stared back and winked knowingly.

"That same year the body of Quillebeuf came into the hands of old Falk," went on the visitor hurriedly. "This man was a little mountebank of unusual talent, who roamed from country to country, miming and jesting, and giving entertainments full of drollery by the way-side. He had never an opportunity of appearing before the better classes, indeed it is said he rarely entered the large towns. He loved the country, and wandered there with tabor and drum, an itinerant maker of mirth, delighting the simple people by his artistic foolery. Had he been given a chance of appearing upon the stage, he must have made his mark as a comedian, but opportunity was not his, and he died a failure. One day he was arrested on suspicion of theft and sent to prison; there he was taken ill and died, wearing to the end a laugh on his comic face. It was subsequently discovered that he had been innocent of the theft, and to do what poor justice was then possible a memorial was subscribed for, and set up in the place where he was born, a memorial which could not have been of any permanent nature, for when I went to see it a few years ago it had disappeared. Quillebeuf's body was sent from the prison to the dissecting-room; and thus Joseph Falk obtained material for his mask of Comedy. There," Biron concluded, "you have the story, as I know it, of the two masks which your great-grandfather made and mine bought."

"Find them, I do beseech you, Mr. Biron," muttered the frightened little toy-maker. "Bury them deep, and get a holy priest to exorcise the evil spirits. Holy Gott! There are horrible things in this world. I shall tremble when I make my dolls. I shall feel that they may go from my hands with the power to work evil upon the minds of little children. I will leave my business, Mr. Biron, and come with you. I do not want my five per cent. I will give it to charity, and more besides, when you have destroyed those awful things."

"I thank you for your offer of help," said the visitor, as he rose carefully from the rickety chair. "But I shall not require it. I am upon the right track I believe. Unfortunately my great-grandfather's notes finish abruptly. There is indeed a tragedy suggested about that termination, and it is curious that no authenticated record exists in my family concerning how, when, or where the old man came to his end. There is however a rumour, entirely unsupported by proof, to the effect that Mr. Biron went to live for a time in a manor-house situated in a lonely English valley, and there left the masks built up inside a cellar, and the harmless copies made by Joseph Falk disposed about the rooms. The latter point is of the greatest importance, for, if there be any truth in the rumour, this pledging of the copies may well lead to the discovery of the originals. England is not a large country, but there are many lonely valleys about the island, and thousands of manor-houses. My grandfather and father both searched in vain for the masks, and bequeathed the duty to me. I have done what little I could, but up to the present without success. Is it not strange that they should now break through the long silence of more than a hundred years?"

"You will find them, Mr. Biron," said the toy-maker with religious confidence. "Cerutti the Jew knows more than he has told to me, and his mouth will open when you show him money. He would not rest until he had found out everything. By this time he has discovered that house, and can point out to you the cellar where the masks are hidden, and directly you go into his shop he will bring before you a receipt for five hundred pounds English money, the reward which your father offered, and you renewed, and will say to you, 'I have the information you require. Give me my money.' Yes, by Gott, he will, and he will not give me my five per cent unless I frighten him with the law."

The toy-maker of Nuremberg unfairly judged the London dealer in curios, but he was prejudiced against the man who had once got the better of him in trade. His estimation of the Jew's shrewdness was, however, not at fault. When, less than a week later, the shadowy figure of Biron flitted across the threshold of the curiosity shop and revealed its identity the shrewd Italian made no mention of the reward, but merely bowed obsequiously, and in a business-like manner produced from his pocket a slip of paper, which he handed to the visitor with a second obeisance deeper than the first. Across this piece of paper was written the three pregnant words, "Thorlund. The Strath."

ACT V

Scene I.—MORALITY

Leave things so prostitute,
And take th' Alcaic lute,
Or thine own Homer, or Anacreon's lyre.—*Ben Jonson.*

It was the day of the dance at the Strath. Early in the morning mist rose before the sun, and a hollow silence prevailed upon the hills. Windy sighs followed, and the trees began to shake, and dead leaves scurried along the roads, and the cart-ridges were brimming with black water. At noon dark clouds raced over the valley to the sound of an anapaestic march. Then a deep haze settled, and the atmosphere was heavy with odours of decaying vegetation.

Never had the valley of Thorlund looked more lonely. Early in the afternoon Maude came to the hamlet and found the rector conducting a funeral. He saw her and with the solemn words of the office upon his lips smiled dreamily. She passed on alone into the Strath, without fear, for the place had lost its terror. She could not remember the incidents connected with her first visit; she only understood that she had suffered of late but the cause of that suffering and its definite nature she had yet to learn. She called herself the same, both outwardly and inwardly, being unwilling to confess that she had changed; although her glass revealed a face where the white predominated over the pink, and her inner vision might have shown a picture, had she cared to contemplate it, of a mind which had been awakened. She went again, and willingly, to the Strath, not dreaming that she too had fallen beneath the influence of the goat-song, to suffer there as one may suffer when a frost-bitten limb is being restored gradually to vitality; but whenever she left the house she believed that this suffering was caused by the troublesome world, and so longed for the Strath where she might be at peace.

A few ordinary preparations had been made for the forthcoming party. The young women had made ready certain delicacies which had been brought from Kingsmore that morning; they had also been occupied over their costumes, and had made themselves masks of silk and lace.

But within the Strath all designs were brought to nothing. Not an article of furniture had been removed from the saloon, the ragged carpet still cumbered the floor, and the impossible harpsichord had not been replaced by any modern instrument of music. Conway was upstairs dreaming, Drayton sat and worked in the ante-room, Nancy Reed sang her old ballads.

Maude entered full of schemes, but when the house had received her she forgot the world and the approaching festivities which she had arranged, and seating herself before the pictures of Hogarth's Marriage *à la Mode* wondered why destiny handled her victims so roughly, so like a thoughtless child breaking her toys and flinging them aside.

She heard the moaning of wind, and dead leaves creeping upon the stone floor of the hall. She passed into the room opposite, and stood between the brown masks, which had watched the recluse Biron ruining mind and body with morbid fancies, and the struggles of the unknown family of Branscombe, before the solitude of a century had come to fill their blank eyes with dust.

The wind was strong on that side of the house. Gloom had already settled. She began to long for a companion, not for Flora who lately had drifted from her, but rather for a strong man who might protect her against that terrible depression, or for a child whom she might call her own, that she might show the spirit of the house how willing she was to conform to the dramatic laws. She thought of Peggy vaguely. As for the man whose name she bore, why he, the voice assured her, had grown tired of her insincerity and had found consolation elsewhere. She stood quite alone and a great fear fell upon her. When Dr. Berry entered in his noiseless fashion he discovered her kneeling, white and shivering.

He came and lifted her by the hands. The dim light fell upon his silvered head and invested each feature of his handsome face with a rare softness:

"The summer is over," he said quietly. "The wind begins to bite. No more long days to walk and think. The time of imagination has gone. The winter comes when we must work."

"That poem I read to you," gasped Maude. "I told you it was my own, but that was a lie. I copied it, word for word. You have been very much mistaken in me. I am a wicked worthless woman, and have always deceived you."

The scholar shook his head with a wondering smile, and answered her, "Are we not all foolish, dear sister? We are not the masters of ourselves. He who is wisest among us is but a copyist. We poets sing as the influence directs. The song is not our own, because nothing that we have is ours. The tongue is a loan, and the mind itself but the tenant of a short-lived body. There is truth therefore in your sublime humility. Your verses are copies, and so are mine; but let us console ourselves with the knowledge that to few is given even sufficient power to repeat an old tale well. No, you shall not answer me. No barrier of false humility should be raised between a brother and sister of Mount Parnassus."

"You will not understand," she cried. "I have no learning—none at all. I could not even understand the meaning of those lines I read to you."

"Still upon that strain," he murmured. "Why then, I must answer you. By your definition I too am false. I am unable to comprehend the great realities which move around us and bend us to their will. I too have no learning, because when I take up that which I have written the finite mind, which has merely suggested the theme, refuses to add an understanding of the meaning. We aim at the clear sky, and find we have only struck the earth. The most inspired poet cannot soar higher than the clouds."

As he spoke Drayton entered, and standing just within the door asked in a scarcely intelligible voice, "What is the first stage of tragedy according to the classical model?"

"The prologue," answered the scholar with his head down. "Why do you ask?"

"We propose to give a representation of Comedy in this house to-night," said Drayton in the same low voice. "I only desire to know the various stages in which tragic destiny moves, so that I may know what to expect. This is the prologue. Well?"

"Followed by the entry of the chorus and the first continuous song," went on the scholar. "Then the first entry of a principal character followed by the second song, and so on, the entry and song alternating, until all the characters have been introduced. Later comes the tragic dirge, sung between a principal and the chorus; finally the solemn marching out."

Drayton bent his head, inclining his ear as though to listen for the repetition of some distant sound, and withdrew, muttering to himself. His voice died away into the house, and the wind and the rain made the continuous song.

"I have forgotten why I came," said Maude, resting her white forehead upon her hand. "I am miserable. I know I have done wrong, and I cannot see how to make amends. I do not even know who it is that I have wronged."

"You have wronged me a little," said the voice of the poet.

"I have deceived you. I have made you believe I am good and clever."

"Cease from this perversity," he cried. "You have wronged me by not confiding in me, by keeping me at a distance, and in withdrawing, as you have done lately, the light of your learning from my work. Do you not see how we suffer when separated, what peace we enjoy when together? Souls are joined by a look of the eyes and the word exchanged. For a week I have been idle, and you—confess now you too have put aside the pen. See how unprofitable the parting has been."

"No, no," she cried. "I have tried to think of my duty."

"Which is twofold," he urged. "The duty of song and the duty of love. By neglecting both you have wronged yourself and me. Do you not remember our first meeting on the warm hillside? I worshipped you then as you appeared before me in clinging white, with the fire of poetry in your eyes. My heart sang to you and yours answered. Let our songs be lyrics always. Let us not descend. Be to me now, as then, as you stood in the sun on the side of the hill."

"What is this?" she murmured, half rising and sinking back.

"It is spiritual love. Perfect love," the poet whispered.

"Tragic love," she cried.

The wind came moaning into the house and the dry leaves were whirled about the hall, and after that a door closed with a hollow sound. Both dreamers were awakened. Both saw themselves. What the man saw was a cold empty life spent among books, with eyes on crabbed characters and fingers upon pen, a life which had never tasted the heady wine of passion nor sought after companionship, an unprofitable life of body-starving, of brain-glutting, of groping after communion with unseen powers.

And the woman saw the wasted heartless career of a butterfly, flitting from flower to flower, neglecting all things but pleasure, making no provision for the future. She saw her husband, knowing that he was her husband, bent by work and lined with care, starting from his occupation of business when she spoke scoldingly, and answering with a kindly word; she saw her little daughter playing alone, asking often in the perplexing manner of childhood why her mother never came. This was a part of her punishment. First the Strath had shown her what might have occurred, had she allowed the evil in her to mature fully; now it put before her the simple truth, shedding across it its own sombre light. Still she saw the captured butterfly struggling to escape, and as she looked all its bright plumage was rubbed away, and there escaped a grey little creature, which somehow seemed a more beautiful object than the pink and white beauty which had been held and bruised.

"It is the love of the soul," a voice said into her ear; and the door fluttered as though with the touch of the eager tragic wind.

"Let me go," she cried. "It is getting late, and it is dark."

"You cannot see the light which you shed around," answered the scholar in rapt tones. "And what is time with us? We are lovers, and for us time and place are of no account. This shall become our brightest day, in spite of the wind and the rain. Beloved, do not tell me you are blind. You have seen in my eyes what I have seen in yours. Together we shall tell the love-tales of the past. And now you shall hear my tale, and I will listen to yours."

"Mine you know," she said.

"I would hear it from your lips."

"You shall," Maude cried coldly and sternly rising and standing in the darkened room between the masks. "I know a man whose every action is unselfish, whose only fault is that he loves me. That man has permitted me to drive him as I would. He has repaid my scorn of him by kindliness. When I rejected some plan which he made for my comfort he has immediately taken the blame upon himself."

"You did not love this man?" he interrupted in his ringing voice.

"I did not."

"Because his soul could never be in tune with yours. Destiny had never ordained that you and he should meet. The same destiny brought you to me."

"I have a husband," she said. "And of him I was speaking."

"Have you not a soul also? That is mine. Day and night it has spoken to me. You have joined your body to a husband, but your soul you shall join with mine. There is no mystery in that union. The body wedded to a body lives under the cypress. The soul united to its affinity soars above the earth."

"Once I might have listened to you," she said.

"You have come out of the darkness, and the first glimpse of the day bewilders you."

"I know myself," she replied. "I have wronged you deeply. I have flattered you and led you on with lies. I have made you believe I am a poetess, while I am, as you see me, a very weak and ignorant woman with nothing to my credit that is good. Pardon my wickedness. I will go out of your life to-day, and face my duty, and you shall never be troubled with me again."

A shudder went through the house as the lyres and flutes of the wind and rain changed from strophe to final antistrophe.

"You and I at discord," the scholar muttered. "Would you throw your life out of tune and mar the harmony of mine? You may go from me, but you shall not forget me. You will come back to me when I call."

"You too have neglected your duty," she said. "You have lived among the dead and forgotten the living. By much study you have lost the body. Wake as I awake, and know that you are still a man treading the stage of life, not a disembodied spirit flying among the hills of Athens or along the valley of Colonus."

These were strange words from ignorant Maude.

He came and seized her hands. She was cold and he was burning, and both were shivering. There was a light in his eyes which she had not seen there before, and she shrank from the sight, because it seemed to her that the man and the mind were drifting apart. She struggled a little, and as her eyes groped into the gloom she saw the door opening very slowly and noiselessly, and she heard the worm-eaten floor giving beneath foot-steps. Then Juxon walked in, pale and bent, with his hands clasped behind.

How ill he looked, she thought. His clothes were hanging to him loosely, and there was upon his face that grey expression which speaks of midnight sleeplessness coupled with days of anxiety. His eyes appeared to glance between them, passing from one mask to the other. There was the knife, the emblem of tragedy, and this was not the time to don the cap and bells. How, Maude wildly wondered, would the new character play his part? There was no good reason for the doubt. Juxon had maintained a high standard of living; he had not rebelled against the dramatic laws; therefore the frown of the tragic mask was not for him.

Dr. Berry looked round when he beheld a hand upon his sleeve. From his height he looked upon the man, whom he recognised, neither as the husband of the woman near him, nor as a principal character. "Who are you?" he asked sharply. "What brings you here?"

"A caprice," said the stockbroker. "Fortune has been hard upon me of late. While I have sat alone during the night a voice has been with me, calling me to the Strath. Is not this the Strath?"

"I do not know," said the scholar querulously. "Let us have light that I may see you."

Juxon stepped forward and lighted a candle. Maude saw his agitated face and marked the trembling of his hands. She called him in a low voice, but he did not appear to hear. He lifted his head and faced the scholar who watched him with hard unreasoning eyes.

"I must ask your forgiveness," said Juxon. "You believe my wife has done you wrong, but I assure you no blame is to be attached to her. What she has done she did unwillingly, indeed upon compulsion. I am the one who has injured you."

The scholar said nothing. There was vengeance on his face as he looked round the walls for some weapon, with which he might strike the man who stood between him and the desire of his soul.

"You may ask why I should wrong one who has never sought to harm me," Juxon went on in a steady voice. "Attribute it to the evil which is in all of us, to an inexplicable longing to make a fellow-creature suffer. I have only to confess my sin and clear the character of my wife."

While he spoke the man was battling with the horrible inclination, which bade him fling himself upon his enemy. He steadied himself by a great effort. All his determination and strength were required. Had he spent in the past an evil life nothing could have saved him then.

"My wife came here to recover her health," he went on hoarsely. "In her letters she told me of you, describing you as a clever poet, completely enwrapped in yourself and your work. I was brutal enough to ask her if she thought she could lure you sufficiently out of your work to make you admire her, and she replied, yet only in jest you must understand, that she believed it would be possible."

Maude comprehended her husband's plan. It was correct. The drama required it. He was sacrificing himself for her.

"In an idle moment I made a wager with a friend, who knew my wife, to the effect that she would succeed in making you believe she possessed knowledge equal to yours. My friend, averring it to be impossible, accepted the wager. I wrote to my wife and entreated her to make the attempt, instructing her to flatter and admire you—in short to make a fool of you—until she had attained my object. I need hardly say she was horrified at the suggestion. She begged me not to press her. The idea was utterly distasteful to her loyal mind. But I refused to spare her. She yielded at last, with what results you know. I won my wager at the cost of my wife's reputation. I dare not ask you to forgive me. I know it must be impossible for you to feel anything but hatred for so mean a creature as he who stands before you. All that I ask is your forgiveness for my wife."

Juxon broke off with a gasp. Dr. Berry towered above him, his face malignant, and its features contorted into a horrid semblance of one of the hanging masks. Suddenly he darted forward, and seizing a candlestick hurled it at the stockbroker. Juxon started aside, and as the missile clattered into a corner snatched his wife's hand and pulled her to the door. The scholar hurled himself against it and the rotten panels shivered into fragments; but the Juxons were gone, into the garden and the wind.

Scene II.—MASQUE

And let the Masquers, or any other, that are to come down from the Scene, have some motions, upon the Scene itself, before their comming down: For it drawes the Eye strangely, and makes it with great pleasure, to desire to see that, it cannot perfectly discerne.—*Bacon.*

The squire of Kingsmore and the rector of Thorlund stood in the latter's study. The clock pointed to forty minutes past seven. Mr. Price looked more solemn than usual, while his companion was haggard and agitated.

"I know now you have spoken the truth," the scholar was saying. "All along you have maintained that the Strath was haunted by an unholy influence, and I would not believe, because I could not feel it. What has come to me now I do not know. I am afraid of the place."

He turned and striding across the room snatched a volume of old English poetry from a shelf. "I was drawn there this afternoon. The house fought against me," he went on. "I was punished there. I was warned that with the falling of the house I too must fall."

"Berry," muttered the old squire. "During all the years of our acquaintance you have strained your brain upon thankless work. I do not know what to say about the Strath. One time I am certain it is badly haunted. Another time I have my doubts. Nothing has frightened me when I have been there, so far as I know, but—and this is the point—after leaving the place it has been impossible to remember what happened there."

The scholar was not listening. He bent the book of poetry open, so roughly that the binding broke, and cried, "'Go, bid the world with all its trash farewell.' Do you hear that? She has deceived me, laughed at me, mocked me. 'Leave it, I say, and bid the world farewell.' I trusted her. Can you not tell me what happened in the Strath this afternoon?"

"I can tell you one thing," said the squarson. "You are doing yourself a lot of harm. Leave your poetry and get out into the air. Why, man, you are shivering from head to foot."

"I am going to the Strath," Dr. Berry muttered.

"I don't like it," said Mr. Price. "I don't want to go, and Flora does not want to go either. My sister has the excuse of rheumatism, and she is the best off. It's a regular wild night, dark as pitch, with a howling wind. If there are phantoms at the Strath they will show themselves to-night. I'll order the carriage and go home. Flora!" he called, to the door. "Here, Flora! We will go back."

The girl came out of the drawing-room with a mask dangling from her gloved hand.

"I want to go now, uncle," she said firmly. "Besides we must. There will be nobody there except ourselves, and Maude—and Dr. Berry." She added the scholar's name as he revealed himself.

"He must not go," said Mr. Price decidedly. "He is going to bed. I'll tell Mr. Conway he is not well."

"I am coming," said the poet.

It was, as the old squire had said, a wild night, full of wind and strange cries. They groped through the churchyard, found the door in the wall, and entered the garden. A heavy beam of light fell from the house and guided their steps. The bridge across the moat swayed perceptibly. The hall door stood ajar. They passed in and saw candles glowing the saloon. Nance was kneeling in the great hall, warming her hands by a fire of logs, and looking up met Flora's eyes without flinching.

"The wind is rough," said Mr. Price in a melodramatic voice, responding as far as his simple nature allowed to the dominant influence.

As he spoke a tall figure crossed the hall, passing from one room to another, clad in close-fitting black with ruffles of yellow lace at its wrists and throat, its face hidden behind a brown mask. This tragic figure went towards the saloon with a dejected step, casting furtive glances to right and left as it disappeared.

"Abandoned and accursed," muttered Dr. Berry. He turned and strode away into the silence of the house.

"Come aside with me," said Flora in a thrilling voice, seizing her uncle and drawing him back. "Put on your mask," she whispered. "They must not suspect who we are. I can trust you? You are my relative. You will not fail me?"

"I will serve you as I can," said the old gentleman, with a wild shiver. "But let us be discreet, let us be watchful. Methinks our plans may be overheard. We will go to some more secret place, but let us carry ourselves boldly, so that no one may suspect we have anything on hand." He stepped away from her and bowed low. "Will it please you to walk with me and study the pictures?" he said; and when she had accepted his invitation they walked away into the gloom, two tragic puppets, like all the other beings who were to cross, or had crossed, the threshold of the house that night.

Presently a little lady in Arcadian costume appeared, and beside her a stout man closely muffled. They were the Juxons. They had been called and could not refuse to come. Strange had been the feeling between husband and wife during the drive homeward after that remarkable meeting at the Strath. On Maude's side there was a novel content; upon Juxon's a sense of happiness. He understood that his wife had changed. While they rattled through the wind she talked, with none of the empty vivaciousness of former days; and had never a scolding word, nor any impatient frown. She inquired after his health with genuine solicitude, and asked fondly after Peggy, stating her intention of returning forthwith to devote herself to her child. And he, jealous of this new-found happiness, did not venture to confess that he had no home, that his business was almost ruined.

She had gained in beauty, he thought, with that pale seriousness. As he felt the wind sweeping in life-giving strength across the hills, he made for the hundredth time the resolution of another effort for her sake. His pretty little wife should have all that she had been accustomed to. As for the scene which had so recently closed it was gone from them both; but Maude knew that Dr. Berry would never fascinate her again. Juxon was not aware that he had been put to the ordeal, that his nature had triumphed, that his character had stood firm for his wife's defence. He only knew that he had gone to the Strath, in obedience to the message, and that his wife had been restored to him there.

The group of tragic characters made a sombre party. The actors were six in number, for the two wearers of the brown masks had ceased to be human entities. They had become conflicting influences. The guests, who had been led to the house under the pretext of a dance, found themselves playing the part of conspirators. They instinctively mistrusted one another. In the saloon Mr. Price was gambling with the figure of tragedy. Upstairs Dr. Berry paced the corridors, biting his fingers, and planning vengeance. Juxon, the object of his hatred, stood with his dazed wife near the fireplace in the hall.

He had told her everything, and to his story of defeat and failure added the words:

"I have played my last card. There is nothing left with which to start afresh. I understand it all now," he went on firmly. "No man can struggle against destiny. It was never intended that I should be wealthy, and though riches were for the time forced upon me it was only that they might be taken away. I am a poor man now, with only these hands, a clear conscience, and a strong head left to aid me in the struggle for existence."

"And I have been a hindrance to you," said Maude gently.

"If we have failed to agree perfectly in the past it was the fault of neither of us," said Juxon. "Riches have been a curse, both to you and to me. For the future there will be no barrier to hold us apart."

"Herbert," she whispered, with a shudder. "You must go your way alone. The warning comes to me now that I have not much longer to live. I am to be punished for my heartlessness."

"Hush," said the man, almost fiercely.

"Only stay with me," Maude entreated. "There is danger here for you, as well as for me."

"There is horror in the very air," Juxon shivered. "Let us go into the light."

They crossed the hall with stealthy movements, and crept into the saloon, there to discover Mr. Price upon his knees, playing his cards madly, while the tragic figure opposite shook with laughter as it won again and again. The squire of Kingsmore had never gambled in his life before, and now he was losing everything he possessed, his invested capital, house, farm, and lands. The perspiration stood upon his face.

"I have an assignation which I must not fail to keep," he cried. "But I will beat you first."

Maude seated herself at the harpsichord, and drew from its

loose keys and clogged wires some fantastic sounds, while her husband leaned beside her, watching and listening, all his faculties keenly alert.

As Mr. Price sent up his defiant cry Flora rushed into the supper room. Filling a glass with wine, she searched in all the cabinets, then snatching up the glass turned to the door. A figure appeared before her with a jingling of bells, a short figure clad in many colours, with a cap like a cock's comb upon its head, a flute in its hand, and the leering mask of Comedy enveloping its face.

"Let me pass," she screamed.

"What do you seek?" demanded the motley figure.

"Poison," she cried.

With his flute he struck the glass from her hand. "You are one of my enemies," he laughed. "You have set before your mind unnatural ideas, and sought to follow them. You have a friend who has been heartless, but she has submitted of her own free-will and shall be happy. You continue to resist and shall be broken. You shall harm no one while I am near."

Flora could not recognise the voice of Drayton beneath the comic mask; but when the figure turned, and the light of the candles fell across the brown face, she shrank from the shape. Was that a mask? If so, it was a mask controlled by muscles, trembling with life, heated by blood: a mask that had grown upon the face like skin, moulding the features that bore it into its own grinning shape.

Dr. Berry was creeping cat-like about the house. He heard a sound of music and the wild ejaculations of the man who believed himself ruined. A smile crossed his face, and he murmured cunningly, "Extreme circumspection is necessary. I will hide in the ante-room, and behold what is taking place." Stealthily descending the stairs he passed through a side door. An antique lamp was burning low upon a table which was littered with sheets of manuscript. The curtains which divided this room from the saloon were closed. The poet halted on the threshold. It seemed to him that he was standing upon the brink of an open grave.

Four of the rotten planks which comprised the flooring had been broken away. Taking the lamp he went to his knees, and lowering the light perceived a small cellar bricked in like a vault. The damp walls shone when the light flashed across them. The lamp-beam saw two iron hooks driven into the crumbling cement; and to one of them clung a twisted fragment of what might have been leather, or rope, or even muscle.

"The grave is prepared," he said craftily. "It remains with me to supply an occupant."

He replaced the lamp, and sat in wild thought beside the table. Some sheets of manuscript lay beneath his eyes. Recognising a portion of Drayton's Tragedy, he bent his head to read a fragment, which had been marked by the author's hand, "Written when Comedy was in the ascendant, and therefore worthless." The fragment ran thus:—

St. James's. A room in the palace. Enter the King, led by a page, singing, and beating time with a roll of music.

King.

They say I'm not the King.
Here, scapegrace! powder-head! let me hear truth!
Who is he whom you lead?

Page.

His Gracious Majesty George the Third, by the Grace of God King of Great Britain and Ireland, Defender of the Faith—

King.

Defender. Ha! Defender is my name.
Old George was not afraid. He mocked the Pope,
Withheld all justice from the Catholics,
Broke up their churches, chased the cunning priests
Back to their Roman cells. He beat them all.
Did he not, boy?

Page.

Yes, your Majesty.

King.

Bah! I do hate great men:
These politicians, with their quips and cranks;
These big-wigs, with their tape and rhetoric,
Brass trumpets of sedition. I stand
Free of the highwaymen, that Pitt, that Burke.

I'll stand alone to fight. I will be king,
Though I lose Colonies. Shall a king kneel,
To beg a favour of his ministers?
A king bow down to seek his subjects' will,
And crave their gracious leave to wear his crown?
Will he not rather drive the rabble forth,
And swear to all the rout he is the law?
Boy, how long have I reigned?

Page.

'Tis fifty-five years, your Majesty.

King.

Has any King of England reigned so long?

Page.

No, your Majesty.

King.

Then get you out,
And call the guard, and bid them cheer the King.

Exit Page. King goes to a harpsichord and sings a hymn, accompanying himself.

The Queen enters, kneels at his side, and sings with him. A cheer from the palace yard, and shouts, God save the King.

King.

Bid them be silent. They have spoilt my hymn.
I am no king. I am a tired old man,
Weighed down with grief. My darling is so quiet!
They snatched her from me. I can smell the flowers
They heaped upon her, and I feel the arms
Of those who drew me from her bed of earth.
That day I lost my crown.
He lifteth up the lowly, and casts down
The great ones to the dust.

Another cheer.

Hark, how they mock me there! Long live the King.
Now let me speak—God grant the King may die.
An uproar in the street. Loud cries of 'Victory' and 'Wellington.'
Queen closes the window.

King.

'Tis time to hold my court. See there the troops,

Who fought in Flanders, waiting for review;
A noble band. Soldiers, I'm proud of you.
Fine fellows are ye, disciplined and bold.
March past, my guards; march past, and sound your drums.

Claps his hands as the ghosts pass.

Right, Left! Right, Left! Aye, that's the English swing,
The tread that startled Louis and his French,
The march that shook the Spaniards. Where are ye?
Gone past already. Soft! What have we here?
I know those faces and those powdered heads:
My House of Commons. I'll see to them straight!
The stubborn knaves, who would have broke my will.
Oppose me if ye dare. I know the means
To break your party, to unseat each man,
And drive him cringing to his rural poll.
I'll do it, if ye force me, and refuse
To aid my plans. Traitor is every man
Who power denies to kings.
Out, villains! Out from here!
What! Must I drive ye forth?

Runs among the ghosts, beating at them.
Noise in the street continues.

Away, place-seekers! Out of this my court.
I will not hear ye. Look now how they come!
Fawning and sighing, each to kiss my hand,
And seek a favour. Bishops sleek in lawn,
Clergy corrupt, and politicians smooth,
Two-faced, four-handed, Jacobite at night,
Cringing before the man in power by day.
They come on, more and more.

Noise increases.

And here we have bespangled generals,
Savage for titles. Here bold Whig-patched dames
Crowd on the stairs, and push some favourite up,
To pay his hollow vows to win a post.
Is this a Court? Call it a market-place,
And me a merchant. Hear those whispered words,
'Give me a Bishopric, and loyal I'll be,'

Or, 'Grant me office, and I'll be your man,'
And there again, 'Hand me authority,
And I will preach the justice of the king.'
Is there not here a man? Are these but masks,
Stamped with some semblance of humanity?
Are truth and honour dead and gone? Away,
Trumpets and heraldry, and power and pomp,
And find me here some loyal flesh and blood.
Away, ye mummers! Out, ye titled clowns!
And hide yourselves in graves. I'm still the King.

Bursts into tears and falls, fainting. The Queen bears him up.

Enter an officer noisily.

Officer.

Great news, Your Majesties! Napoleon
Has met defeat. His army is destroyed
By the allies, and he, a fugitive,
Must soon be taken.

Queen.

Go with your tales of battle,
And shout to them that live.

Officer goes out sneering. Queen goes to window and opens it.

Queen.

They do not look this way. For fifty years
I've been the Queen of England. They forget.
The Prince goes on his way to Carlton House;
The crowds close round his carriage, crying out,
'God save the King,' and 'Victory.' The King!
There lies the King.

The curtains were drawn apart. The reader started up to behold a fearful face with drooping mouth, cruel and thin-lipped, narrow forehead and sunken cheeks, quivering and palpitating with all the passions of evil. It was the figure of Conway; but the face was the face of Tragedy.

"I have ruined the old man yonder," he mouthed. "Hear him howl! I have won everything that he possessed, and now all he asks for is a pistol that he may shoot himself. Tell me, friend, where I may find that young woman who lately entered this house. I would decoy her outside to a lonely part of this garden, and there—nay, but I was ever too free with my tongue."

"I need your assistance," muttered the scholar.

"It is yours," came the answer. "I see you are a brave fellow, accustomed to use the knife."

"See that man!" exclaimed the other, pointing out Juxon through a rent in the curtain. "He has made me a laughing-stock."

"Trust in me, friend. We will despatch him together. Do you go into the long corridor and conceal yourself, while I engage the man in conversation. Presently I will bring him that way, and as we pass do you leap out upon him. I will have him held. He shall not have time to shout."

"I will procure a knife," the poet chuckled.

The garden of the Strath was plunged in total darkness outside the shafts of light proceeding from the windows. There was no rain, but the wind howled and worked havoc among the trees and shrubs. The few labourers of the hamlet, safe inside their shuttered cottages, were convinced that the Strath had never been so noisy before.

October blasts had howled as fiercely over Thorlund; but the grim influence of the house had never predominated as upon that night when all the ways were shaded.

The miserable squire of Kingsmore rushed into the hall, shouting the one word, "Ruined!" He saw himself a dishonoured man, deprived of the lands and house which his family had held for generations. He was half-mad to know that he should have come to this in his old age. True there were rumours in his family of an ancestor upon whose career the gambling element had been plainly marked; but even he was never so deeply dipped as to have forfeited the estate. He hung to Juxon and implored him for a loan upon easy terms, and when refused sought Dr. Berry with a like request. The scholar pushed him back with a curse. When Flora came to him, the miserable old man snatched her hand and tried to drag the bracelet from her wrist. She caught his hand and whispered a fierce reminder into his ear.

"Ha! I had forgotten," he gasped. "Say, child, has she money? Let us go in search of the trollop."

A sound of flute-play entered their ears. They looked up to see

Comedy descending the stairs. Recognising an enemy they shrank back against the draperies. He cast his grinning eyes upon them and cried, "Do your will. Do your worst. You shall find me near."

That instant Tragedy came out and stopped, shivering with fear and fury, when it saw the motley. During that moment, while the two masks were glaring at each other, the hearts of the watchers seemed to cease. Then the fiend slunk abjectly away, and the merry flute piped onwards like a bird.

The Juxons were alone in the saloon. Maude was clinging to her husband, still haunted by the terrible prospect of death by violence. Beside them the table was overturned and the cards were scattered about the floor. While Juxon was attempting to calm her fears with words of consolation Nance fled into the saloon pale with terror, and screaming for help. Flora and Mr. Price pursued her with murder upon their faces. They caught the girl as she reached the Juxons and bore her to the floor; but as the old gentleman, whom his own sister could not then have recognised, hissed out, 'Strangle her!' a tinkling of bells was heard, and Comedy jumped through the curtains with his mocking laugh. The tragic characters fell back. The figure in motley lifted the girl and led her away, leering upon the baulked couple and saying, "Did I not promise I would follow you?"

"We are foiled, child," muttered the old gentleman with a ghastly smile. "But no matter. We can bide our time."

The atmosphere of the Strath was charged like the thundercloud which is about to break. The two forces, through which destiny works her will, were fighting for supremacy. In the presence of Comedy, Tragedy had so far been powerless. Wherever the spirit of destruction went with its frown, the spirit of protection followed with its laugh. It was a battle between despair and and happiness. It did not occur to any of the characters that safety might be found in flight. By the laws of the drama, they were compelled to remain upon the scene, until the entry of the final character and the exodic march.

A dark figure glided into the saloon. Taking its stand beside the Juxons, it engaged them in conversation with the subtility of Mephistopheles. Its tongue was full of flattery, and they yielded to it. There was a picture in the corridor above which deserved their attention, and he, the soft speaker, sought the privilege of conducting them there, having some poor knowledge of the arts, that he might point out its merits and its beauty. They went with him, and as the figure stopped in the dimly-lighted corridor and pointed with a horrible laugh towards a dark copy of The Plague at Athens, Juxon was held and a cry of exultation rang down the house.

"Blunderer! The knife," hissed Tragedy.

But the bells again jingled. Through the gloom of the house danced Comedy, to strike down their hands with his flute and to hunt his enemy before him; and with the dark figure fled the scholar hand in hand.

For the greater part of another hour the struggle continued. Maude and her husband were also absorbed into the maelstrom and sought to be avenged. The Strath was occupied with conspiracies and stealthily moving creatures filled with the lust of slaughter. The dark spirit of tragedy hounded them on. And whenever the blow appeared certain to fall the bells jingled. Amid the frowns and screams and muttered words sounded the laugh of the flute-player. And the wind howled and beat upon the house in a wild chorus heralding the approach of the final character.

Apart from that final entry the supremacy of one of the opposing powers was inevitable. Although Tragedy feared its rival, the time came when repeated defeats goaded it to fury; until it dared to attack the motley figure, and the characters drew round to watch the fight.

The wind fell and there was silence throughout the garden. The old house seemed to be aware that its last hour had come. A stranger had passed through the gates, one who was able for a time to resist the influence, because he understood the secret of the power and his mind was not open to receive impressions but resolutely set upon the removal of the cause. This was the final character, who came in ignorance as to what was taking place at the crucial moment ordained by the dramatic laws.

The spectators of the struggle between the rival powers marvelled at the courage displayed by the last principal character of the drama when he entered and drove them aside to pass and fling himself upon the figure of Tragedy. The stranger's body seemed to them a mere frame of bones, and his arms were like wire-ropes for strength and thickness. He held the dark shape upon the floor, one hand clutching its throat, the fingers of the other tearing at the hot palpitating mask, raising it by the edges where it adhered less powerfully to the skin, dragging and peeling it away. Off came the limp horrible face; and the stranger pressed it upon the fire and held it down, until the room was full of odours and a nauseous soot, and all its occupants shivered and grew sick, and the house seemed to thrill with groans. Then came the turn of Comedy; and with the consigning of that mask also to the flames the power fled from the house, the influence came to an end; and the two men who had been controlled that night by those rival influences, which beat with fierce activity upon actors on and off the stage, were lying unconscious upon the floor, their faces blistered and their limbs rigid.

Then the wind arose and with it came a noise of thunder. A portion of the roof had fallen in. The Strath was a rotten carcase. It had lost its power of evil and its power of good. Biron, for he it was who had reached Thorlund at the time appointed, turned to the astounded guests, introduced himself, and briefly explained why he was there, and how he had served them.

"Destroyed the masks!" exclaimed Mr. Price feebly. "What masks? God bless my soul! what has been happening?"

PROSCENIUM

Tragedy is an imitation, not only of a completed action, but also of an action exciting pity and terror.—*Aristotle.*

Drayton and Conway were carried into the hall where they could receive the benefit of the cold wind. The little party abandoned the saloon in silence, Flora being supported by her uncle. Biron, after bending once more over the charred remains in the fire, joined them, closing and fastening the door behind him. The late mummers regarded each other with a curious suspicion, scarcely daring to speak, and feeling as though they had awakened from a drugged sleep. Already one of the company was missing. Dr. Berry had gone back to his solitude; and after a short interval the Juxons followed.

At last the survivors were able to regard the Strath with undistorted judgment. It appeared to them an impossible residence, damp, windy, and tottering. It had no more romance than an old barn filled with curiosities; it was a tumbledown museum, filled with draughts and dust, a place for owls and rats like the ruined parsonage house of Queensmore.

Drayton was the first to recover and stand upon his feet. Several more minutes elapsed before Conway was restored to consciousness. Both were depressed, troubled by nausea, and tormented by blistered faces. Neither had the slightest recollection of what he had undergone. Indeed the entire life of those past months remained a blank sheet unwritten on by time. There were memories of a dream-like nature, which could not be framed in words.

Refreshments were placed in the dining-room, and there the company betook itself, sane, human, and no longer theatrical. Presently Mr. Biron gave the tale, as he knew it, of the masks, from their creation by Joseph Falk, toy-maker of Nuremberg, to his own unexpected and dramatic arrival that night. He told them how his great-grandfather had entombed the horrible things in the vault—where, owing to decay of the flooring in the ante-room, Drayton had discovered them—and then had disappeared leaving the Strath to become impregnated with the rival influences. "From certain records handed down to me," Biron proceeded, "I am convinced that these masks must have exerted a fearful power. They would have influenced not only this house and garden, but the surrounding country and its inhabitants also."

"You have told us a strange story. You must forgive me when I say it is not easy to accept," said Mr. Price in a bewildered voice. "I knew there was something unnatural here, indeed everybody knew that, but the curious part about it was that no one ever thought of organizing any active crusade against the Strath. I do not know what has been going on to-night. I am only painfully conscious of my aching limbs."

"Do you suggest that my friend and myself have been under the control of these masks all the summer?" asked Conway.

"I say also you may consider yourselves fortunate in having escaped," Biron answered. "Fine weather would have been favourable to you. During the long dark nights of winter you might have lost your reason and committed suicide. I speak from my small knowledge of the masks."

"What brought you here in time to save us?"

"I can answer that," said Drayton, coming forward, his face still bearing the comedian's leer. "I pawned the masks which used to hang in your room in town. I wanted to tell you, but for some reason or other could not. It was a mean thing to do, but I wanted to reach you, and had no money."

"You could not have rendered your friend a better service," said Biron. "It is owing to your action I am here. I had offered a reward for information which might lead to the discovery of the originals. It was the least I could do to atone for my ancestor's irresponsible conduct—I do him the credit of believing it to have been so. Unfortunately I was away from my home in Naples when the information was sent, or I should have been here much earlier."

"You are right when you suggest that this neighbourhood has suffered," said Mr. Price thoughtfully. "Everyone has left it, except those who are tied to the land. A little village yonder called Queensmore lies in ruins. Sheep-farming has been a failure. As for this valley of Thorlund it has remained indifferent to everything. The villagers could talk of nothing but the Strath."

Conway moved across to the wall and taking down the wooden copies of the masks turned them thoughtfully between his hands.

"They are harmless," said Biron with his cadaverous smile.

Conway made no reply. Removing one of the logs he placed the masks in the hottest part of the fire and savagely watched the process of immolation.

"Flora, we must go," said the old squire, lifting himself stiffly. "Take your last look at the inside of the Strath, for I doubt if you will ever see it again."

"Indeed you may not, Miss Neill," said the owner. "The house is coming down, and the wilderness outside shall be reclaimed."

As the uncle and niece were about to take their departure Biron bent his bony figure to whisper into the squire's ear, "If this young lady has been much under the influence of the masks I should advise you to send her away for a change of scene."

At that warning the old gentleman looked at his niece and noticed the heaviness of her eyes. He dimly wondered what would have befallen her, and himself, had the masks been permitted to live, but dismissed the thought because it was not a pleasant one. He wished the men good-night and turned to leave the house for ever.

But Flora as she shook hands with Conway could not refrain from confessing in a low voice, "I think I have learnt something here."

Biron, who was near, overheard and said, "I have always believed that there was good as well as evil in the power—or shall I call it the teaching?—of the masks. Unfortunately they could only impart that teaching, or we could only receive it, in a manner that was full of danger both to body and mind."

"And we never knew anything about it," said Mr. Price solemnly. "That is the strangest thing of all."

"We know nothing of the influence which controls us in the state before birth or in the conditions after bodily death," said Biron. "I have discharged the duty of my life," he went on. "The masks are destroyed. Results must live after them, but I am content to know they cannot claim any more victims. I rejoice with all my heart at your escape."

When Mr. Price and Flora had gone the three men continued to speak upon the subject which was uppermost in their minds; and presently it was Biron's turn to listen while Conway spoke upon his uncle's fate. When he had concluded, having indeed very little to state, the attenuated man took up the matter with interest.

"You tell me your uncle was found dead in this place, under conditions which precluded the possibility of anyone having placed violent hands upon him. You say also that the police, after making every effort to discover a murderer, were forced to relinquish their search for lack of material upon which to work. But surely the truth is obvious. Your poor uncle came to Joseph Falk's end. He destroyed himself."

"No," cried both the listeners together, and Conway added, "it was shown at the inquest he had been strangled."

"Not hanged?"

"He was discovered lying across the threshold of the hall-door."

"Then here we have a mystery," said Biron. "Some material influence must have been brought into requisition that night. You must give me time to think over it. And now with your permission, I will walk through the house."

"We will go with you. It will be as new to us as to you," said the owner grimly.

They made a tour of inspection throughout the Strath from cellars to attics. Upstairs the walls were mildewed and gaping with cracks. Room after room of the dead house they examined, scarcely venturing to speak during that solemn survey; until they entered a bedroom which contained an immense four-post bedstead hung about with a filthy valance. Part of the wall had broken away, and the wind howled inward, lashing the ivy against the loosening brickwork. Upon a table they saw a floriated cross and near it a book in shagreen covers. Conway picked up the book, and glanced through it idly, and pushed it into his pocket. Biron drew back the draperies and looked into the bed which was piled with clothes half-eaten by grubs. "My faith," he muttered. "There should be some remote influence haunting this house even now."

"I will tell you what I know of its history, if you will come downstairs," said the owner. Then he turned to his friend and asked, "Drayton, do you think we have been living here without anyone to look after us? You may remember, but I cannot."

"Wasn't there a girl, or an old woman?" said the writer dubiously. "I seem to remember a tall girl, with a very serious brown face and a quantity of black hair, and an old woman who was always grumbling."

Upon going downstairs part of the mystery was solved; for the found in the kitchen the rachitic dame, who had served them, fast asleep in a crazy chair. Nancy Reed had gone, and at that time was running with the wind back to her late home at Kingsmore, a wild girl again, and her mind in borderland.

Venturing to re-enter the saloon the men found that the atmosphere had cleared. The fire which had destroyed the last remains of the criminal and the mountebank was burning low. More logs were piled upon the rotten irons, and then Conway gave his visitor a true account of the history of the Strath down to the end of the eighteenth century, mentioning what he knew of Sir John Hooper's villainous career and punishment, and the story of his daughter's misery. "This book, which I picked up in the bedroom above, seems to be Winifred Hooper's journal," he concluded.

The guest reached out his arm and having taken the tragic record passed his eyes hurriedly across its pages. Presently he began to read extracts aloud. Their interest increased. Biron lingered over a page, and from that point read on continuously, wherever the writing was legible. The two men drew closer and leaning forward listened intently, while the candles guttered down to their sockets, and the fire burnt to an angry red.

It was midnight, and the wild wind was at its height, rushing overhead and howling down the passages. Still the three men sat motionless, and Biron's voice, enriched by its foreign accent, read on, lifting as it neared the last pages because of the noises in the house. Occasionally Conway started, or Drayton averted his eyes hurriedly from the black window. For the first time the Strath appeared to them haunted indeed. The shadowy visitor's voice faltered once, then sounded strongly as it read:

"And now I am alone with the God who called me upon this scene. My dog is dead. He has been ailing for many days, and this evening when I went to care for him as my poor skill permitted, he lifted his head and licked my hand, shivered and moaned and died. The body lies beside me. No longer will he spring up and growl when a footfall sounds along my passage. No longer will he stand before me to protect me from my father, snarling and showing his white teeth when he beholds the whip which is not for him. Dear faithful friend, good-night.

"It is strange that while we cannot by any means foretell the future we may yet feel the approach of calamity. During this last week, when listening in the silence of this room, I have felt the nearness of disaster. Will the omen fail? It matters so little. I am able to bear misfortune because accustomed to it, but any unexpected happiness might stop my heart for ever. Were Geoffrey to stand before me now I should neither laugh nor speak. Like my poor dog I could only kiss his hand and die. I would embrace a phantom were it his. I am a philosopher, and my crucible is filled with adversity out of which I strive all night to win knowledge, not of the world, nor of its hidden forces, nor of the stars which shine above, but an answer to my heart which goes on asking, 'What is love?' Is it a morning cloud melted by the sun, or a flower scattered by the breeze, or is it a rock which defies the storm? Is it made of dreams, loose-clinging stuff, falling from the body at a touch? Or is it an immortal essence, imbruing the soul through time and space and change?

"None can answer me, and indeed I care not. I doubt whether to-morrow's sun will rise upon the hills. I fail when I try to trust in life eternal. I resign my confidence in ministering spirits and my hope in Heaven. I am not even assured of my own existence. I pass to and fro, without sound, with so little substance, haunting this house like some unhappy ghost. Have I indeed ceased to be material? Is there anything that I may believe in? Yes, there is one thing. I believe in the reality of fear.

"Geoffrey is but the memory of a long past time. I must speak to that I see and feel and hear, to the indifferent and unresponsive objects of this daily prison, to the drifting clouds and the whirling wind. There is life in the wind and strength. It passes on, the same, yet not the same, changing its cry, now howling, now falling to a sob, now rushing like a madman, now crawling snake-like. And I can hear the trees roaring like the sea. So I address the wind, and the trees, and my poor friend's body, and all else that I can see and hear, because faith can do no more.

"It must be hard on midnight. I dare not think what may be taking place outside. The house is filled with shadows. It is like a cave beaten by the waves. Walking in the garden to-day I heard voices beyond the wall, and three strange men rode beside the gates, cloaked and long-booted, and one had a deep scar along his cheek, and all were armed. One muttered, as he nodded to this garden, 'We may trap the old fox to-night.' They passed on, along the high road in the direction of Kingsmore, and I knew it was I who had brought them. The villagers will not warn my father, because they hate him. His fate rests with me, his only child, and he is condemned for Geoffrey's sake.

"I have been to the head of the stairs because I thought I heard a disturbance. Old Deborah is walking about the hall, beating her hands together. Deborah loves my father, because she nursed him as a boy. She saw me, and frowned, and began to snuff the candles that she might persuade me she was not anxious. She muttered, ''Tis a mighty wind, and bad luck to him who's caught in it!' Then she went to the door and I heard her say, 'That's the coach. And that's the noise of—get you to your room,' she cried, starting back and shaking her hand at me. 'Get you away.' So I came back, and am now straining my ears at every sound.

"Now I could hear were I stone deaf. The end has come. The terrible night! First the noise of furious galloping. There was the clang of the iron gate, the galloping again, and voices shouting; and after that a lantern flashed its light upon the side of the house. One horse crossed this light, my father's flecked with foam, then another and that was Reed's big grey, and then a third. What have they done? There has been murder upon the highway. The third horse carried a body slung across the saddle. They passed, were gone, and then a voice I know too well shouted, 'Rub the mare dry, unsaddle her, and turn her into the field. Here, fool, you have dropped your mask. Burn it, and throw these pistols into the moat, and clean that sword. Then come into the house, for you and I must have a word together.'

"I can hear the beating of my heart. The awful night! Why did

I not escape. Better the cold plantation than my father's fury. All is silent now, apart from the wind—but there! It is the door. A wild voice shouts, 'Deborah, bring brandy-wine and plenty of hot water.' God grant he may forget me.

"Again I have listened in the passage. The hall-door was pushed open and the man Reed entered—I knew him by his oaths. He was breathing thickly and struggling with some burden, which he let down upon the floor, or dropped it rather, for I heard it roll and settle with dreadful heaviness."

As Biron spoke that last word, there came from above the sound of a body, falling heavily, so as to shake the house. Without lifting his eyes, or moving in his seat, he read calmly on:

"Then a brawling began between the man and the master. Their words I could not often catch, but I heard my father's voice, shaking with fear and rage. 'Burn it,' he shouted. 'Or, if there be not time, hide it away in the girl's bedroom.' What Reed replied I could not hear, but I imagine he told my father there could be no cause for hurry, as he is a dense besotted creature, with a mind set upon strong liquors, a man too incapable of feeling to know fear. Their voices became hoarse mutterings, and now I hear the clinking of glasses and the rattling of flasks. I can write almost unmoved, and yet that horrible feeling of calamity impending remains, and when I look upon my bed I seem to see a cold sheet, and a shape, and a solemn candle burning at the head. Is that the shape of the poor wretch they have murdered to-night? No, it is too thin and small, and I think I discover a lock of fair hair upon the pillow. Well, there is but one more page remaining to this book.

"Again I hear the note of disagreement. They have always been violent in their cups. The voices are raised higher. There is none here they need fear. Still no sound from without. They have been favoured by the wind and the darkness of the night, and thus have again escaped. But there—a blow. Surely a blow, and now, 'Traitor! Spy! Informer!' There is death in that voice. The clash of swords! Oh God! they are fighting like beasts. Let me not be the cause of any man's death, be he highwayman or murderer. Now I understand the reason of that fight which must end in death. My father knows that his guilt has been discovered. His return was a flight. Those cloaked long-booted men are perhaps even now upon his track, and he believes that his companion has betrayed him, and, half-drunk, half-mad, cannot listen to denial. And I am the informer. And I dare not go down, dare not face him as he is, dare not tell him that his accomplice is innocent, dare not tell him it was I. Oh, the clamour, the ringing, the clashing of those swords! The shrieks of the wind, and that awful breathing! Silence, but the whole house seems to shuddering. There is a hollow sound in the hall, rising and swelling along the passage, louder every moment, and now, 'Open in the King's name.'

"Torches are flaring in the garden. The house is surrounded. That beating upon the door continues, or is it the beating of my heart? But the same stern voice demands admission, and my wretched father shouts in terror, as he feels the shadow of the gallows creeping across his head, and blunders about the saloon, and now into the hall, past the rebounding door, and now he is upon the stairs, and I can hear a dragging and a heaving and two dead heels rattling from step to step. Oh, merciful God! He is coming here to hide the body, and I cannot bear it, I cannot look upon it. They are breaking down the door, battering it in with a heavy log, and now it gives with a noise of thunder, and the avengers rush in shouting at their loudest, 'Surrender, in the King's name!'"

The three men started fearfully, but not a sound escaped their lips, when there rose above the wind a terrific noise in the neighbourhood of the hall-door, a crashing thunderous riot, as though that door had indeed been crushed inwards and the human hounds were hunting in the house. The reader's thin face quivered, as his tongue concluded the last wild words upon the final page:

"Let them seize him upon the stairs. He has reached the corridor, gasping in his terror. He is dragging no longer, but carrying. He enters this passage, shouting my name. They hear him. The house rocks as they rush up the stairs. 'I have brought him. Take him. Hide him away.' What does he mean? Will he reach the roof and fling himself down? He is here, panting outside my door. Again he is dragging the dreadful thing, and now I must look upon that, and upon him. He flings himself against the door . . ."

As the record ended with that blotted word, a fearful crash

shook the ground, the house tottered, and suddenly the saloon wall opened peacefully, and the men caught glimpses of a wild watery moon between two lack shuddering fringes of ivy.

"Run!" shouted Biron, dropping his hands and the time-worn book. "The house is falling upon us."

EXODE

He had no brains for the Royal Diadem to cover; and if Zeus should give him his Lightning and Thunder, he would be no more Zeus for that.—*Plutarch*.

The vacarme had ceased and the Strath was abandoned to its decay. The influence had done its work upon the minds of those brought beneath its sway. Punishment, sharp and summary, had been meted out upon Henry Reed with the cruelty for which Nature is notorious. A like punishment was to fall upon Dr. Berry. Both were weak men, although in other respects eminently dissimilar; the one a dull material creature, the other a sensitive spiritual being. The former attempted to arrest the working of the influence, while the latter essayed the equally impossible task of establishing himself as an active principle of that power. The active and hostile scepticism of the one was no whit more dangerous than the complete resignation of the other.

Mr. Price, a man of very simple nature who clung to his belief, never adding to it nor subtracting from it, emerged from the ordeal unchanged. Juxon found himself equipped with a knowledge which had come unsought. He was further rewarded by the affection and constancy of his wife. Even when wealth came to him, and he was pointed out with some awe as a man endowed with uncanny gifts, little Maude kept her head and her resolutions. The Strath had been kind to her, because her faults had sprung from weakness and vanity, not, as in Flora's case, from a malignant growth. The latter was punished by being compelled to know herself; and that punishment endured.

Conway had been shown that idleness and debauchery are serious infringements of the laws of nature. He carried away with him from the ruined Strath a bitter hatred of his former life. As for Drayton when his inheritance came, late in life, he knew he had not himself to thank. He had always done his best, but the parrot-like nature of his former labour had stunted his mind, and poverty had sapped his physical powers. He acknowledged to himself, when his fame as a dramatic writer became fully established, that those ideas which enriched his brain had been born in him during the weeks of dream and languor spent in the garden of the Strath.

After those days of the change Conway found for Lone Nance a congenial home and a kindly guardianship. In that condition her wild beauty increased and her face softened, although her mind never recovered the even balance to which it had attained during her stay in the Strath.

It was Maude's last day in the country, and she walked—donkeys, cart, and silver bells having been consigned to the auctioneer—to Kingsmore, that she might say good-bye to Mr. Price, also to Flora and her mother who were about to leave. The little lady had sobered down her exuberance of colour; she wore a grey skirt with coat to match, and a black hat, where a trace of the old Eve survived in the shape of a small pink bow nestling as though ashamed beneath the brim. Her husband had gone away, full of confidence, by reason of the new strength which had been vouchsafed to him at the Strath; and Maude was about to follow, having a wild desire to live in two rooms, and cook her husband's dinner with her own ignorant hands, and be nurse to Peggy, and lady of work generally. "For I am going to be a wife now, Herbert," she had declared. "And not a caricature. I am very stupid and shall have to learn everything. If you will just be as good to me as you have always been, I don't mind getting old and I won't be afraid to lose my looks." Such was Maude's new and liberal doctrine.

The squire came riding in from the farm as the little lady entered the drive and seeing her lowered himself stiffly from his horse. She noticed for the first time that he was looking old and fragile; his legs, crooked by years of riding, were weak and unsteady, his shoulders were bending, his cheeks were growing hollow, and the fringe of hair above the nape of his neck was as white as wool. She ran forward and offered him her arm with a pretty smile.

"Why, young lady!" he cried in his hearty manner. "I did not recognise you at first. So you have come to say good-bye. Well, I am sorry to hear that, because at my age it is a serious matter to say farewell. Do you mean to say you have walked all the way? Come into the house and rest yourself. Flora is not well, I'm afraid.

She will be glad to see you, and you may cheer her up. There is something on her mind, but she won't tell me what it is. I hope and pray she is not going into religious mania, like my poor eldest sister who went and made a useless nun of herself. In my young days girls were not allowed to have opinions. They were given their religion, just as they were given their husbands, and very much happier and more useful they were."

"Flora wants a change," said Maude. "Autumn is so depressing."

"You don't look particularly downcast," said the old gentleman. "The autumn seems to agree with you."

"That is because I have made a heap of resolutions, and I am going to stick to them," said the little lady. "I have done nothing all my life, except dress and laugh, and now it's time to work."

The squire was about to chaff her, but one glance at her face convinced him that she meant what she had said.

"There is nothing like work," he said, with more feeling than was usual with him. "There is no happiness in life without work. The preacher, who advised his fellow-creatures to follow the example of the ant, knew what he was talking about, even if he hadn't the sense to put his teaching into practice. I lose money every year over my farm, but it gives me plenty of healthy work, and it affords a living to the people of my village. I hope to go on working to the day of my death and to pass from the saddle to the grave. That is how my grandfather went. He came in from the hunt at six o'clock, and was dead by dinner-time."

"Don't," said Maude gently.

"Ah, you think we are here for ever," said the squire. "We all think so when we are young. But when past seventy we feel the ravages of time and lose our roast-beef stomachs, as somebody once said. Fill in your years unselfishly, child. Fill them in with work and laughter, help those who are in trouble, and do your duty elsewhere, and you will be happy when you're old."

The old man tramped away, gave his horse to a boy, then went round the yard, ferreting out eggs from the hen-houses, poking his riding-crop into the sides of fattening porkers, and replacing the hay which wasteful cows had tugged from their rack and were trampling underfoot. As he stood in the raw autumn afternoon, with his dogs jumping round him, and the pigeons fluttering down for a portion of the grain he always carried in his pockets, he looked what he was, the last of the plain old squires.

Flora was alone in the drawing-room, lying on a sofa, reading a book, which she tried to smuggle away when her friend was announced; but Maude jumped upon the volume and secured it. She merely opened her eyes a trifle wider when she read the title, 'Plato's education of the young,' and dropped the book without a word.

"I thought you would come, Maude," said Flora in a heavy voice. "I am going to Italy with mother next week. I may very likely never see you again."

"My girl!" cried Maude. "What do you mean? Why, of course we shall meet again. Do you know I am going to learn house-keeping—yes, it is rather late in the day—and when I am proficient you shall come and stay with me, and I will give you lessons. Herbert is fearfully hard up just now, but he is going to make heaps of money presently."

"I may stop in Italy," said Flora, in the same dull voice.

"Then I shall come and worry you," said Maude with decision. "But, my dear, you won't. You will come back in the spring, and marry a nice husband, and be a nice wife. And then you will be as happy as I am."

"Are you happy?" said Flora. "Really happy?"

"Happy enough to whistle on a foggy day," said the grey lady.

"You have changed, Maude."

"I have found out Herbert's good points, and some of my bad ones," said Maude. "And you have changed since that day when we sat in the punt on the river, and you tried to persuade me you were horrid and unnatural. You have changed all that, haven't you, girl?"

Flora flushed a little, and by way of reply introduced a fresh topic.

"I have received a letter since I last saw you," she said hurriedly. "It is from—well, I need only say that I led him on, he proposed, and I refused. He must be fond of me if he wants me still."

"You will say yes?" said Maude softly.

"I have said no."

"You shall, you must, change your mind. Write the letter now. Or let me send a telegram as I go back through the village. You would be happy if you were married. And if you had a little girl like my Peggy, you would so proud of yourself you would turn up your nose if you met all the queens in the world at a street-corner."

Flora had never been demonstrative, therefore when she suddenly flung her arm round Maude's neck the little lady was considerably astonished; but this was nothing compared to her consternation when she heard the communication which the fair-haired girl proceeded to whisper into her ear.

"Flora!" she exclaimed. "It is not true. You have always been imaginative. That is your idea because you are not well. When you get away from here you will soon change all that."

"Don't you know that the neglected faculty dies for want of use?" came the answer. "I cannot love now. The power is not in me. And without love I will not marry. I am as cold as any stone and my heart will not respond. When I read that letter not a pulse in me stirred. I have repelled the blind boy too long, and now he has left me for ever."

"He will come back," said Maude earnestly. "He will come back in the spring and shoot a sharp arrow right through your poor little heart, and then you will forget all that has passed, and be a good wife—a much better one than I have ever been."

"I called myself an asymptote and tried to live up to the part," went on the girl. "Now I am the curve, and Cupid plays the asymptote. And yet it really matters very little," she added firmly. "Love and marriage are, after all, only incidents in life. There is so much besides."

"Oh, my dear! Take away love, and life is a tragedy. But I don't know how to preach," said the little lady with a laugh. "I will just hand you over to the mercies of time. Only promise that you will come and stay with me when you return."

"If I return I will," replied Flora; and with that delphic utterance Maude had to be content.

She never saw her friend again. The following year Flora offered her services to a mission society, was accepted, and sent to Ceylon to work among the natives. There she became a Buddhist, accepting the religion she had gone out to fight against, an action which was typical of her. Maude gasped with horror when she heard, through Mr. Price, the news, for Buddhism and cannibalism were with her synonymous terms. She wrote several frantic letters to

Flora, entreating her to leave the savage state and return to civilization. No answer came. Mrs. Neill lapsed ungrammatically to the grave; Mr. Price, with tears in his simple eyes, altered his will; and Flora, the original and strong-minded, was never heard of again.

Two characters remained upon the scene, the former leader of the dramatic mysteries, and he who had entered last. Biron would not leave until the whole of his duty had been accomplished. He conceived it incumbent upon himself to unravel the mystery of Reed's end, that he might atone as completely as possible for the trouble brought upon the place by his great-grandfather's actions. The day after Conway's departure he drove to Thorlund and entered the dripping garden. There, hard by the sundial, he encountered the rector, closely muffled, and walking slowly with the aid of a stick. They greeted one another and fell into a conversation, which Biron quickly turned towards the subject he had at heart.

"This is a mournful sight," he said, indicating what had been the house.

"And this a hateful wilderness," replied the scholar weakly, waving his stick across the garden. "Once, I believe, I loved it."

There was little remaining to inspire affection. The Strath had fallen. All that was left of the standing ruins were two blank walls, one gable, and a mass of ivy. Beyond were heaps of bricks, torn draperies smeared with mud, and shattered furniture. The unsupported walls appeared to sway gently, waiting for the blast which should level them with the ground; and the saloon window, still bearing the unbroken escutcheon of the Hooper family, stared vacantly across the unromantic tangle of garden. Illusion had left that haunted ground for ever.

"I can tell you nothing," said the scholar, in answer to his companion's question concerning Reed's death. "Perhaps there are circumstances which later on I may recall, but at this present time my mind refuses to work. I have been very ill. There is a pain in my head as though my brain was wounded. It is strange to know that I was once so happy here. Now the whole place repels me."

"It is certain that Reed came to a violent end," urged Biron. "It is equally certain that no one was suspected of the crime of murder. I imagined that you, being in this garden so often, might have formed some theory."

"He afforded an instance of a man whose folly brought its own punishment," answered the rector. "I warned him that it would so happen, but he laughed at me. I do not believe that any man had a hand in his death. His life was removed by supernatural powers."

"Those powers of which you speak can only work their will through human agency," said Biron. "The masks might have supplied the influence, but the act could only have been consummated by material hands."

"Come back with me," said the scholar restlessly. "This damp wind cuts through my head."

The fire was burning low when they entered the study where the scholar had dreamed his life away. So soon as Biron had seated himself his host emptied two drawers of a quantity of manuscript, and this mass he piled upon the glowing cinders, laughing foolishly when the flames blazed up. "Draw your chair near," he cried to his guest. "That log of dry wood will soon warm the room."

"Log of wood!" Biron muttered, with a quick glance at the scholar's white face. "Do you call that paper wood?"

"Paper or wood, the chemical constituents of the two are alike," came the answer. "Fire reduces each to carbon. I have finished my work," he went on, with a touch of the old dreaminess. "I have nothing more to do. It is a false heat we find in poetry after all."

"You have burnt your work?" suggested the other, his eyes fixed upon the stooping figure.

"It is wood that is burning there," said the poet irritably. "Dry, rotten wood. Let me show you my books. I have some rare books here."

The short autumnal day drew on, but the visitor did not rise to go. His host was talking wildly, yet never mentioning the Strath, nor its owners, nor his own griefs. Psychology was the subject he dilated upon. So great was his tongue's activity that Biron was given no opportunity for replying to the distorted theories which tumbled one upon the other from the scholar's mind. He conjured up all manner of phantasies, delighting himself with them as the child with new toys, diving far into abstruse beliefs, passing from one problem to another, his mind never seeking after cause, never pausing to grope for a solution, but glancing off lightly and speeding into fresh whirlpools of theory. The accumulated learning of a life burst from his brain, deluging the ears of his listener, who sat amid a library of books which had been piled around him.

At length Biron was given a chance of speaking. Seizing the opportunity he opened his lips hastily to put the question, "What are your theories regarding involuntary action and the secondary personality?"

Straightway the scholar was started upon fresh roads leading into stranger realms; but as he talked unceasingly the words "bodily insensibility" detached themselves from the general outpour and struck Biron's ears with a sinister sound. Also the word "sleep" became bracketed constantly with the phrase "unconscious action," and the word "premeditated," came with an ominous ring in conjunction with such expressions as "natural fear" and "subliminal self."

As darkness crept into the room and the firelight grew more pronounced Dr. Berry's eloquence failed and he sank back exhausted in his chair. Then Biron began to talk, but his mood was neither argumentative nor controversial; he spoke gently and soothingly, avoiding the subject of the Strath, merely describing certain of the places he had visited in the course of a life mainly devoted to travel, Venice, the Campagna, the secret ways of mediæval cities, the ancient castles of the Rhine; and when he saw that his purpose was likely to be fulfilled his musical voice went on to picture Athens, the calm Aegean, and the tombs of Grecian heroes. His voice sank into a whisper when he understood that the poet had succumbed.

Fifteen minutes passed—thirty, but the sleeper made no sign. Biron watched the white face with its sealed eyes until a mist formed before his own. Outside, darkness had settled. Within a long flame darted from the midst of the burnt paper flashing across that set face and brightening the silvered hair. Forty-five minutes, and no movement, although the bony watcher still exercised the hypnotic power. When the hour was proclaimed by a little marble clock some sense of shame entered Biron's mind. The knowledge that he was grievously abusing the laws of hospitality forced itself upon him. Half rising he called gently, "Doctor Berry," then sank back with a thrill. The poet was standing upright before him, his hands swaying loosely at his sides, his eyes wide open.

"Show me what took place upon that night when Reed died," said the hypnotist firmly.

Dr. Berry moved to the writing table, and his fingers rustled among some papers. Then he turned to the window, put out his arms, and at once evinced what might have been surprise or annoyance when he found it closed. Biron approached the casements and flung them open. They passed out, one after the other, the scholar taking the well-trodden path through the churchyard which led to the Strath, walking quickly and without hesitation, while Biron groped and blundered behind.

The ragged wall streaming with ivy lifted before them. They reached the muddy moat, choked with dead leaves and rotting branches, but as they neared the edge Biron saw that the bridge had disappeared. The sleeper was walking on. The hypnotist sprang forward and seized him; there was a slight struggle, and Dr. Berry awoke.

He did not show any surprise at finding himself in that place. He had in the past awakened beside the sun-dial, or in the orchard, without any remembrance of having left his study; but he was clearly dismayed to see the ruins looming out of the gloom, and he was irritated at discovering Biron close to him, pointing to the handkerchief which he had twisted like a rope. He laughed unpleasantly when Biron addressed him, and turned away still laughing; but the traveller stood before him whichever way he would have gone.

"What would you do with that handkerchief?" he demanded. "Why have you twisted it?"

"To beat back those who follow me," the scholar shouted, with a sudden burst of anger, stepping out and flicking Biron across the face. "Why are you with me now?" Then he laughed again, and said quietly, "Go your own way, my friend, and I will go mine. The Strath has fallen. I had resolved never to come here again."

Biron seized the speaker's wrists in his bony fingers. "You have much to forgive my family," he muttered. "Had my great-grandfather not lived those masks would never have been here. Had you only been strong enough to abstain from this garden your mind would not have suffered. Had Reed not incurred your ill-will he might have been alive to-day."

"Folly," cried Dr. Berry angrily. "That Reed was a monster, who wanted to turn this place into a farm and keep pigs and poultry. But the Strath was well able to take care of itself."

Biron gulped down the answer which was ready on his tongue. "I entreat you," he said loudly, "I implore you to leave Thorlund, and that quickly, and try to forget all that has taken place here."

Dr. Berry's laughter ceased. Taking a match from his pocket he struck it, and held it above his head without moving, until the flame burnt his fingers. Then he dropped the glowing fragments, and said in a choking voice, "Go away! You have frightened me."

Biron made one step back, then hesitated. Again he advanced and muttered, "After all there may be nothing to forget. You have been all these years under the influence of the masks. You are not guilty. It was the eighteenth-century monster Cagliari who controlled your body and made use of your hands. He alone is guilty, and no man can call him to account."

"Go!" shouted the scholar. "You white-faced shivering creature, you bone-faced ghost!"

He stumbled forward with threatening motions, and Biron backed away, his feet ploughing through the leaves. That moment the dark clouds parted and a glimpse of moonlight passed, revealing the wild features of the one man and the bony face of the other. Suddenly Biron started round and ran towards the road, alive to the knowledge that alone he would be unable to restrain the scholar, who began then to comprehend how that garden and fallen house had used his mind and brain.

Many minutes passed before the rector presented himself at the iron gates, and passed from that scene for ever. The moon had vanished; the muddy road wound away like a black river; there was not any creature in sight, nor within hearing of his mumbled complaint; and upon the hills all was silent. He walked out. From the gates, beside the lichened wall, and so round to his home, was a distance of three hundred yards, past some ruined barns, a deserted farmyard, a standing pool, and the worn patchwork of turf and mud known as the green; and so to the churchyard and the mossy little Bethel which was his official, but had never been his spiritual, charge.

He paced along the centre of this road his fingers knotted

together. And as he went there flickered across his vision a fantastic object, something which resembled a small white tassel, shaken violently at the corner of his eye. When he turned it was gone, but only that it might appear upon the other side. And opposite the pool his foot trod upon and snapped a rotten stick, which cried out to him as though in pain. And when near the churchyard a phantasm started from the wall of the Strath, and walked beside him. At the lich-gate this apparition vanished, and the ghostly tassel quivered wildly between his eyes.

Later the old housekeeper of the rectory heard strange noises in the house and a voice which she could not recognise. Lifting the lamp, she left the kitchen. The study was unoccupied. The sounds proceeded from the dining-room. And there she discovered her master. He had placed a chair upon the table, and was seated upon it, with a paper crown on his head and a ruler in his hand. And as she stood and trembled before him he bade her have no fear, because he was Zeus, king of gods and of men, sitting in judgment upon the world.

"Open that door which leads down to the world and you shall hear the din of cries ascending to me," he cried. "All are asking for riches, honour, or long life. Not a single voice supplicates me for wisdom or for charity. Do you not wonder how I restrain my anger and allow my thunderbolts to lie idle?"

In the grey of the morning, when the wet hills were wrapped in mist and the valley was full of gossamers, a closed carriage entered Thorlund, Biron accompanying it, and presently rolled away, removing Dr. Berry from his charge. The scholar was seated between two grave black-coated men, who held their hands upon his wrists and only spoke to humour him. The poet's mind, which had always sought to soar above the world, had left it altogether. He was equal with the gods. He was destiny, able to use men and women according to his will. He had been lifted to the stars. "I will teach you," he murmured from time to time, as the carriage wheels jolted through the mud. "I will lead you into the ways of happiness. I will be merciful, for I know how weak you are. I was once a man myself."

EXEUNT OMNES

THE AUTHOR, MR. E. G. HENHAM.

From a Photo.

This rare photograph of the author appears on the first page of a short story, "The Conquest of Joe Beveridge," by "E. G. Henham, formerly Factor of the Hudson's Bay Company," in *The Wide World Magazine*, vol. 7, no. 41, August 1901, pp. 438-442. (*Courtesy of Gerald Monsman.*)

ALSO AVAILABLE FROM VALANCOURT BOOKS

Michael Arlen	Hell! said the Duchess
R. C. Ashby (Ruby Ferguson)	He Arrived at Dusk
Frank Baker	The Birds
Walter Baxter	Look Down in Mercy
Charles Beaumont	The Hunger and Other Stories
David Benedictus	The Fourth of June
Paul Binding	Harmonica's Bridegroom
Charles Birkin	The Smell of Evil
John Blackburn	A Scent of New-Mown Hay
	Broken Boy
	Blue Octavo
	A Ring of Roses
	Children of the Night
	The Flame and the Wind
	Nothing but the Night
	Bury Him Darkly
	Our Lady of Pain
	Devil Daddy
	The Household Traitors
	The Face of the Lion
	The Cyclops Goblet
	A Beastly Business
	The Bad Penny
Thomas Blackburn	A Clip of Steel
	The Feast of the Wolf
John Braine	Room at the Top
	The Vodi
Jack Cady	The Well
Michael Campbell	Lord Dismiss Us
R. Chetwynd-Hayes	The Monster Club
Isabel Colegate	The Blackmailer
Basil Copper	The Great White Space
	Necropolis
Hunter Davies	Body Charge
Jennifer Dawson	The Ha-Ha
Frank De Felitta	The Entity
A. E. Ellis	The Rack
Barry England	Figures in a Landscape
Ronald Fraser	Flower Phantoms

Gillian Freeman	The Liberty Man
	The Leather Boys
	The Leader
Rodney Garland	The Heart in Exile
Stephen Gilbert	The Landslide
	Monkeyface
	The Burnaby Experiments
	Ratman's Notebooks
Martyn Goff	The Youngest Director
	Indecent Assault
F. L. Green	Odd Man Out
Stephen Gregory	The Cormorant
John Hampson	Saturday Night at the Greyhound
Ernest G. Henham	Tenebrae
Thomas Hinde	The Day the Call Came
Claude Houghton	Neighbours
	I Am Jonathan Scrivener
	This Was Ivor Trent
James Kennaway	The Mind Benders
	The Cost of Living Like This
Cyril Kersh	The Aggravations of Minnie Ashe
Gerald Kersh	Fowlers End
	Nightshade and Damnations
Francis King	To the Dark Tower
	Never Again
	An Air That Kills
	The Dividing Stream
	The Dark Glasses
	The Man on the Rock
C.H.B. Kitchin	The Sensitive One
	Birthday Party
	Ten Pollitt Place
	The Book of Life
	A Short Walk in Williams Park
Hilda Lewis	The Witch and the Priest
John Lodwick	Brother Death
Kenneth Martin	Aubade
	Waiting for the Sky to Fall
Michael McDowell	The Amulet
	The Elementals
Michael Nelson	Knock or Ring
	A Room in Chelsea Square

Beverley Nichols	Crazy Pavements
Oliver Onions	The Hand of Kornelius Voyt
J.B. Priestley	Benighted
	The Doomsday Men
	The Other Place
	The Magicians
	Saturn Over the Water
	The Thirty-First of June
	The Shapes of Sleep
	Salt Is Leaving
Peter Prince	Play Things
Piers Paul Read	Monk Dawson
Forrest Reid	The Garden God
	Following Darkness
	The Spring Song
	Brian Westby
	The Tom Barber Trilogy
	Denis Bracknel
George Sims	Sleep No More
	The Last Best Friend
Andrew Sinclair	The Facts in the Case of E.A. Poe
	The Raker
David Storey	Radcliffe
	Pasmore
	Saville
Michael Talbot	The Delicate Dependency
Russell Thorndike	The Slype
	The Master of the Macabre
John Trevena	Sleeping Waters
John Wain	Hurry on Down
	The Smaller Sky
	Strike the Father Dead
	A Winter in the Hills
Hugh Walpole	The Killer and the Slain
Keith Waterhouse	There is a Happy Land
	Billy Liar
Colin Wilson	Ritual in the Dark
	Man Without a Shadow
	The World of Violence
	The Philosopher's Stone
	The God of the Labyrinth

WHAT CRITICS ARE SAYING ABOUT VALANCOURT BOOKS

"[W]e owe a debt of gratitude to the publisher Valancourt, whose aim is to resurrect some neglected works of literature, especially those incorporating a supernatural strand, and make them available to a new readership."

Times Literary Supplement (London)

"Valancourt Books champions neglected but important works of fantastic, occult, decadent and gay literature. The press's Web site not only lists scores of titles but also explains why these often obscure books are still worth reading. . . . So if you're a real reader, one who looks beyond the bestseller list and the touted books of the moment, Valancourt's publications may be just what you're searching for."

MICHAEL DIRDA, *Washington Post*

"Valancourt Books are fast becoming my favourite publisher. They have made it their business, with considerable taste and integrity, to put back into print a considerable amount of work which has been in serious need of republication. If you ever felt there were gaps in your reading experience or are simply frustrated that you can't find enough good, substantial fiction in the shops or even online, then this is the publisher for you."

MICHAEL MOORCOCK

TO LEARN MORE AND TO SEE A COMPLETE LIST OF AVAILABLE TITLES, VISIT US AT VALANCOURTBOOKS.COM

www.ingramcontent.com/pod-product-compliance
Lightning Source LLC
Chambersburg PA
CBHW011427010726
47494CB00011B/2540
* 9 7 8 1 9 4 1 1 4 7 0 7 8 *